WHAT SHE FOUND IN THE WOODS

WHAT SHE FOUND IN THE WOODS

JOSEPHINE ANGELINI

Cover design by Mark Swan
Cover images © Maria Heyens/Arcangel; Clement M/Unsplash
Internal design by Danielle McNaughton/Sourcebooks

Published by Sourcebooks Fire, an imprint of Sourcebooks
P.O. Box 4410, Naperville, Illinois 60567-4410
(630) 961-3900
sourcebooks.com

Originally published in 2019 in the United Kingdom by Macmillan Children's Books, an imprint of Pan Macmillan.

Library of Congress Cataloging-in-Publication Data

Names: Angelini, Josephine, author.
Title: What she found in the woods / Josephine Angelini.
Description: Naperville, Illinois : Sourcebooks Fire, [2020] | Audience: Ages 14. | Audience: Grades 10-12. | Summary: While summering in her grandparents' small Oregon town, where a serial murderer lurks, eighteen-year-old Magdalena faces recovery from a scandal at her Manhattan private school, schizophrenia, and falling in love with "Wildboy." Told partly through journal entries.
Identifiers: LCCN 2020027391 | (trade paperback) | (epub)
Subjects: CYAC: Love--Fiction. | Schizophrenia--Fiction. | Serial murders--Fiction. | Drug abuse--Fiction. | Forests and forestry--Fiction. | Diaries--Fiction.
Classification: LCC PZ7.A58239 Wh 2020 | DDC [Fic]--dc23
LC record available at https://lccn.loc.gov/2020027391

Printed and bound in the United States of America.
VP 10 9 8 7 6 5 4 3 2 1

Content warning:

This book contains depictions of
mental and physical abuse,
drug abuse, racism,
eating disorders, and self-harm.

For further information, please see
the back of the book for resources.

July 11

I'VE ALWAYS FELT RELAXED IN AIRPORTS.

I don't know why, but the chaos that eats away at everyone else's well-being creates a dome of serenity around me. I guess that's a terrible thing to say, but it's true. In airports, I'm compact. Boiled down to the few items I've chosen to take with me. I know where I'm going, I know what I have with me, and I don't need anything else.

Airports used to be my favorite place to write. The solitude that I feel when I'm completely surrounded by strangers is better than uppers. I have a notebook hidden in my coat pocket, but I don't take it out. I don't have time, anyway. My grandparents are already at the airport, driving around so they don't have to park. I poke my head out between other travelers and find them.

Always there's that jolt—that moment when all the features come together, and a stranger becomes a relative. Makes a person wonder how big of a difference there actually is between the people they've known their whole life and someone they've never met. I wave, and they pull over.

Hugs first, and then, "You've gotten so thin!" from my grandma.

"I haven't lost a pound," I say, shrugging. "They weigh us every morning."

My grandfather shrinks away from me, and from the unfortunate circumstances that have brought me to stay with them for the summer. And, possibly, forever. But he soldiers on, tacitly letting me know we will not talk about it. Not even if I need to.

"Let's put your bags in the car," Grandpa says cheerfully. "Where are the rest?"

"This is it," I tell him, wheeling my carry-on to the back of their Range Rover.

"But you're staying for the whole summer, right?" Grandma asks, confused now. She's the type of woman who changes her clothes multiple times a day. Her morning ensemble is always business casual, though she's never had a job. Then comes the gardening gear, complete with a wicker hat and mud clogs, even if she's just going out to stand there. And she still dresses for dinner. Always wears jewelry to the table. Nothing ostentatious, but enough to be noticed.

My grandfather tries to help me with my bag, but I won't let him. "I can do it, Grandpa," I say with a smile, and then I hoist it into the trunk easily.

"You pack light," Grandma says, while I settle into the back seat and put my seat belt on.

"Summer clothes," I say. "If I remember right, it gets hot out here when it isn't raining."

Trust the weather to soothe their WASPy souls.

Grandma and Grandpa eagerly launch into a diatribe about the weather in the temperate rain forests of the Pacific Northwest. They have all their descriptive adjectives honed. Every simile has been carefully chosen. They lavish the never-ending rains of western Washington State with all the fiery contempt of true love. The weather is their solace. As a topic of conversation, it safely delivers us back to their summer home on the edge of the forest.

It's not the largest house set back from the street. There are other big constructions dotting the fringes of the wild, but my grandparents' Tudor revival place has a cozy storybook feel to it. And it's buried the deepest, tucked right in between the ocean and the forest, which are the two things that make this a summer destination for the stupid wealthy. The working-class people who live in this town year-round would never have a house right here. They couldn't afford it. We go down their long drive, and the updated two-story springs into view among the tangle of trees and moss.

"Your garden is lovely, Grandma," I say. It looks almost wild, except for the artfully placed splashes of color and the perfectly tiered native ferns and perennials.

"I could use some help with the vegetables out back," Grandma offers, making it clear that the flowers in the front are hers.

"I'd be happy to help," I say.

My grandmother punches a long code into the alarm panel, and we go inside. We have Long Island Iced Teas in the salon. Mine is virgin. Theirs definitely aren't. My grandparents hold firm to their inalienable right to cocktail hour, like it's written somewhere in the Constitution. I look around at the Chippendale furniture, Great-Grandma's collection of Fabergé eggs, and...oh yes, the Degas that hangs so casually on the far wall in its hermetically sealed protective frame as I listen to my grandparents talk. They're thinking of selling after this season and buying a new summer home in Santa Barbara.

"Are you really thinking of leaving?" I ask, just to make conversation.

"The area's changed a lot... That reminds me—I'll have to give you the code for the door," Grandma says primly. "It's not like it used to be when we summered here with your mother, or even when you were younger, and you used to spend July with us."

"I'm sorry to hear that," I tell them. "Everyone says

Santa Barbara is lovely, though," I add. It's bad manners to linger on depressing things. I've grown up changing the subject as soon as anyone says anything unpleasant. It's expected.

When I've finished my refreshment, I take myself to the guest room I used the last time I stayed with them four summers ago. As soon as I open the door, it's like I'm thirteen again.

I laugh under my breath at the frilly bedspread and the smell of powdery, girlish perfume that still emanates from a neon bottle left on top of the vanity. I was so determined to make it my signature scent back then that even the walls soaked it in.

All the furniture is white. The wallpaper is thick, alternating pink and white stripes. It's not a tacky room. My grandparents would never allow me to choose tacky furniture. But how strange that this used to be me. Or the me I wanted to be, I suppose.

"There are still some clothes in the dresser," my grandmother says quietly. "And a lot of pretty sundresses in the closet that you could still wear."

I open the closet at Grandma's urging and notice that, yes, it is stocked with very pretty sundresses. They're young-looking, but they'd still fit. I grew up, not out, as I got older, and most of that length was in my legs.

"Everything is perfect," I say. "Thank you for keeping it just as I left it."

Her eyes shoot over to the writing desk, tucked snugly into the dormer window, betraying her misgivings about leaving it.

"Did they give you a schedule for your medication?" she asks quietly.

I smile reassuringly. "I take all of them once in the morning. It's not like it was when Mom was my age."

She looks relieved, but still troubled. "She had to take so many..." Grandma breaks off and smiles back at me suddenly. "Come down when you're ready, Magdalena. We'll play cards tonight after dinner."

"Great."

Grandma finally leaves me. I take my phone out of my bag and plug it into the wall, but I don't bother to turn it on. Nothing to check, anyway. I deleted my social media accounts months ago, and I have no friends anymore.

I sit on the bed and think about being thirteen. I'm not going to change anything about this room, I decide. I'll let it stay frozen on the inside. Like me.

July 15

I SLEEP A LOT.

It's the pills. They knock me out. That is what they're designed to do, I guess. I'm also getting more exercise than I've ever had before, so I need the rest. I garden in the late morning with Grandma, and after lunch I usually go for long hikes in the woods.

I'm not super outdoorsy or anything, but it's hard not to get swept up in the magic of this place. Every day, I pack up one of those picnic blankets with the water-repellent bottoms, some books and a canteen, and I hike up into the hilly rain forest. My grandparents' property is right next to the edge of a lovely trail. Of course. Why buy a summer home that's so far away from the trail that you're too exhausted to hike it once you've gotten there?

There are a few set paths I usually take, but today I go left instead of right, thinking about that Robert Frost poem.

And I find it.

A stream cuts its way downhill. A small, flat bank fans out to the side of the tiny waterfall, creating a shelf of green oxalis among the moss-covered Sitka spruces. Perfect for a picnic blanket. I wade through the little stream and spread out my blanket on the soft bank. The hill raises sheer behind me to nearly a seven-foot drop, and the waterfall sluices down the rocky face of it pleasantly. I nestle into this little cove of green and listen to the water.

I take out *Walden* by Henry David Thoreau and think about what it means to "live deliberately," as he'd intended when he moved into the woods. I'm not really reading. I don't know if it's because I don't like transcendental philosophy or because Thoreau is boring as hell, but I wish I liked this book better. I wish I had the sort of mind that could slog through the dull bits and follow along with the navel-gazing of a philosopher.

But I don't. I need plot. So I'm just letting my eyes pick out phrases here and there to mull over. Things like *to suck out all the marrow of life, to live so sturdily and Spartan-like as to put to rout all that was not life*. I like how high-minded Thoreau is. How deeply he believes in the innate goodness of conscious individuals. I like to pretend I agree with him.

I try to read, but it's page after page of this guy obsessing about the beans he's growing in his garden. I skim for a pithy quote to think about, but I've lost the thread. There's always my notebook. I take it with me wherever I go out of habit, but I haven't written in it since it served its final purpose. I have to admit, it scares me. It scares everyone around me. But that's so silly. They're words, not bullets. I could just jot down a few lines about this place. I only want to see if I can describe it accurately. I pick up my pen and hold it over the page.

The dappled sunlight and the sound of falling water overtake me. I sleep.

When I wake, all I can remember of my dream is a sense of fellowship. I'm smiling while I pack up my things and head back to my grandparents' house.

I see an unfamiliar car parked in the drive. I don't know a lot about cars, but I know it's a Porsche. I have no idea what year it is or anything like that. I saw one like it in an eighties movie once, I think. *Top Gun.*

"You're finally back," my grandma calls. I take off my hiking sandals and join her in the living room. A young man stands and turns to face me. "Do you remember Robert Claybolt?" Grandma asks. "His family has summered down on the beach for years."

I smile at him as I enter the room and join my grandmother. "Hi. Wow. Robert."

He laughs, rolling his eyes. "You don't remember me," he teases.

"I do," I say defensively.

I blush, because I don't remember his face, but the name is familiar. Whoever he used to be, he didn't used to be this good-looking, or I definitely would have paid more attention to him. That and the meds I've been taking for a year have left gigantic gaps in my memory.

I barely remember who *I* am most days, let alone some random guy I haven't seen since puberty.

"But it's been years, and you've…filled out," I say, trying to turn my faux pas into a compliment. That seems to please him.

"You never come here anymore," he says, letting me off the hook. He already has a tan, and his teeth are white and straight as he grins at me. "I guess New York City is tough to leave."

I'm nodding a lot. Too much. I must look like a bobblehead.

"You want to get coffee?" he asks.

"Yeah, but I think we're about to have dinner," I say, turning to my grandma.

"Oh, there's plenty of time," Grandma says, pushing me toward Robert. "You go and enjoy yourself."

She's awfully eager. "Ah, okay," I say. I look down at what I'm wearing. Frayed shorts and a dirty T-shirt. "Let me wash up real quick? I was hiking."

"Hiking?" Robert makes a face. "I still haven't figured out why people do that."

Something clicks in my head. "Rob! That's right! You're the kid who refused to go camping with all of us because you hate the woods. You always wanted to do something on the beach."

He rolls his eyes. "Finally."

"I'm sorry," I say sheepishly. "You've changed a lot."

"You haven't." His eyes warm. He definitely means that as a compliment. Oh boy.

"I'll be right back," I say, bolting up the stairs before the silence can get any more fraught.

I strip down and rinse off, holding my long brown hair out of the shower spray as I turn a few times under it, and then I quickly towel off. It's warm out, so I opt for one of my old sundresses. It's a little tight around the bust and a little short along the hemline, but not egregiously so. I slip into flat sandals before I run out of my room. As I'm going downstairs, I feel a long-forgotten tube of lipstick in the pocket of my dress. On a whim, I swipe a bit of it over my lips. It's the first time I've worn any kind of makeup in months.

Rob is sitting and talking with both my grandparents in a comfortable way. He looks up at me and grins. His eyes crinkle up when he does that.

"I remember that dress," he says. "Fourth of July."

I look down at the blue dress with the red whales embroidered on it. I have no idea what he's talking about, but I go along with it anyway.

"I'll be back in an hour," I tell my grandparents.

"No rush," says Grandpa. "You two should catch up. Don't worry about dinner."

"Okay," I say uncertainly. "Bye."

I'm frowning as we walk to Rob's car. He opens my door for me, but I don't get in just yet.

"Did my grandparents call you and ask you to take me out?" I ask.

"Yes," Rob answers. I turn away from him and make for the house. He grabs my arm to stop me. "And I almost crashed my car twice, I was so excited to see you again." I breathe out a surprised laugh, and he laughs with me. "Yeah, so, that's pretty much *all* my cards on the table," he mumbles. He realizes he's still holding my bare arm and lets go.

"What did they tell you when they called?" I press.

His brow creases with concern. "They told me your parents are going through a brutal divorce, and you're having a really hard time with it."

I widen my eyes at him, urging him to continue. "And that you got into some trouble at school."

"Is that it?"

He shifts uncomfortably. "Is there more?" I don't respond, so he makes a frustrated sound and runs a hand through his hair. "Look, I'm not here to do a good deed and comfort the sad girl with asshole parents," he says, making me laugh again. "I'm here because I want to see you."

I smile and look down. “Okay,” I say.

“Okay.” He gestures to the open car door. “Let’s get something greasy to eat.”

Rob takes me to a little place by the ocean called the Snack Shack. We sit outside. The sun takes forever to go down while we eat french fries and drink iced tea. He tells me about his parents’ split when he was thirteen. He shows me a photo he has in his wallet. Most guys would just keep a picture in their phone, but he went to the trouble to make an actual print. Something he can hold in his hands. He’s a tactile guy. I notice he takes good care of his nails as he shows me the photo. Buffed, but low shine. Still masculine.

“This is the last picture of all three of us,” Rob says.

“Your mom’s gorgeous,” I say, because she is. Long brown hair like mine. His dad is handsome, too. Strong jaw, charismatic eyes. “You look just like your dad now,” I say, although the Rob in the picture is an awkward kid. “When was this taken?” I ask.

“Five years ago? You and I met this same summer,” he tells me.

Now I really remember him. He was always one of us “summer” kids, as opposed to the “year-rounders” who weren’t what I’d consider dating material back then. Meaning: he came from money, but he had no style. He was a good kid, but I wasn’t interested in that. I went for Liam. The cute boy who wore all the right clothes.

"My parents split up a few months later." Rob looks one last time at the photo before putting it away. "I don't know what was worse. The screaming or the silence after." I nod and hold his gaze, offering what little comfort I can by listening.

"My dad took our place out here, and my mom is at the Seattle estate. I go between them because my mom is alone, but I prefer it here. Anyway," he says, shaking his head and sighing. "We were supposed to be talking about you. I'm usually the shoulder to cry on, and here I am spilling my guts."

"It's good. I'm tired of my story. I'd rather hear someone else's."

He leans forward, nodding understandingly. "I bet you've talked about it a lot with all your friends in New York."

"No."

He gives me a disbelieving look. "Come on. You're probably the most popular girl in your school. I bet you throw friends away."

It's a little cruel of him to say, but I can't contradict him. "I used to," I admit. "I don't have friends anymore."

He realizes I'm telling the truth. "What happened?"

I look out at the sun that just won't set. "I told a very big lie," I say. I look back at him. "And I got caught."

His eyes pop with intrigue. "You *have* to explain that."

I shake my head and poke at the ice in my glass with my straw. “Some other time, maybe.”

He doesn’t push. Instead, he keeps talking. Filling the silence with information about the town of Pinedale, our current home. We finish our tea, and he pays. I offer, but he shrugs me off with a “next time,” and then he walks me to the car and opens the door for me.

“Tomorrow I’ll take you to a barbecue so you can get to know everyone again,” he says, climbing into the driver’s seat.

“Tomorrow?” I ask, raising an eyebrow. “We’re going out again tomorrow?”

“Definitely.” He starts the engine and backs out with a smile. Like he’s daring me to contradict him.

He walks me to my door, even though it’s a little silly and completely awkward. I put a lot of space between us, just in case.

“Give me your number,” he says, pulling out his phone. We exchange digits, and he pockets his phone again. “Tomorrow,” he says firmly. His eyes dart down to my lips, like he’s thinking about kissing me. I turn away from him to unlock the door.

“Maybe,” I reply, pushing my way inside.

July 16
Morning

I USED TO BE REALLY POPULAR.

But the problem with having a packed social schedule is that you can't always go where you say you're going to go. You make promises to acquaintances, to parents, to guys, and you mean to follow through, but then things happen. And before you know it, someone is hurt or angry or disappointed.

It's hard to be perfect *and* popular. When everyone wants something from you, eventually you reach a breaking point. Someone is going to be let down. But I thought I was so clever. I thought I came up with the perfect solution. Actually, it wasn't just me, but that doesn't matter anymore. I'm the one who took the fall. "Are you going for another hike today?" Grandma asks, interrupting my reverie. "By yourself?"

"Do you need me to stay here and help you with something?" I ask.

"No, it's not that," she says through a forced smile. I notice she looks fluttery and anxious, like she either skipped one of her pills this morning or took one too many. "You spend so much time alone. Aren't you going to see your friend?"

It takes me a moment to understand. "Oh, you mean Rob? I think he's taking me to a barbecue tonight," I say, threading my arms through the straps on my backpack.

Her face relaxes. "How nice," she says. "Well, enjoy your hike." In her mind, as long as I'm social, as long as I'm "getting out there," then she shouldn't worry.

"Thanks, Gram," I say, because there's no point in trying to explain to her that some of the sickest people I've ever known were also some of the most social. And I put me, as I was a year ago, at the top of that list.

It's not her fault. My grandparents take everything at face value. The scary part is, I don't think they realize how shallow that makes them. That sounds mean, I know, but it's true. They only go so deep, and asking for more from them is pointless. They're easy to live with, as long as I fit into their picture-perfect idea of what life should be like. As long as I seem happy, they'll be happy to have me here.

So I play along. I smile, I joke, I follow their rules—which is easy to do because they don't ask much. When I came here, I knew what kind of contract I was signing. Only perfect and pleasant will be tolerated. Just like my dad. Don't make it hard, or you have to go.

I hike back to the place by the river with the flat green bank and the little waterfall. I don't have a name for it. I just think of it as *there* in my mind, and I picture it rather than name it. I don't feel like I have the right to name it, actually, because it doesn't belong to me.

I think the whole way, which is a terrible mistake.

I set up in my spot and take out my books. *Walden* is not happening right now. Neither is the Longfellow I've brought. My eyes keep scanning the words *This is the forest primeval*, but they can't seem to get to the next line in the poem.

I look at my notebook.

I hear a pounding sound, and I startle.

It's coming from behind me, so I twist around and look up the sheer wall that rises about seven feet above where I'm lying.

The pounding stops, and a deer comes flying over the edge. I scream and duck and cover my head as a few hundred pounds of terrified animal lands on my picnic blanket and narrowly misses crushing me to death.

"Oh, shit!" I hear. And then something big and heavy lands on top of me. I realize it's a large, dirty boy.

He rolls, keeping his weight off me as we tumble across the blanket. The deer struggles to get her legs under her. She kicks and makes an almost human sound as she screams. The boy drags me as far away from her thrashing hooves as he can and protects me with his body until the deer hauls herself up and trots off with a labored, uneven gait.

I'm too stunned to speak.

"I'm sorry. I'm sorry," the boy keeps repeating.

"What the hell?" I manage to choke out.

"Are you okay? Did I hurt you?" he asks, and he starts inspecting my head and upper arms.

"I'm fine. I mean, I'm not fine, but I'm not hurt," I say, pushing on his bare chest. Wow. He's really solid.

He looks down at my hands, touching him. He shakes and pulls back. Then he jumps off me as if stung. He sits back on his heels and nervously starts handing my books to me although that makes no sense.

"I got it," I say, gesturing for him to stop. I look at my blanket. It's streaked with mud and blood. "What are you doing out here?"

"I live here," he says with a shrug. "What are you doing here?"

"I was reading," I say, gesturing to my books.

He looks at *Walden* and scoffs. "Wasting your time is more like it. You know Thoreau left the woods every Sunday to have dinner with his mom?"

I did *not* know that. I stare at him. "Well. Doesn't that just kill all the romance?" I say dryly.

He stands, and I see a brace of arrows is strapped across his back. There's a huge knife tied to his thigh over a pair of worn camouflage pants. I look at his face. He's about my age, maybe older. I can't really tell what he looks like because of all the mud on his face, but his eyes are two bright blue-gray discs. He turns the way the deer went and then back at me anxiously.

"Are you sure you're okay? That deer is injured and in pain. I can't leave her like that," he says.

"Oh, right," I say, frowning at the thought of that poor animal. "I'm fine. Go kill the suffering deer."

But he hasn't waited around to hear the catty ending to my response. He's already running off yelling, "Sorry!" In moments, he's disappeared in the underbrush. I stare after him, my mouth hanging open. I look down at myself and realize I'm filthy. There's blood everywhere. I should be disgusted, but I'm not. I'm definitely feeling something, which is remarkable, but it isn't disgust. My heart takes forever to stop pounding.

I rinse off as best as I can in the river and pack my things up while they're still a little damp. Luckily, these water-repellent blankets also repel a fair share of blood. The scent lingers. Musky and metallic.

On the walk back to my grandparents' house, I can't

stop wondering about the wild boy. He was out here, hunting I guess, with no rifle and no one to help him. He just had a bow and some arrows and a giant knife. How would he even carry a dead deer back to wherever it is that he lives by himself?

I mean, seriously. Who is this guy? Slaying deer with his bare hands by day and reading philosophy by night… Who does that? Not that I'm into the whole Tarzan thing—or the smarter-than-thou philosopher thing, either.

I mean, it's nice to know a guy is tough enough to chase down a deer. And that he's smart enough to do more than just hit things with rocks. And the way he shook when I touched him…

It's dark by the time I get back to my grandparents' house. I see Rob's car in the driveway and mentally kick myself. The barbecue.

"Sorry!" I call out as soon as I open the front door. "I fell asleep! I'll be right down."

I go straight up the stairs and run to my room. I hear Grandma calling after me, but I don't reply. My clothes are irreparably stained with blood. I take them off and throw them into the very back of my closet. I'll have to get rid of them when my grandparents aren't around.

I rush through a shower and quickly dab on lipstick, and then I'm down the stairs again wearing another one of my old dresses.

I can't apologize enough as I enter the living room. "Rob, I'm so sorry," I say as he stands to greet me.

He looks me over. I've twisted my damp hair on top of my head in a bun, and the dress I'm wearing has a low neckline, showcasing my long neck and toned arms.

"Worth it," he says, making me and my grandparents laugh.

We chat with my grandparents for a little before we head out the door. I don't know why I don't say anything about the deer and the wild boy. I don't feel like trying to explain it, I guess. I can't really explain it to myself, let alone anyone else.

Wildboy said he lived there. Does that mean he lives in the woods? It's illegal to live on public land. He must have meant in town. For all I know, he'll be at the barbecue, and then I'll have him there to explain it to everyone else, because I don't even know where to start. A deer fell on me, and then a guy did? My grandmother is anxious enough as it is. No. This I'm going to keep to myself until I get a little more information from Wildboy. If I ever see him again, that is.

When we get in Rob's car, I notice him checking his watch. It's a Patek Philippe, I'm sure of that, but it's got an obscure complication I've never seen before. It must be very rare.

I apologize again for being late and ask, "Did we miss it?"

"No," he replies, but I can tell he's annoyed. "It's not that late. It's just a little rude."

He lets the word hang there. I realize he's implying I'm rude. He's either expecting me to insist that I'm not rude or he's expecting an apology. But I already apologized. Come to think of it, I don't think I ever actually agreed to come out with him in the first place.

I'm starting to think up a convenient bellyache, maybe a migraine. I'm contemplating going for the gold by saying I have massive period cramps so I can have him bring me home, when he completely changes the subject.

"So, you fell asleep?" he asks. "Were you writing?"

"Reading," I reply, shaking my head.

"What were you reading?"

"*Evangeline.*" I cringe at how pretentious I sound.

"*This is the forest primeval,*" he quotes in a stage baritone, "*with the murmuring pines and the hemlocks.*" He looks over at me as he stops at a sign. "Very fitting."

"I'm impressed," I say. "And, yes, I do realize that I am a giant cliché."

"You don't believe that," he says like a statement, not a reassurance. And he's right.

"No. I don't," I reply. "Nothing about me is a cliché." He's quiet for a moment. His eyes are on the road.

"That's why we're both still here."

I don't quite get what he's saying. I can feel an

undercurrent to his words, something deep and murky, but I don't know him well enough to take any guesses about what it is.

"Who's going to be at the barbecue?" I ask him.

He smiles to himself. "Don't worry." He looks at me. "Whoever they are, they'll love you. Everyone loves you." I'm not going to argue with Rob, although I know from the expectant way he's glancing at me that he's waiting for me to.

Here's how this normally pans out. If I were to say something like, "No they don't," he would accuse me of false modesty. Or if I accept it and say, "Okay, yes, most people love me," his next move would be to accuse me of vanity. Either way, it would lead to him taking me down a peg.

If I were to skip a step and simply point out that there is no way for me to answer a loaded statement like that, all he has to do is say something like, "I was just teasing. Can't you take a joke?" or some such passive-aggressive nonsense, when we both know there's no way for any girl to win an argument like this. And that's why guys start them. So they can win.

See, I've had this argument before. Many times. Usually with guys who know I'm not that interested in them. They're looking for a way to get in my head. Call a girl rude or phony or vain, and she'll do anything to prove to you she isn't. By my count, Rob has implied all three of these things in less than a minute. I get it. He's offended I think so little of him, and he wants to punish me. If he were wrong about any of the things he's implied, I'd think he was a dick.

But he's not wrong. I think he's kind of hit the nail on the head here. In fact, I know I am far worse than rude or phony or vain.

Instead of getting into all that, I look out the window.

July 16
Night

I was not the most popular girl in school.

That was Jinka Pritchett. Jinka was the one everyone wanted to be close to. It wasn't just that she was beautiful with light brown skin, hair for days, and an impossible figure. It wasn't even that she was valedictorian-smart, or unfailingly funny. No. *Everyone wanted to be close to Jinka because she was, hands-down, one of the nicest people you'll ever meet.*

In my school, there was none of that mean girl bully shit you see in teen movies from the nineties. Not with Jinka around. She would defend any geek to any jock, and vice versa. She was patient with even the most annoying, socially awkward kids who invariably say something that they shouldn't and make everyone uncomfortable. She included even the most forgotten members of our graduating class in at least two parties a year, and she genuinely tried to get to know them.

Jinka reached out to everyone. Jinka cared about other people. Jinka made everyone around her be the best versions of themselves because she wouldn't tolerate gossip, cruelty, or petty gripes. And Jinka was almost my best friend. I say almost *because, with someone like Jinka, everyone wants the best-friend job, and I was just one of the select few who was in on the rotation.*

The thing about Jinka was that while she was all of those lovely things I said, she was also incredibly shrewd.

There were five of us. Five beautiful, smart, funny, sweet girls who did everything together: Jinka Pritchett, Scarlet Simpson, Olive Wentworth, Ivy O'Bannon, and me. Jinka was the lynchpin, and the rest of us subbed in as her best friend in a sort of round robin, depending on how arrogant any one of us was getting.

For example, if I was rising high and mighty, Jinka would schedule in some one-on-one time with Scarlet and leave me out. I'd get the hint pretty fast. Scroll back your ego or get replaced.

Jinka was the center because she kept the rest of us a tiny bit off balance. We had no choice but to spin in her orbit, but we didn't care because having Jinka for a sometimes-best-friend felt better than anything.

But it wasn't just Jinka. It was the Five of us. Having friends like that was more important than any guy or any teacher or any parent, and we didn't really care what anybody else thought. Because we were perfect.

And perfect is hard to do. Impossible, in fact.

Rob and I arrive at the barbecue fashionably late. His charm offensive begins as soon as we pull up to the Craftsman-style house. A college-age guy is chatting up a younger girl on the wide front porch.

"Tay-dog," Rob calls out to him.

Tay-dog lifts his beer and starts to howl at Rob in greeting. "There he is! Robert the Bruce!"

Rob looks at the girl and waves politely, but he doesn't seem to recognize her. He introduces me to Taylor, or Tay-dog as Rob had called him, and he leads us into the house and through to the back deck. There's a great view of the ocean and coolers of beer between the comfortable but not expensive deck furniture. The grill is still going, but the burgers and dogs on it are all charcoal.

There's a mix of teens and college-aged kids here, but there's no more than three or four years of an age difference among them. It's obvious that the core of this group has known each other for many summers. These are the vacation friends I gave up for the Hamptons set.

Olive's family has a house in Southampton, and by the time we were freshmen, the Five of us couldn't bear to be separated for a whole month. I traded my grandparents and this woodsier West Coast clique for the posh and polished teenaged spawn of the rich and famous on the East Coast. I traded microbrew beer for mimosas, and real hugs for air-kisses. I never even thought to think about it.

I don't know Taylor from the old days, or at least I don't think I do. He's one of the year-rounders, and I didn't meet many of them back in the day. But the next guy they introduce me to I *do* remember.

"Liam?" I say to the tall, blond guy in a button-down shirt and swimming trunks. It's an odd look, but he's got an amazing body, so he can pull it off.

He turns and faces me, and there's a blank moment that is quickly replaced with disbelief. "Magda," he breathes. "You're back?"

Liam gives me a hug, and we both laugh. We had a *thing* the last summer I was here. We were only thirteen, so it never progressed past hand-holding and a few regrettably limp-lipped kisses that promptly ended my interest in him, but he was a nice guy. Can't remember how we lost touch. I probably just never texted him back.

"It's good to see you," I say. "You look great."

"You look amazing," Liam replies, and I notice a touch of disappointment.

"Okay, okay, break it up," Rob says laughingly. He takes my hand. "You already have a girlfriend," he reminds Liam.

Liam looks away, and an awkward moment passes between him and Rob. Liam turns to me. "Did you ever meet Mila?" he asks.

I've got an unreliable memory at the best of times lately, but I'm still good at reading other people. A quick glance at Rob tells me that *he* knows I haven't met her.

"No. I'd love to, though."

I know who she is before we join the group of girls chatting over a tin bucket full of iced and fruited Blue Moons. She glances at me, and I almost call out the wrong name. They aren't dead ringers by any means, but the essence of them is the same. Mila ticks every box—impossible body, flawless skin, and a luscious mane of hair, although hers is a natural lemon blond. Her sandals are Prada, her earrings are Tiffany's, and the way she dresses is five minutes more stylish than the other girls around her. They all tilt toward her slightly, even when she isn't talking. They all want to be her.

Mila is their Jinka. The way she stands, the way she listens, the way she smiles...the way she *is*... The resemblance is almost overwhelming.

She looks right at me before Liam interrupts the group and introduces me. I compliment her, so she knows I'm not going to be any trouble. She does the same, calling my dress a "throwback" but with genuine appreciation. The other girls' names flash past, and I smile and nod. A curvaceous little Earth Mother hippie named Aura-Blue, probably a year-rounder, asks me if I want something to drink.

"I can get you water," Rob offers, gesturing back inside the house.

"You know, I'll go with you. I need to use the restroom," I say, and then make a swift getaway.

Rob takes my hand again as he leads me through the crowded house. "That was masterful," he says with a raised eyebrow. "Already eluding your competition?"

"I'm no competition for her," I say, shaking my head.

"No," Rob says, coming to a stop in front of the bathroom. He regards me thoughtfully. "She's no competition for you."

"I appreciate that," I say. I untangle my hand from his. "But this isn't a competition. And I don't want anything she has."

"Including Liam?"

"Rob," I warn, "I don't play like that." And I close the door between us.

Rob spends the rest of the night showing me off. He tells everyone stories about things he remembers "the old gang" doing. I don't remember half of the memories he recounts, but that's my new normal since I started taking the meds. He talks about how I was the center of everything.

His stories are hilarious, and since I'm past caring what anyone thinks of me, I don't mind that he tells a story about me getting drunk at the country club and puking in a senator's golf cart. I don't remember it, and I've done way worse since. Things I *do* remember. Things I wish I didn't.

I laugh along with everyone and ask if the senator was a Democrat or a Republican. That gets another laugh and an appreciative smile from Rob. I'm playing along. His dutiful backup singer, making him sound great.

At the end of the night, Rob takes me home. There're a few moments of silence when I can feel him gearing up to say something before he sighs heavily and jumps in.

"Look, about earlier this evening," he says. He glances over at me and gets specific. "When I picked you up and acted like a jackass?"

He really is a funny, charming guy. I laugh, and he smiles and reaches for my hand.

"I guess I was feeling insecure because, let's face it, you like me, but I'm way more into you," he continues, rolling his eyes self-deprecatingly. "But next time if I'm upset with you about something, like being late, I'll just talk with you about it, rather than try to make you feel bad. I'm sorry I acted like that."

"I get it," I tell him, because I do. "And I appreciate the apology."

I let Rob kiss me on my grandparents' doorstep. I keep

it short, but not because I'm not enjoying it. He's a good kisser. Practiced. But for some strange reason, I'm thinking about the wild boy and how his bare chest felt under my hand. How he shook when he realized I was touching him.

I say goodnight to Rob and go to bed, thinking about Wildboy chasing deer.

July 17

I go *there* again the next afternoon.

I lay out my blanket and wait, although I tell myself I'm not waiting. I'm just here to read and enjoy the sound of falling water. It rains. I pretend that sitting in the rain was part of my plan all along. I'm not waiting for Wildboy.

Wildboy doesn't show.

I'm not disappointed, I tell myself. And why would he come back on the off chance that I would, too, anyway? It's not like I impressed him with my philosophy-lite reading choices or my pretentious poetry. We didn't even tell each other our names.

When I get back to my grandparents' house, there are two cars in the driveway. One is Rob's and the other is a black Mercedes coupe I don't recognize, but that just screams Liam to me.

I'm not wrong. I go inside and find Rob, Liam, Taylor, Mila, and Aura-Blue chatting with Grandma and Grandpa and drinking lemonade. Apparently, showing up at my house is now a thing.

"Hi," I say, waving a desultory hand. "Did we make plans?"

"We just stopped by to see if you wanted to come out with us," Mila says. She's got such a sweet smile, I find myself smiling back at her.

"I didn't hear from you all day," Rob says, annoyed.

"I was just hiking," I reply.

"I love to hike," Mila croons. "We should go together someday."

I pretend I didn't hear her while I say, "I'm all sweaty. I'd have to clean up."

"We'll wait," Liam says.

I look around for a way out and see Grandma's eyes flash with worry that I'll turn them down. I have no choice but to say, "Great! I'll be right down."

Another rushed shower, another sundress, a swipe of lipstick, and I hurry to join my uninvited guests. "Have fun," Grandma and Grandpa call out from the doorstep as Rob holds open the passenger door for me.

Rob gets in the car to avoid the faint drizzle that is left after the rain, but he doesn't start the engine right away. He waits for my grandparents to go back inside and for Liam,

Mila, Taylor, and Aura-Blue to pull out before he turns to face me.

"Not even one text?" he asks. He looks hurt.

"I..." I stammer, but he's not done.

"I thought after that kiss last night, you'd at least answer the phone and talk to me, but I would have settled for a text." He sits back and runs his hands through his hair. "There are a lot of girls who actually take my calls, you know."

"Rob, you're a catch. I can see that. *I'm* a mess. Save yourself," I say through a laugh. Despite himself, Rob laughs with me.

"Are you this hard on every guy who's into you?" He taps the steering wheel in agitation. "I promised you I'd talk with you when something bothered me, rather than play head games, but are you just playing with *me*? You saw that I called, didn't you?"

"No. I usually switch off my phone unless I'm going to use it. Half the time, I don't take it with me at all when I go hiking."

He looks utterly baffled. The thought of being separated from technology is unthinkable. "Why?"

I don't have to give him an explanation, but I decide he deserves one anyway. He's really trying to be straight with me. I respect that. I respect him, I realize, because he's earning it.

"A year ago, I was getting a lot of nasty phone calls,

and I had to change the way I live. It has nothing to do with you. And I apologize that I left you hanging. I'm not playing with you."

"Why were you getting a lot of nasty calls?" he asks. All his frustration is gone now, and he looks concerned.

I shake my head, refusing to answer.

He sighs and stares at me for a long time. "God, you're beautiful," he says quietly.

I smile. "You realize that's the worst reason to be interested in someone, right?"

He starts the car. "So I'm learning," he says ruefully as he pulls out.

The rain stops, so we play mini golf. It's silly and fun and it works great because there are three guys and three girls, and everyone can pair up. We joke around for a while, taking selfies and saying ridiculous stuff, but it's clear this is an intelligent group of people. The conversation inevitably turns to more serious things.

"Did you hear about the woman who was mauled?" Mila says.

"No. Where?" I ask.

"The woods," Rob says with a shrug, stepping up to the tee. "You know, where you love to read or write or hike or whatever it is you're doing."

I'm stunned. "But I've never seen a bear."

"Just because you don't see them doesn't mean they're not

there," Rob says, putting his ball between the whirling blades of a windmill. "You all tease me for never going into the woods, but there are no bears in the ocean. No Lyme disease, either."

"What happened?" I ask. I turn to Aura-Blue, who seems to know what's going on. "Who was she?"

"Some hunter from out of state," Aura-Blue says sadly. "They found her rifle first by the side of the river. She'd discharged it a few times, and the authorities think she must have made a bear angry. I mean, what did she think was going to happen? Bears have a right to defend themselves. They live in the woods; we don't. We're the intruders."

Liam, Taylor, and Mila share a knowing look. They're obviously used to Aura-Blue's earthy-crunchy indignation. "You know, she was found partially eaten," Taylor says, reveling in that gory detail.

The thought makes me sick. "No way," I reply, covering my mouth.

"Taylor," Mila chides. She turns to me. "She was found in the river."

"Yeah. Partially eaten," Taylor insists, and both Aura-Blue and Mila smack one of his arms. "Ow!" he says, rubbing his big bicep.

Everyone is ready to change the subject at this point, but I can't let it go. "When did she die?" I ask.

"Yesterday, they think," Rob answers. "They found her this morning."

I'm thinking about Wildboy. If that woman couldn't stop a bear with a rifle, how could he defend himself with a bow and arrow?

"Magda?" Rob touches my arm. "Are you okay?"

"Yeah." I shake myself at how maudlin I'm acting. I don't know Wildboy. I'm not invested. "It's just sad."

"Hunting is sad," Aura-Blue insists. "Murdering animals with guns is sad."

Liam leans in conspiratorially. "She's vegan, if you hadn't guessed."

We talk about hunting and then slide into a lively debate about gun laws. Taylor is adamant about his Second Amendment rights.

"No one's going to take my guns," he says. That's when I know he has never read the Second Amendment.

Aura-Blue rolls her eyes. "It takes months of classes and two separate tests to get a driver's license because cars can kill. Don't you think we should at least have the same setup for something that is specifically *designed* to kill?"

"I don't kill people with my guns," Taylor grumbles without answering Aura-Blue's question.

"I think the one thing we can all agree on is that people who have a mental illness shouldn't be allowed to have guns, right?" Rob says. Even Taylor agrees with that. I stay quiet, but I can feel Rob's eyes on me.

"Will you teach me to shoot?" I ask Taylor.

He looks stunned. "Yeah. Sure. Rifle or handgun?"

I shrug. "Both, I guess." He laughs, and I take the golf club out of his hand and step up to the tee. "What is it?" I ask, off his look.

"You just don't seem the type."

I line up my shot. "Well, you know." I tap my ball directly into the pirate ship, down the ramps, and into the hole. My father spent lots of money on my swing. It's impressive. "Bears."

We get pizza and beer after. Everyone has fake IDs except for me.

"You can put your glass down here," Mila says, pointing under the table to the space between us on the bench. Her Van Cleef & Arpels bracelet flashes on her wrist. "I'll watch out for the waiter while you drink."

"Thanks, but I can't have alcohol," I say. I grimace mournfully. "Unfortunately."

Mila smiles. "Antibiotics?" she asks. I laugh and look down, letting her think whatever she wants.

They kill a pitcher of beer before the pizza even arrives. Rob is the only one who has barely even tasted his first glass.

"Do you ever drink?" he asks me.

"I used to," I admit. "But not anymore."

He hands his beer to Taylor. "Here, man. I'm done."

"You don't have to..." I begin, but Rob leans forward

suddenly and brushes my long hair behind my shoulder. "If you don't drink, neither do I," he says. The pizza arrives before I can tell him the gesture, although sweet, is not necessary.

It's not New York pizza, but nothing is. I wonder if I'll ever have another real New York slice, standing on a corner, midtown traffic lapping like waves around me, the sky humming with the urgency of the city. I doubt it.

"How's your pizza?" Aura-Blue asks as she bites into her salad.

"Great," I say, shoving the greasy cardboard between my teeth. I chew for a bit.

She watches my expression skeptically.

"Not so great," I admit. "I should have gotten one of those." I point to her salad, and she smiles.

"I think there might be another vegan among us," she sings teasingly. Everyone else groans.

"First alcohol, now I've got to give up meat, too?" Rob says.

And we're all laughing and enjoying this and tucking our performances away so we can rethink them and wonder if we could have been a little more charming in this moment or a little less ostentatious in that one.

At the end of the night, I let Rob kiss me for a while in his car, but that's it. I stop him and tell him I'm not ready for anything else—we're just getting to know each other. He understands. He doesn't push. He walks me to the door and tells me to call him tomorrow. Or at least turn on my phone so he can call me.

I'm waiting to feel something. It's the meds, I tell myself.

July 19

The next two days, I dodge Rob and go *there*.

I need alone time, I tell him. I'm not lying, either. Toward the end of the second day—and that makes it a full three afternoons I've spent waiting by the waterfall—Wildboy still hasn't shown. So technically I've been alone this whole time. Although I wish I wasn't.

My notebook sits next to me. I touch the cover, but before I can pick it up, I hear a snap behind me. I jump to my feet and look up the sheer wall. The first thing I think is—*Bear!* Mostly because my grandmother has been a nervous wreck about that woman who was mauled, but also because I've seen Animal Planet. Bear attacks are horrifying. Do I run? No. They eat you if you run because you look like prey—thank you, Animal Planet. I'm supposed to yell. But how can I yell when the fear in my throat is as thick as sand?

"Who's there?" I call out. I hear movement and back away from the wall so I can see over the crest of it. "Come out!"

"Okay," I hear behind me.

I whirl around, a scream halfway up my throat, and there he is.

Wildboy.

No mud this time, so I can see his face. He's fair with closely cropped blond hair. He's not magazine beautiful, but he has nice features and a strong chin. His teeth are a little crooked. He's muscular and tall, but he's not puffed up and sculpted like Taylor, Liam, and Rob. He doesn't have a gym-rat body. He has a functional body—limber and lean. If I were to pass him on the street in New York, I'd think he was definitely above average, but not light-your-panties-on-fire sexy. At least, my former friends wouldn't think he was. So why am I hot all over?

"Were you watching me?" I ask.

"Yes," he says, looking down. He's blushing. "You came back."

"I've *been* coming back," I admit.

"I know."

"Wait. How long have you been watching me?"

He smiles but doesn't answer. "What's your name?"

"Lena." It just pops out. But that's what I want him to call me. "What's yours?"

"Bo."

The sound of the river fills the silence. I still can't believe he's here. He's *real.*

"Did you catch that deer?" I ask at the same time Bo asks "Did you finish *Walden*?" We both laugh. I say "No," the same moment he says "Yes."

"You know, if we both keep talking at the same time, our conversations will take half as long," I remark.

He thinks for a moment. "I don't want our conversations to take half as long," he replies. "Maybe instead we can both say twice as much."

I smile at him because while that might have sounded like a pickup line from a different guy, from him it's genuine. Because he's genuine, I realize. He's a real person. I wonder how long it's been since I've met one of those. Another long silence. I could stay like this with him all day, comfortably quiet as I watch the filtered light morph across his face, but he looks anxious. Embarrassed, even, so I say the first thing that pops into my head.

"Why do you hate Thoreau?"

He smiles slowly. "I'll get you started on some John Stuart Mill. We'll go from there."

"Really?" I say, laughing. "That sounds serious. What are you? Some sort of wild boy philosopher?" It sounds silly coming out of my mouth, but that's how I picture him.

He shakes his head. "My mom is the philosopher. Or she was a professor of philosophy. I just read what she tells me to read."

"She *was*?" I ask, emphasizing the past tense as delicately as I can.

"Oh, she's alive," he replies. "She just doesn't teach any more, although sometimes she still writes for some political journals. She loves to write." He looks down at my notebook. "Like you."

"No," I say, waving a dismissive hand at my long-neglected notebook. Why do I even carry that thing around anymore? "I'm not a writer."

He gives me a searching look. "Then why do you spend so much time out here alone?"

"I'm not alone, am I?" I say, gesturing to him. He laughs with me. He's got a great laugh.

"You're making this easier than I thought you would," he says. And then he blushes. "I mean, you're nice." He looks like he could kick himself. "No—nice isn't what I meant." He realizes he just implied that he'd assumed I wasn't nice, and he looks like he wants to turn inside out with shame.

"It's okay. This should have been much weirder than it's turning out to be," I say. I gesture to my stuff again. "I mean, I'm the one who sat in the middle of a forest for the better part of a week just in case you showed up." Now I want to kick myself. "Just forget I said that."

"Only if you'll forget I was watching you the whole time," he admits sheepishly.

I nod and laugh nervously. What is wrong with me? Guys never make me nervous. "So we're both creepy," I say.

He shakes himself and takes a step back. "It's getting late. You've usually left by now. And—listen." He looks tortured again. "This is a national forest, and my family is out here illegally."

"I haven't told anyone about you," I say immediately. "And I won't."

"Thanks," he says. And then he's gone. A few rustling ferns and—*poof*.

I can't believe it. "Bo!" I shout.

I see his head peek out from the underbrush. "Yeah?" he says, sounding almost hopeful.

"Meet me here tomorrow," I say.

He smiles and does the *poof* thing again.

I've got Grandma on the ropes.

"Give me all your sevens," she says, like this is some kind of holdup.

"Go. Fish."

I get up and dance. Grandma has lost. I am not a

graceful winner. Not since this is the first game of Go Fish I've ever won off that conniving old cheat.

"I won! In your face with a can of mace," I chant.

I am five years old. I am taunting an old woman. I can't sink any lower.

"Hi!" a cheerful voice calls from the front of the house. "It's Mila and Aura-Blue!"

"Come on in!" Grandpa calls back.

I'm still dancing around Grandma as they enter. "How lovely to see you girls," Grandma says as she catches me and pulls me down next to her on the settee. "You owe me one dollar," I remind Grandma. I look at Mila and Aura-Blue. "What can the reigning queen of Go Fish do for her subjects?"

"We wanted to know if you, um...had a job?" Aura-Blue says haltingly.

Mila's lips purse with displeasure at Aura-Blue's lack-luster opening pitch.

"Summer kids don't apply for jobs while we're in town because that could potentially take money away from people who live here and need the income," Mila explains.

"People like me," Aura-Blue adds without a hint of embarrassment. She's working class, but obviously secure enough in herself to know she's got way more to offer than a trust fund. I smile with her. I could really get to like this girl.

"But it gets boring just hanging out for three months, right?" Mila continues.

Um, sure? I nod for her to continue.

"So instead, some of you summer kids volunteer a few days a week at the women's shelter the next town over in Longridge," Aura-Blue says. "I'm doing it this year, too, for college credit, and we thought you might like to come with us."

"Oh, how wonderful!" Grandpa exclaims.

"Girls, it is just so special that you do that," enthuses Grandma.

I give one mirthless laugh at the irony of being asked to volunteer.

"I'd love to," I say firmly. There's no making up for what I've done. I'm not stupid enough to think I'll ever find redemption. But still, it's better to do something positive than nothing at all. "Thank you so much for inviting me."

"Excellent," Mila says as her face lights up. "I knew you'd be into this. You've probably done a lot of volunteer work in New York."

I shrug and look away. "Some," I say. "Not nearly as much as I should have."

"We can't go," Jinka said. "There's no way we can blow off my mom."

Scarlet looked at me. Egging me on. She rolled over on my bed and snapped her gum pointedly.

"Hold on," I said. I went over to my desk and sat down. "Let's think this through."

"There's nothing to think about. We promised my mom weeks ago that we would volunteer this Saturday at the soup kitchen with her." Jinka shrugged. "There's no way we can back out now."

"Backing out to go to a party would be terrible. But not if someone needed our help more," I said, smiling.

"What are you talking about?" Ivy asked. "Noah doesn't need our help throwing a party. He does it every year when school starts."

I shook my head and started over. Better to paint a picture than to just say what colors are in it. "Imagine there was a new girl at school this year. Shy. Underprivileged."

I looked around. Ivy was still confused, but Olive and Jinka were starting to get it. Scarlet got it, of course, because I had already told her what I thought we needed to better our junior year of high school. And she had agreed with me.

"This girl has no friends yet," I continued. "She's just moved here from India, and she needs a group of nice girls to take her to a beginning-of-the-year party or she won't make any friends. She's poor, but she's so sweet. Smart and pretty," I said, looking at Jinka. "But she needs to borrow clothes."

"Oh, that's good," said Scarlet.

"Her parents don't speak any English," I said.

"That's even better," Scarlet chimed in. "My parents

are terrified of running into one of our housekeepers because she can't speak English."

I nodded. "Our parents have to have a reason other than that they're poor to never try to meet this imaginary family."

"Oh, definitely. If it was just that they were poor, my mom would feel like she had to throw them a parade probably," Jinka said.

We set it up carefully. We preyed on our parents' classism. Their racism. The Five of us absolved ourselves of both of these things. Jinka was African American. Our best male friend, Noah, was Korean—adopted at birth—but still ethnically Korean. We were careful that our parties always had a visually pleasing mix of every color, like a soda commercial. We told ourselves there was no way we were racist. And although none of us were friends with a poor person, we couldn't be classist, either, because that wasn't our fault. We'd totally be friends with poor people if we knew any.

I remember feeling a twinge of guilt, and I stopped for a moment. One look at Jinka's excited face, and whatever guilt I felt disappeared.

"Her name will be Ali Bhatti. Our alibi," I said.

While my four former friends squealed with excitement, I took out my journal and started writing down the details.

The details. That's where the devil lives.

July 20

THIS RIFLE KICKS LIKE A MULE.

I'm not about to complain, though. Taylor already suggested that we switch out the 7mm for the .243, but I'm being stubborn.

"The .243 has less kick," Taylor says again after I miss the target he's set up on the edge of the woods by his house.

"I just want to see if I can do it," I reply, and I take another shot. My arm is numb, but I hit the target.

"Not bad," Taylor admits.

I take another shot, and it hits center. I can hear Rob laughing behind us.

"If you tell her she can't do it, she'll end up doing it better than you," Rob shouts to his buddy.

I take six more shots, all of them clustering in or very near the bull's-eye. I hand the rifle back to Taylor.

"I don't see what all the fuss is about," I say. "It's not hard to hit the middle once you get used to it."

Taylor looks at the rifle and then back at me. "You've done this before," he says.

"No," I say, shaking my head. "But I am good at darts." *And golf. And bocce ball. And shuffleboard. Anything that involves hand-eye coordination and a projectile*, I add silently. I don't say all that out loud, for obvious reasons. "I can hit targets. Maybe it's an aim thing."

"Maybe you're just a natural born killer. Look at that *shot*!" Taylor shouts, truly impressed. "Dang, girl. You want to fire off a few rounds on my handgun?"

I pause, shaken. There's no way he can know. And it seems like he's honestly praising me. If he knew, he wouldn't be doing that.

"I can't," I complain, rubbing my arm. "I'm so done."

He tries to talk me into it, but my arm really is just killing me. I join Rob and sit down in the lawn chair next to him as Aura-Blue steps up for her first lesson with a rifle. She balks at even holding it, and Taylor basically takes over and starts showing off.

Rob looks at me with a strange expression. "Are you good at everything?" he asks.

"Beginner's luck," I say. "I doubt I'll ever win any

competitions, like Taylor over there, but I guess I can hit a target if it's not too far away." We watch Taylor become increasingly more testosterone-addled with every crack of the rifle. Some people really get off on guns. "Do you shoot?" I ask Rob.

"I don't see the allure," he replies, making his ambivalence clear. "Too noisy."

"What?" I say because of the noise and get a begrudging laugh.

"Are you going to start carrying a rifle on your hikes?" Rob asks out of nowhere.

"I hadn't thought about it," I reply.

"Think about it," he urges. He takes my hand. "I'm not trying to tell you what to do, but that woman who got mauled—"

"Had a rifle," I finish.

"Good point," he concedes. "But will you think about it anyway? I'm sure your grandparents have something you can take if you're going to keep hiking alone. I'm really worried about you out there."

I smile, but don't say anything. Handing me a firearm is the last thing my grandparents would do. Besides, on the slim chance anything ever happened to me out there, it would only be what I deserved.

"You can't shoot guns sober!" Liam shouts from the driveway. We turn and see him hold up a six-pack.

Another round of greetings and jokes and smiles as Liam and Mila join us. And the gang's all here.

Mila is dreamy and chatty. I notice she's not wearing any jewelry or much makeup. I wonder how many of those beers she's had already.

I wait a half hour and start saying I have to go.

"You want to go home to write some more?" Rob asks me.

I give him a puzzled look. "Why would you say that?" He gestures to my hand. I'm holding my journal. I must have put it in my handbag before we went out, but I don't remember doing that.

"You really don't realize how much you write, do you?" he asks me. He doesn't blink.

I shrug and laugh. "I haven't written in weeks," I say. But then I notice where the silk ribbon marking my spot lies sandwiched between the pages. Half-full. "That can't be right," I whisper.

Rob's eyes glitter with fascination. "That must be some read," he says. He takes me by the elbow and starts shouting his goodbyes to the gang before I can respond. He takes me home and doesn't mention it again, but I know he's curious. I hide my journal in my closet. It's not for Rob, really. It's not like he has ever been, or will ever be, in my bedroom. I hide it in a difficult spot so I don't accidentally scoop it up again and put it in my purse when I don't mean to. It's just such a habit, I guess. It's a habit I need to break.

I don't see Bo anywhere when I arrive at our spot.

I put my stuff down. I spread out my blanket. I wait. Finally, I start to pull out my journal. Wait—didn't I just hide this?

"You're early," Bo says. I look up and see him slipping his way toward me through the ferns.

"You sure you're not late?" I ask, smiling. He stops on the edge of my blanket and shifts from foot to foot. "Sit," I say, offering the place opposite me. He doesn't.

"So… What did you do today?" he asks stiffly, like he's trying to follow a script.

"I learned how to shoot a rifle," I reply. "You?"

"You've never shot a rifle before?" he asks, his surprise loosening him up.

"No." I laugh. "Not a lot of reason to shoot rifles in New York City."

Bo's eyes widen. "That's where you're from?"

"Uh-huh," I reply. "Please sit down, Bo. You're making me jumpy." He sits but looks even more uncomfortable. "Have you ever been to New York?" I ask.

He laughs nervously. "No."

"Do you really live out here?" I gesture to the woods. "Or do you live in town?"

"We live here in the woods—my family and I," he

replies. "We go into town maybe once or twice a month to pick up mail and supplies and drop off the herbal medicines my dad makes."

I don't know how to ask this, so I just do it. "Do you live in a house?"

"Not exactly," he says. His face is turning red.

"So, like, tents?" I press. He shrugs, unwilling to talk about it further.

I know my mouth is hanging open rudely, but I can't help it. "How many people are there in your family?"

"My mom, dad, me, two brothers and three sisters."

I do some quick math "You have *five* siblings?" I nearly shout. He smiles uncomfortably and looks away. "Where are you? I mean, what order..."

"I'm the oldest," he says. "My youngest sister is only four."

"How old are you?"

"Eighteen."

"Me too."

Silence again. Bo looks like he's being tortured. He stands up.

"Where are you going?"

He wanders away and then comes back. "I don't know." He sighs with frustration. "I don't know what to say."

"Well, neither do I." I rub my sore shoulder absently, and he peers at me knowingly.

"Does that hurt from the rifle?" he asks. I nod. He

looks down at the bow in his hand. "Have you ever shot a bow and arrow?"

"No," I say, perking up. Finally, something to do other than stare awkwardly at each other. "Are you offering to teach me?"

"Yeah." He grins.

I stand up. "Let's go," I say.

He leads me off the trail and into the undergrowth.

We talk more freely now that we're moving.

"My dad was a doctor. He got turned off by the hypocrisy of Western medicine and the parasitical pharmaceutical companies and started studying Eastern traditions and philosophy."

I love how he uses "hypocrisy" and "parasitical" as if they were facts and not a matter of opinion. He's second-generation self-righteous. It's not annoying because he isn't trying to be inflammatory. It's just all he knows.

"Is that how he met your mom?" I ask, remembering that his mom was a philosophy professor.

Bo looks back at me and smiles. "Yeah. They met at Berkeley when my dad was getting his second PhD."

"Wow. Smart," I mumble under my breath. "Do you go to school?"

"Our parents are our teachers," he says tightly, speaking for himself and his siblings.

"Oh. And how is that? Being homeschooled?" I ask.

He stops and comes back toward me. "They're really good teachers. I can go to any of the best colleges if I want."

He's offended. I realize he must think I was making fun of him for being homeschooled.

"I think it's amazing your parents cared enough to be your teachers," I say. He still looks wary and defensive. "My parents couldn't even be bothered to teach me how to drive, and I can't get into *any* colleges, let alone the best ones."

He frowns at me, but his eyes are soft. "Why can't you get into college?"

I said too much. I don't want Bo to know all the horrible things I've done yet. I push past him, into the undergrowth. Not that I know where I'm going. Bo eases his body through the tangled vegetation, and in three steps he's in front of me, blocking my path. He's so close, he's practically touching me, but I don't mind.

"Why won't you get into college?" he repeats. His face is so honest and open. Like mine isn't.

"Because I was stupid and selfish and I thought I was smarter than everyone else and I thought I could get away with pretending to be a better person than I was actually willing to be," I say in a rush. "I ruined my life, and there's nothing I can do about it now."

I'm two seconds away from crying. I cross my arms and take a few breaths to calm down. Bo backs up, giving me space. He doesn't try to tell me that I'm not a bad person or that I couldn't possibly have ruined my life or any of the other empty platitudes a stranger would usually feel compelled to say. He's not trying to force me into his idea of me. He's just letting me be who I am and feel what I feel. I don't think anyone's ever done that for me before. Socially, he's awkward as hell, but he's probably the most emotionally intelligent person I've ever met.

I look up at him, and I don't have to force a smile. I don't have to force anything with Bo.

"So, how far do we have to go to get to this archery lesson you're supposed to be giving me?" I ask.

"We're here," he says.

I look around and realize we are on the edge of a small glen where a giant has fallen. A great, mossy log lies across the center of the opening in the canopy, and light fills the narrow stretch of forest floor. Saplings are already trying to beat their neighbors to the sun, but I can see that deer have been at them, keeping this space open with their nibbling.

"I come here to hunt sometimes," Bo tells me. "Deer like the grazing."

I think of Bo running after that deer, and I try to imagine what it would be like to chase down something and kill it with my bare hands. There is something so intimate about it—the hunter and the hunted. It's a relationship. I mean, I eat meat. But I never knew it first.

Though, now that I consider it, I think Bo's way is more

caring than mine. It seems gentler to me to kill something myself than to have a dead animal passed to me through a fast-food window. Bo's way is cleaner, somehow. I want to be clean again.

"Do you eat what you hunt?" I ask as nonchalantly as I can, although this is the first time those words have ever crossed my lips.

Bo gives me an odd look. "Of course," he replies. "My family uses every part of the animals we take from the forest."

I nod, and then something occurs to me. "You don't expect me to hunt anything right now, do you?" I ask.

He tries not to laugh. "Let's just work on learning how to shoot for today."

Bo slips the quiver off his back and puts it at my feet.

"Okay. First thing is holding the bow," he says. "Oh, wait. You're going to need my arm guard."

He unties the thick piece of leather covering the inside of his right forearm and starts to tie it around my right arm, then he stops, like he's realized something.

"Are you right-handed?" he asks, looking at me.

He smells faintly of—not a perfume, exactly, but some blend of natural oils like lavender and sage mixed with cedar and sandalwood. It's feminine and masculine at the same time. Under that, he smells like a guy who's been walking around in a forest, but that doesn't smell bad to me. He notices me leaning toward him, and he freezes, terrified.

"Yes," I say, but he's forgotten the question. "I'm right-handed."

He takes a long time to recover, and that's when I realize he must have thought I was going to kiss him. He's blushing and shaking so badly, it makes me wonder if he's ever been kissed before. I don't think so. And I don't think I've ever wanted to kiss anyone more.

But he's done tying the guard to my left forearm and he's handed me the bow already and taken a step back from me. And now he looks mortified again. And I remember my first date. I was thirteen and he was fourteen, and Jinka set us up. I didn't really know him or particularly want to go on a date with him, but Jinka liked his friend, and she chose me to double date with her. Of course, I was so thrilled to share this bonding moment with Jinka that it didn't matter what boys were with us. We had our first dates together. We had our first kisses together in the back of the same movie theater. We'd be best friends forever.

I didn't choose the first boy I made out with. In fact, I didn't really choose any of the boys I've dated, because since then I've only dated boys that made sense within our group of friends, and that's more political than it is romantic. Either that, or I've dated guys like Rob, who chased me so spectacularly that saying no to them would have been, well…rude.

I've never kissed a boy I've actually wanted to kiss. But I want to kiss Bo very much. And now I'm the one who's blushing and shaking. I take a mental step back, and I see us—Bo and me—two idiots standing in a forest thinking about first kisses. I start laughing.

"So, where's the safety on this thing?" I ask.

Bo laughs with me, and all the awkwardness is gone. "Right," he says, a teacher now, "let's see you plant your feet."

I had no idea how hard it was to stand. Definitely a skill I've taken for granted since I was about a year old. Bo keeps sticking two fingers into different points of my body, and with almost no effort at all, he's able to tip me over.

"Enough!" I say, after about fifteen minutes of this. I turn and nudge him to give him a taste of his own medicine, but he doesn't budge an inch. "Oh. That's annoying. You didn't tip over at all."

"I'm not doing this to annoy you," he tells me evenly. "You'll see when you draw the arrow back. Go ahead. Give it a try standing just like that without your weight distributed."

I try. "Ouch," I say. I shake out my fingers. "That's really hard."

"Yeah. You have to pull from between your shoulder blades. Like this."

He turns his back to me, plants his feet, nocks an arrow, raises his bow, and draws. His whole back ripples under his worn T-shirt.

"Brace your shoulders and back with your legs, or you'll

hurt yourself after two or three pulls. It's all in your legs. You see?" He turns to face me.

"I see, but I don't have...what you've got going on under there," I say, gesturing to his shoulder-chest area. I hold out one of my skinny arms as proof.

"My sister Raven isn't that much thicker than you, and she's a better shot than me," he says, and then he sees something. He takes my arm and turns it gently. "You're all bruised."

I twist the underside of my right arm up so I can see what Bo's looking at. The crook of my armpit is purple. And now Bo looks angry.

"What moron taught you to shoot?" he asks, eyes blazing with protective indignation.

"No, it's my fault," I say. "I should have used a different caliber, but I was feeling stubborn." That's not the right word, so I shake my head and rethink it. "I guess I was feeling like I needed something." I'm struggling. Why did I do that? And why did I say it wasn't that hard afterward? It was hard. "I think I did it because I wanted to set myself apart from the other people I was with. I wanted to prove..." I break off, completely at a loss. "Something," I finish weakly.

Bo watches me for a moment, but I can't read his face. "We'll do this in a few days," he says. He picks up his quiver and slings his bow behind his back.

"What?" I say, stunned. And a bit hurt, actually. "Why won't you teach me now?"

"Heal first," he says.

I'm just standing here, staring at him, because even though what he said makes perfect sense, I just told him something real and not very flattering about myself, and he tells me to go home. Why do people bail on me when I tell them what I'm really thinking? He starts to get uncomfortable. He looks like a little boy when he's uncomfortable.

"Fine. Whatever," I say, turning away from him and heading back to where I left my stuff.

Bo follows me quietly. I can feel words jamming up his throat.

It starts to rain. The soothing staccato of water hitting leaves does nothing to calm my anger. I eventually find my blanket and start rolling it up. Bo stands behind me, shifting from foot to foot. He looks miserable.

"Bye," I say, purposely not making any plans to see him again.

I'm wading through the river when he shouts, "Because you wanted them to know you were more." I stop and turn to face him with the water halfway up my legs and freezing cold. "You wanted them to know that they're underestimating you."

I nod and start to wade back. "Yeah," I say, but I doubt he can hear me over the rush of water.

"I'm the same with my dad," he admits. He laughs at himself and pulls up his shirt, so I can see a huge bruise on his ribs that goes all the way down to his hip.

"Oh my God," I gasp. I close the distance between us and reach out toward the contusion before I catch how inappropriate it would be to touch him and pull my hand back. "What happened?"

"We were rappelling, and I fell. I told him I was fine because he was expecting me to say I wasn't." Bo gives me a wry smile. "He always turns moments like that into a series of questions. You know—asking me what I'm going to do to get out of it. How would I get back to camp with a broken rib? How would I solve this problem to survive?"

And from just the look on his face, I can see the whole scene—Bo, injured, and needing a father, but only being given a lesson. "What a dick."

Bo shakes his head, suppressing a laugh. "No." He looks past me, almost wistfully. "He's just worried about us. I'm the oldest. If I can't survive out here, then he made a mistake."

I watch Bo for a while in case he wants to continue. When he doesn't, I ask, "Why do you live out here in the woods?"

Bo shrugs. "Well, now, for a lot of reasons. But originally my parents wanted us to be free from the prison of capitalist consumerism that perpetuates the institutionalized torture of both the body and the soul."

He's not joking. If he had a zealot's gleam in his eyes, or if he were trying to convert me in any way, I would be running. But he doesn't. So I nod, because who am I to judge?

"Okay," I say.

"Okay?" he asks, like he knows what he just said is off the pale.

"I grew up Protestant. We worship a guy who said you have to give away everything you own in order to follow him and find peace. Nobody I know has actually *done* that, but it's not the first time I've heard of people chucking everything and living off the land for spiritual growth. It's supposed to be the ideal."

He narrows his eyes at me. "You don't think it's strange?"

"Of course it is," I say with a smile. "But lately I've been thinking maybe strange is more normal than I once thought it was."

Silence builds, and he starts to look uncomfortable again. He takes a deep breath. "Can I see you soon?" he asks a little too quickly, like he's ripping off a Band-Aid.

"Of course," I say. "You still have to teach me how to use that." I gesture to his bow.

"Okay," he says. He turns away abruptly, like he has no idea how to say goodbye.

"I can't tomorrow," I shout. "How about the day after?"

"Sure," he says, and we both go.

I look back once and catch him watching me.

July 21

MILA PICKS ME UP IN HER MINI. SHE LOOKS ME OVER thoroughly, almost as if she expects to have to tell me to go change.

Despite the heat, I'm wearing long jeans, close-toed shoes, and a T-shirt (not a tank top). My hair is pulled back, I'm not wearing any kind of jewelry, and I'm not carrying a purse.

"Did Aura-Blue tell you how to dress?" she asks me.

"I've volunteered before," I admit.

"I should have figured," Mila says as I settle in.

I smile, but not too much, because I can't really read if she meant it as a compliment or a jab. Her tone teeters somewhere just in between, and her face gives away nothing. Just like Jinka, Mila likes to keep you off balance. But that's okay. And because it's okay, I can look out the window and sigh contentedly. It feels good to not crave approval from someone who won't fully give it so she can stay a few steps ahead.

"I know, right?" Mila says in response to my sigh as she takes the turn to Aura-Blue's house. She completely misinterprets it, though. "Volunteering is the best job there is."

Only if you don't need money, I think, but I don't need to say that to Mila. She's trying to be a good person. And at least she didn't say something ridiculous like, "Everyone should do it." The Five of us used to say ridiculous stuff like that all the time.

The truth is, before I created something that got us out of it, all Five of us volunteered regularly. Our mothers were big on charity, or more accurately, charity parties. Socially, you aren't someone unless you have a cause and throw a star-studded ball to raise money for it.

I think about Bo and what he would say about us rich girls volunteering. Probably, "I'll help." For some reason, I don't think Bo judges anyone, including rich girls.

"Thinking about Rob?" Mila asks teasingly.

I'm so thrown I actually sputter. "What? I don't... What are you talking about?"

Mila laughs. "You're love-struck, honey." She slaps the side of my leg as she pulls up in front of Aura-Blue's house. "I get it." She pulls the emergency brake and faces me. "Listen, before anyone else tells you, I want you to hear it from me." Her lovely heart-shaped face is solemn. "Rob and I used to date. Long time ago, though. I've been with Liam for half a year now."

I recall the tension that brewed between Liam and Rob at the barbecue at the first mention of Liam's girlfriend. "Ooohhh," I say, like I just got a joke. "*That's* what that was."

Just then Aura-Blue shouts to us from the house, "Do you guys want some of my mom's fakeon and egg-substitute wraps?"

I roll down my window and shout back, "I'm fine!" I look at Mila. "Did you want some...kind of vegan breakfast wrap?"

"No," she says, thrown. She intended her confession to create more turmoil in me. Rookie. I can't remember the last time I dated a guy that hasn't dated one of my friends first, or the other way around.

"We're both fine," I shout to Aura-Blue, who nods and starts toward the car biting into her wrap. Damn. That actually looks delicious. I should have accepted.

"Wait," Mila says, pinching her eyes shut to give her brain a chance to pan back to our pre-Aura-Blue conversation. "What *what* was?"

"Nothing," I say, waving it away because it would take me too long to explain. "Full disclosure, I used to date Liam."

Oops. From the look on her face, I guess Liam didn't tell her. But Mila doesn't get a chance to reply because Aura-Blue bustles into the back seat of the car in a flurry of tie-dyed clothes and coconut-oil-scented hair.

"Did you hear?" Aura-Blue asks breathlessly.

"What?" I say, twisting in my seat to give her my full attention. I'm done playing this stupid power game with Mila. Hopefully forever.

"The police don't think that woman—you know, the one who got mauled?" she asks, and I nod my head to keep her talking. "They think everything the bear...you know... did to her..." She glances at me in the rearview mirror, trying to not say anything too graphic. "Anyway, the bear's bites happened hours after she was already dead. So the cause of death wasn't the bear. He just happened upon her body in the woods, and..."

"Ate part of her," Mila finishes for her.

"Yeah." Aura-Blue is holding her breath, waiting for us to beg her to continue.

I comply. "Do they know what killed her, then?" I ask.

Aura-Blue goes back and gives us a little exposition to build the tension. "My grandpa was the old sheriff, and he's still really close with the new sheriff. You know, they have a student-sensei relationship. It's really cool," she adds. Too much exposition in my opinion, but she gets back on track. "Anyway, and the new sheriff, Sheriff Whitehall, told my grandpa last night that the FBI is launching a murder investigation."

"Shut *up*," Mila says.

"The FBI?" I ask. "Why not just the sheriff station?"

"She was from out of state, so the FBI has to get involved," Aura-Blue explains. "The coroner said that her injuries weren't consistent with a mauling, but he did find something that *might* be a stab wound."

Mila glances back in the rearview mirror at Aura-Blue. "So you're saying there's a murderer somewhere in the woods just outside our town?" she asks in a too-calm way.

"Yeah," Aura-Blue replies, deflating. On that realization, she's not so happy to be the bearer of all this information. She shakes herself, brightening. "But my grandpa always thinks there's a serial killer lying in wait somewhere in the woods. It's kind of his hobby."

I laugh weakly at Aura-Blue's attempt at a joke, but I notice that Mila does not. She's staring straight ahead, her jaw clenched.

I'm suddenly relieved that I've never mentioned Bo and his family to any of the people in town. The radicalized family living in the woods and hunting deer would be the first suspects.

We drive the rest of the way to the women's shelter in silence. It's not far from our town to Longridge, but the difference is noticeable. Everything is a bit shabbier, less geared toward the adventurous type's picture-perfect seaside vacation. There are more strip malls and gas stations. The spaces between traffic lights have some houses with overgrown lots—a sure sign of foreclosure.

It's still a middle-class town, and a few cheerful mom-and-pop shops in the center are clinging to the tourist appeal of the town's original architecture and its placement on a states-long nature trial, but something's happening to this place. Some kind of rot has set in, crumbling the framework.

When we get to the shelter, I find out what it is. Many of the women sitting out front smoking cigarettes and trying to swallow coffee have pockmarked faces and too-early rotting teeth. Meth. The others are just as skinny as the meth users, but have hollowed-out eyes and wear the dark long-sleeved shirts favored by heroin users everywhere. Meth and heroin have swallowed this town whole.

It's like a plague. So that's why my grandparents are thinking of selling. There was always a line between the summer people and the year-rounders, but I can't imagine any tourist town keeping its appeal with this many addicts. Crime must be off the charts here.

As we get out of Mila's shiny Mini and walk in the back door of the women's shelter, Aura-Blue slips her hand into mine and rests her head on my shoulder for a brief moment.

"It's *so* hard," she whispers.

I put my arm around her and give the tenderhearted girl

a quick squeeze. "Let's find the coordinator," I say brightly. No whining allowed. Mila knows that. She's already marching in the back door with a smile held rigidly on her face.

We show up just as the full-time staff is standing in a circle, holding hands, and saying a prayer to each of their individual higher powers. They end with the chant, "*Keep Coming.*"

Since I'm new, the coordinator, Maria, puts me in the back of the kitchen chopping vegetables. They don't want a newbie out front staring at the women's destroyed faces or bursting into tears when they see one of the blank and starving children that some of these women have with them.

I've chopped before, so I put on my hairnet, apron, and gloves, and get to work. The only rule is to go as fast as you can without slicing off your fingers. I chop. And if it weren't for the onions, I'd love this job. But there are always onions. I'm so blinded by the fumes that my fingers are in danger. I'm relieved when Maria tells me I'm done chopping for the day, and it's time for me to move on to pots and pans. Lunch is over, and the time just flew. I was *busy*. There are a lot of people at this shelter. Too many for such a small town.

As I switch stations and change out my cloth apron for a rubber one, I can't believe the day is half done. And I didn't even think about anything. Nothing. Just…vegetables, I guess. Working one afternoon in a shelter is not restitution. There is no restitution for what I've done. But I do feel something that's almost like peace.

Mila and Aura-Blue are doing the side work out front. I nod to the older woman who supervises pots and pans. She's wire thin, her skin is rough, and she has the ever-shifting gaze of a recovering addict. She doesn't talk to me, but she does call out to one of the other women at another station. Their conversation carries.

I take up a lump of steel wool and scrub a pot big enough for me to crawl into. I try not to butt in. They're talking about who is showing up to meetings and who is back out there. They ask each other when was the last time either of them saw so-and-so. They aren't surprised that Sandy, who's still pretty enough to trick, took off a few weeks ago and didn't come back. They talk about who has died, and who hasn't died yet. Neither of them expects anyone to get out of this alive. Not even themselves.

I finally run out of pots and go look for Maria. She flips through pages on her clipboard and checks my work.

"Good job," she says, her eyebrows raised in surprise. "You work hard."

"I like it here," I tell her. I try not to sound too desperate, but now that I know what an afternoon of almost-peace feels like, I'm not sure what I'd do if I had to give it up. "Can I come back? Regularly?"

"Yeah," she replies.

"Thank you." I turn to go find Mila and Aura-Blue, and Maria stops me.

"They sell these goggles to protect your eyes for when you're chopping onions. Cost about twenty bucks, but you don't tear up," she tells me. And she's smiling now. I haven't seen her do that all day.

"I'll get a pair," I say, and I walk out back where Mila and Aura-Blue are waiting in the car.

July 21 and 22

I GET HOME FROM THE SHELTER, SHOWER, AND FALL ASLEEP.

In the downy haze of a guilt-free sleep, I hear voices. They pull me up, fighting, and I roll over, trying to grasp at the imageless sensation of being worth something again. But it's gone.

I wake up drowning, as usual. I take my meds and gulp down two glasses of water. I stand in the bathroom and wait to feel nothing again. I look out the window.

When I go downstairs, Grandma and Grandpa are still lingering over coffee. I pour myself a cup and greet them. "Rob came by last evening," Grandma tells me. I nod, only now recognizing the sound of his voice at the door. "Thank you for not waking me," I say. "I was exhausted after yesterday."

“He wanted to let you know that he was going to his mother’s place for the next two weeks,” Grandpa tells me.

“Oh yeah,” I say. “He mentioned something like that.”

I trawl my turbid memory and dredge up our first date when Rob told me about his divorced parents. “His mom lives in Seattle, right?”

As I talk, the details, which have become more fluid for me lately, take shape based on the context I’m pouring them into. Now that I think about it, I can almost remember Rob telling me about this.

“Rob goes back and forth between his parents so his mom doesn’t get lonely,” I say, to prove to no one in particular that I was listening to him.

“Nice boy,” Grandma says, like she’s reminding me.

All I can think about is two weeks with Bo minus the irritating thought that Rob will be waiting for me in my grandma’s living room when I get back. And I know that’s not right. I’m going to have to do something about Rob when he gets back, regardless of whether or not anything ever happens with Bo.

Grandpa misreads my dark expression and says, “Don’t be too disappointed, dear. Absence makes the heart grow fonder.”

“Oh my Lord,” I groan. “You’re worse than a greeting card.” I go back up to my room with their snickering trailing behind me.

I can hardly dress fast enough. I throw on a shirt and shorts and tie my hair into a low braid. I put on my hiking sandals when I get downstairs and I see that my grandmother has gone out to the garden. I stop to say goodbye to her on my way to the trailhead.

"Please don't stay out after dark. There are some bad characters in that forest," she tells me.

I pause and shift under my backpack. "What do you mean?" I ask.

She looks up at me and purses her lips, reluctant to talk about unpleasant things.

"You know," she says, and lowers her voice. "*Druggies.*" She looks back down at the row of berries at her feet. "Some bad characters are out there making all sorts of things from the mushrooms and the weeds and heaven knows what else. I don't want you running into any of that sort," she says. Then a thought occurs to her. "You haven't seen any of those people out there, have you?"

Actually, I think I might have. Bo did mention that his father made holistic remedies that he sold in town. But my grandparents don't have any concept of gradation when it comes to drugs that aren't prescribed by a doctor. Put it in an orange bottle with a printed label on the front, and Grandma will chug her uppers and downers religiously, but smoke a little pot, and you may as well carjack a nun.

"No," I lie. "Just me and nature."

"Well, I'm glad. Nature can be very healing," she says, indicating her garden with a proud smile. Gardens aren't nature any more than a tree by the side of the road is a forest, but there's no point in arguing with her. "I've been worried about you out there," she says. "You come straight back here if you do see any druggies, and we'll report them to the authorities."

I don't say I will. I feel bad about lying to her already, and I can't make myself do it again. I thought I was done with that, but there's no way I'm going to narc on Bo just because my grandmother is old-fashioned.

"I'll be back before dark," I promise instead. That appeases her, because everyone knows "druggies" only come out after sundown, and then I'm racing down the trail to the woods.

There's no reason for him to be *there* this early. I'm fully expecting to have to wait for him, but I don't mind the thought of waiting for Bo. I wade through the river, spread out my blanket, and take off my sandals to let them dry. I pull some books out of my backpack, fully intending to read the John Stuart Mill Bo had suggested, but the only book that seems to stick to my palm is my journal. It flops open automatically to where my pen is sandwiched between the pages, like a dog rolling over to show you its belly.

I'll have to get a new notebook soon. This one is nearly full. That can't be right.

"You're early," Bo says.

I look up, and there he is, standing in the ferns like he grew there. He's wearing the same camouflage pants I first saw him in and an old T-shirt that's so faded, I can't tell what color it used to be. Although I've only met him twice before, I'm starting to realize all of Bo's clothes are so old and out of style they're almost in again. Not quite, but you could make a case for him being mistaken for cool by someone. I don't want him to be cool, though.

"You're early, too," I reply.

"I couldn't wait to see you," he says. Then he blushes, second-guessing his honesty. It's as if someone's coached him to hide what he feels from girls, but it doesn't come naturally to him.

"Me neither," I admit.

Another awkward silence that we have no idea how to fill up. He looks around, growing more uncomfortable.

"You know, we don't always have to be talking," I tell him. He looks at me skeptically. "I'm serious," I say. I stand up and go toward him. "If you don't have anything you really want to say, you don't have to say anything."

He frowns, like he knows that can't be right. "But women find emotional connection through dialogue," he says. "They are impressed by a man's ability to express his thoughts and feelings." He speaks in a clinical way, like he's learned all this stuff out of a book. It's adorable.

"Because that's what women want in a man," I tease. "A large...vocabulary." He looks confused. I try to recover from the failed dick joke. "So, what do I do to impress you?" I ask him.

He laughs. "Um...stand there?"

"Like a decoration?" I say, raising an eyebrow, inviting a rebuttal from him.

But he doesn't bite. Instead he shifts from foot to foot, looking miserable again. "I was trying to give you a compliment. I don't think you're...inanimate."

"I know. I was just..." I break off, and I realize that Bo doesn't do banter, sexy or otherwise. I don't think he's ever learned how.

I've never had to work this hard to talk to anyone, and conversation is my forte. I'm good at making people feel comfortable. That's part of the reason I've always been well liked. Well, until you get to know me, that is. What a disaster. I'm going to have to totally switch gears, or this is not going to work out. And I realize that I *really* want this to work out. I've never cared enough about a guy to want that before.

"You know what?" I say. "I'd rather just learn to shoot, and if we don't talk, we don't talk."

He doesn't look like he buys what I'm saying, and I'm not sure I buy what I'm saying, either. How do I connect with a guy when I can't make him laugh, or subtly compliment how he takes a selfie? I wonder why anyone would want to spend time with me if I'm not entertaining him or making him feel like he's an entertaining person. But Bo accepts my no-speaking terms and starts to lead me back to the clearing of the fallen giant.

What follows is two hours of us not saying anything except small exchanges directly relating to the task at hand. I learn how to stand, how to draw, how to aim, and how to release an arrow.

I also learn how patient Bo is. How respectful he is of other people's personal space. How he knows how to correct you without implying that you're doing something wrong first. I also learn that when he's not worried about coming off as a misfit, he has all the self-assurance of an alpha, but none of the swagger. Bo is capable of being entirely himself. It's a brand of confidence I've never seen before because it doesn't require a witness. It's humble. It's magnetic.

I'm sure time passes, but I don't notice a change in the light. Bo must have, because at some point he looks up to the canopy and says, "It's getting late. You should probably go."

"Okay," I reply. We start to walk slowly back toward my blanket. "Thank you," I say.

"You're a good shot," he replies, like I'm the one who did him a favor, although I'm not too sure what he's gotten out of today. "That was fun."

"It was fun," I agree. "I've never learned so much from someone who said so little," I say, and I mean it. I learned more about Bo just by standing next to him for a few hours than I have about myself after years of self-obsession.

Bo is quiet the rest of the way back to my blanket. He helps me pack up. His hands shake a little every time he has to touch me to give me something. I strap on my pack and face him.

“May I see you tomorrow?” he asks haltingly.

He’s still so nervous about asking to see me. “I’d like that, but I have to work tomorrow,” I tell him. He deflates. “The day after?” I offer.

His face brightens again, and he nods shyly, still not trusting that I really want to see him. I come toward him and place a hand over his heart. I feel a seismic heaving in his chest, and I lean forward and kiss him very softly on the lips. It isn’t until after I’m kissing him that I realize my mistake.

I thought this kiss would be a small gesture—my lips briefly brushing past his in a way that is somewhere between friends and more than friends. I know what a tiny kiss like this means in my strata of the world. It would leave a guy not sure where we stood, giving me the upper hand.

Now, kissing Bo, I’m going to have to start all over again. Go back to the beginning and reshape the way I’ve classified physical contact. Because my knees almost give out and I’m falling against him and he’s holding me up, and a little kiss is not so little anymore.

I rest my head on his shoulder and wait for the trees

to stop tilting. I'm wearing a backpack, so he doesn't know where to put his hands, and that's a good thing, because I don't know how I would react to him touching me. I'm going to have to get out of this or...actually, I don't know what. I don't know what will happen if I stay.

"The day after tomorrow," I say, and my voice is too breathy and strange to be mine. And I pull away quickly and bound through the river and I'm running home.

July 23

I'M ONLY HALFWAY THROUGH MY PILE OF DIRTY POTS WHEN Maria comes over to me and pulls me aside.

"I wanted to talk to you for a minute," she tells me.

"Sure," I say. Nervous acid rising up the back of my throat makes the word come out like a chirp.

Maybe Maria found out about me, and she doesn't want me here anymore. I fumble with my rubber gloves, wondering if I should take them off or just leave them on. "Do you need me to move to another station?" I ask, hoping that if I offer her an innocuous course of action, she'll take it rather than tell me I can't come back.

I like it here. No. More than that. I need this. I wipe some perspiration off my brow with the back of my wet glove and smear greasy water across my face.

"I wanted to ask you if you had some more days you could spare?" she asks, almost sheepishly, like she's not comfortable with asking for favors from others.

"Yeah," I say, and then frown. Because then when would I see Bo? "Um, how much more time were you thinking about?"

"I need someone to help me with stocktaking." She's lowered her voice, and she's looking around to make sure none of the resident volunteers hear. "Someone I can trust with the keys, you know? The girl I used to trust took off."

I nod, thinking that she definitely did not find out about me, or she wouldn't be trusting me with anything, really. "When would you need me? It's just I have someplace to be most afternoons."

"You could come in the morning. Early is better. We get some shipments as early as 5 a.m." She hesitates. "Is that a problem?"

"Not at all," I say. "Mornings work better for me, actually."

"Good," Maria says. I feel like that's the end of the conversation, so I start to move away, but Maria stops me. "Maybe don't mention this to your friends," she says, glancing to the front of the house where Mila and Aura-Blue are chatting while they load dispensers with napkins. "They might not understand why I asked you and not them."

I nod, although I don't really understand why she's

asked me, either. Maria and I take a few more minutes to sort out when the shipments come and which mornings I'll need to be here to give Maria a break. I finish up with the pots and meet the girls out by Mila's Mini. That reminds me. I still have to figure out how I'm going to get to the shelter without a ride.

After volunteering, the three of us girls have gotten into the habit of going out for ice cream together. The best ice cream is on the beach at the Snack Shack Rob took me to that first date.

As we wait in line for a scoop, I have the decency to feel guilty about kissing Bo, but not for very long. I'll take care of it when Rob gets back. I don't want to do it over the phone because that's how all my relationships have ended. Usually by text. Rob has been really good to me. In fact, he's been one of the best boyfriends I've ever had, if you could even classify our time together as a relationship. I want to show him the courtesy of making my break-up with him something special, at least. I squash the twinge of guilt I feel and bring my attention back to the conversation in progress.

"It's USC for me," Aura-Blue is saying. "It's in a terrible part of the city, but I don't care. I'll live in a nice area and drive like everyone else in LA. What about you?"

Aura-Blue turns to me, and I realize I'm supposed to supply my chosen college.

"I'm not going this fall," I tell them.

"Year off?" Mila guesses. I don't correct her.

"My dad was set on me going to his alma mater. Yale. My mom always wanted me to go to Vassar, like she did." We reach the counter, and I shrug. "I'm thinking neither."

Mila and Aura-Blue laugh and turn to order.

"Oh, I forgot to put cash in my wallet," Mila says.

"Don't," Aura-Blue says warningly. From the tense look that passes between them, I can tell Mila forgets to put money in her wallet more often than she should for a rich girl.

Mila glares at Aura-Blue before she faces me. "Can you spot me? I'll pay you back."

"Don't worry about it," I reply as I hand her some bills. "I owe you more than this for gas anyway."

All talk of my college choice is buried for now. Technically, I haven't lied to them. Lying is too hard. Lying takes too much energy, and eventually you get caught. It's so much easier not to lie, but instead to have a different truth. The Five of us realized this.

Jinka threw her schoolbag down on Scarlet's shag rug and flopped down on to the beanbag chair beside it.

"If I have to go to one more stupid decoration committee meeting and listen to PMSing prom queens argue about how large fairy lights should be, I am going to lose my mind,"

Jinka said. "Can't we make up something Ali needs us to do every Thursday after school?"

Everyone looked over at me. At that moment, we were ostensibly at Ali's house because all our parents knew that Scarlet's parents were in the Seychelles. The lie we told our parents was that we always went to Ali's after school, rather than her coming to one of our houses, because she had to babysit her younger brothers. Both her parents worked insane hours because they were poor, but we said we didn't mind babysitting with Ali. We liked her brothers because they were cute and sweet.

Our parents loved the idea of us babysitting these pretend children from India for free, and this fake job opened up our schedules, so we could do what we wanted with that time—all while seeming to be the most generous of young ladies, of course.

The contact number that we gave our parents for Ali's house was an Indian restaurant that always answered the phone in Hindi. If our parents tried to call "Ali's house," they wouldn't understand a word of it. Not that any of our parents ever called that number. While they loved the idea that the Five of us were open-minded, that was as far as their involvement with other cultures went. The truth is, none of us would have gotten away with this if all of our parents didn't have their heads firmly up their asses.

Parental heads being as deeply implanted as they were,

the Ali Bhatti alibi had been working for us for over a month now. We went where there were no parents, and one of us almost always had parents who were taking a week in Paris or going on safari in South Africa, so we would always have a place to ourselves. Sometimes we invited boyfriends and other acquaintances over, and sometimes we didn't. We partied a lot that month. It was, without a doubt, the best time I'd ever had in high school.

But this was different. Up until now, Ali was just for our parents. Using Ali to get out of stuff in school could be tricky. Everyone looked at me to figure it out.

"I don't know how we're going to pull that off," I said. "If we want to start using Ali at school, obviously she can't go to school with us, so what school does she go to? How do we know her? Why do we have an obligation to her that would supersede our obligations at school?"

Jinka stared at me with an eyebrow raised.

"I don't have any answers for those questions," I replied defensively.

Jinka threw a pillow at me. "You'll figure it out," she coaxed. "You always do."

I looked around at Scarlet, Olive, and Ivy. They looked between Jinka and me. Jinka's ultimatum was clear. Figure this out or one of them will be my new best friend.

I went over to my bag and pulled out my journal. I opened up a fresh page and started to write while I spoke.

"It'll have to be a club. A club that helps welcome people from foreign countries," I said, but I was just vamping because the pressure was on.

And then I had what I thought, at the time, was a brilliant idea. I actually smiled while I wrote and spoke aloud. "It's a club that not only helps introduce foreign kids to American students so they can make friends, but a club that helps American kids learn more about foreign cultures. The Cultural Outreach Club."

"The Cultural Outreach Club?" Olive said, nearly squealing the words, she was so excited. "That's brilliant! My parents would literally force me to join that club if it were real."

Confidence flared in my chest as I wrote down the bullet points. "We'll need a charter if we're going to register the club with school so we can cut classes," I said. "And we'll need to make up a teacher from another school to be the advisor. We don't want to have to choose an advisor from our school, for obvious reasons. Oh. And a web page. Yeah. We need to upload lots of pictures."

"Of what?" Scarlet asked. I could hear the challenge in her voice, and it only pushed me harder.

"Of our dear friend Ali in a sari for some Indian festival, or Yander from Angola doing whatever rite of passage people in Angola do. The club is just a blog, really." I shrug and keep writing. "I'll just write a few lines about some lesson

learned, download tons of culturally diverse pictures from the web, and post them in between pictures of us dressed up like we're attending some function. Cultural outreach achieved."

A slow clap started. I looked up to see Jinka beaming at me while she clapped, Scarlet glaring at me with barely repressed envy for impressing Jinka, Olive giddy with the thrill of danger, and Ivy shying away with a hint of fear in her eyes that this elaborate lie had come to me so easily. Ivy was the only one who had it right.

The Cultural Outreach Club is where we proved to be more racist and more classist than our parents. We treated other people's cultures as if they were there solely for the purpose of serving our most frivolous whims—fake proof we were enriching lives when really we were somewhere else partying. At least when our parents threw one of their charity balls that were really just an excuse to wear couture gowns and make the society page, some deserving cause got a fat check at the end. We served no one but ourselves.

And I poured myself into it. Writing that blog became my un-journal. It was an account of exactly where I hadn't been and the people I hadn't met.

I stopped writing in my real journal and wrote lies for the Cultural Outreach Club instead. But even before the blog for the Club, I used to write things in my journal that weren't true. They weren't better or worse; they just weren't what happened.

Silly stuff, like I'd lie in my journal about getting a deli sandwich when really I'd had pizza. Or that I'd gotten into an argument with Jinka when I hadn't. I'd lie about the most random things. Maybe it was to embellish my life a little. To smooth out the uglier bits. But sometimes I'd just replace one ugly truth with an equally ugly lie. Honestly, I don't know why I did that. It's not like I expected anyone else to read my journal, not before the blog, so I don't know what the lies were for. Maybe they were for me. Maybe they were what I'd wished I'd done and hadn't. Or maybe it's easier to own up to an ugly lie than the ugly truth. I can't remember.

It's easy to forget what's real when you've spent so much time and care describing what isn't.

July 24

I'm early getting *there* again. But Bo is already waiting for me.

The saying is that your heart leaps, but to me it feels like all of my insides do, which is disturbing. Uncomfortable, even. I have to stop myself from skipping, because skipping is for little girls with pigtails. I almost skip, though.

His lips part in a crooked-toothed smile, and I can see his chest bellow in and out with deep, fast breaths. I'm in the river and freezing from the thighs down, and he's already at the bank to take my hands and help me up the other side. He's so close to me, but still straining just a few inches closer, and then away from me again before his chest touches mine. He does this toward-me/away-from-me vacillation over again, and it's like I can see two halves of him running in opposite directions.

So I kiss him to answer that silent question he's asking me. *Yes*, my kiss says. *You may.*

But he has no idea how.

"I've never kissed anyone before," he admits, frustration and embarrassment flushing his skin. I giggle a little and open his mouth with mine. His hands come up to my face and then drift down to my shoulders. He slips the straps of my bag off them, and he laughs when he finally gets my body free from my backpack. Now he can hold me against him, and now I can show him how to kiss me, but I don't need to anymore because he's already figured it out. He makes a noise somewhere deep inside. It sounds like waking up or remembering.

I don't need anything but this. This kiss is big enough to fill a whole day—a whole day doing one thing so completely it's like you've done everything.

When we finally break apart, Bo helps me open my pack and spread out the blanket. He's still so nervous, I can see that his eyes are unfocused like a sleepwalker's.

"Are you hungry?" I ask.

He nods, and I start to pull out some trail mix I have in my pack, but he catches my hands and draws me to him again. We lie down together, food forgotten, and I rest my head on his shoulder.

He looks up at the canopy and touches my hair. I can feel him getting shy again. I feel shy. I'm never shy.

"This is the strangest thing that's ever happened to me," I say.

He chuckles uncertainly. "Strange good, or strange bad?" he asks.

"Strange perfect," I reply.

He rubs a strand of my hair between his finger and thumb. "Yesterday, when I couldn't see you, I kept telling myself there was no way you were real," he says. He tilts his head so he can see my face. "Where do you work, by the way?"

"At a women's shelter," I say. "I volunteer there."

"The one for addicts?" Bo asks.

"You know it?"

He nods, his forehead creasing with troubled thoughts. "It's one of my father's favorite examples of the failings of Western medicine," he says.

I lift my head and prop myself up on his chest. "I don't see the connection."

"A lot of the women there started on pain pills. Prescription drugs lead to addiction."

Technically true, but an oversimplification. "Your dad knows they have addicts in the East, too, right?"

Bo laughs, his eyes sparkling. "You should tell him that."

We both stop laughing. "You want me to meet your dad?" I ask.

"Yes," he whispers. "I want you to meet my whole family. Is that okay?"

I nod and rest my head on his chest again. I fall asleep.

I wake alone.

"Bo?" I say, looking around, but I already know he's not here. I can feel that he's gone. It's an unnerving thing to fall asleep with someone and then wake up alone. It's like there's a hole in your day—a swath of time where you know something important happened, but you can't remember what it was. I hate that feeling.

As I start packing up my stuff, the initial surprise I felt at his absence turns to anger. Just as I'm working myself up into the thought of never seeing him again, I find a torn-out page from my notebook with blocky, masculine handwriting on it.

> I TRIED TO WAKE YOU UP, BUT YOU WERE SLEEPING TOO DEEPLY. I HAD TO GO. SEE YOU TOMORROW?

Though the page he used to write on is from my journal, I know he didn't peek at my writing while I was asleep—that's not what worries me. Bo has too much respect for others and for himself to trespass in such an underhanded way. What worries me is that I can't see him tomorrow. And now I'm imagining him waiting here for me and me never showing. I imagine his anticipation turning to worry turning to disappointment, and it actually hurts me to think of him being hurt. I tear out a fresh piece of paper and write,

I can't tomorrow. The day after?

I leave the slip of paper under a river rock, right where I usually put my blanket. That's when I notice that he's left me the bow, arm guard, and a few arrows. I smile, thinking how awesome it would be if I practiced nonstop and became amazing enough to impress him.

I put on the arm guard and nock an arrow. I pull back in the long, drawing motion he taught me. My feet are planted. My breathing is steady. I think I'm actually better at this when he isn't with me. I'm calmer. Everything is still. I close my eyes and just hold fast, letting the posture sink in. Letting the wilderness teach me to do something wild.

I hear a rustling in the underbrush and turn to it. I don't think. I don't feel. I loose the arrow.

Something shrieks. The ferns twist in circles as something I can't see struggles among them.

"Oh shit," I whisper.

I realize I'm frozen to the spot. I drop the bow, wrench my numb feet into action, and blunder into the ferns. All I can hear is Bo's voice that first time I met him, when he fell on me, chasing the wounded deer. He said, "I can't leave her like that," and the words echo in me until they become all.

Whatever it is I hit, I can't leave it to suffer, but how am I going to kill it? I don't have a knife.

A rock. I'll use a rock.

I find a sizable rock and clutch it tightly in one hand as I push the ferns back with other. There's blood. A lot of blood. This isn't a rabbit. I picture a fawn, and my stomach heaves. I try to follow the path of blood. The poor creature must have been running in circles.

Whatever it was, it was big. It looks like there are buckets of blood smeared on leaves and ferns, enough so that it's transferred to my clothes as I've been circling. And then—nothing. I double back and try to find a few drops trailing in a new direction, but I can't see anything.

I start stamping down the ferns so I can see more clearly where I've been. I can't find the trail.

I'll do it in quadrants. I have to find this animal and put it out of its misery. I start sectioning off areas, looking for the trail leading out of the panic circles. Nothing.

I start calling out to it. Begging it. Saying it's going to be okay in my most soothing voice as I heft my killing rock.

I don't find it. I find the arrow. Must have come out in the mad whirling circles the creature made. I pick up the arrow and realize I'm covered in blood.

I go to the river. I wash Bo's things first. I leave the bow, arm guard, and arrows with my note. I can't bear to take them home with me. Then I wash my body. Blood has soaked into my clothes and stained my skin. I can't tell Bo. Something in me says he'd be furious with me for doing something so thoughtless, even if it was a million-to-one shot.

I never should have done that. Careless carnage. I thought I was through with that. Shame stains me more deeply than the blood.

By the time I get back to my grandparents' house, dusk is turning into dark.

"I'm here!" I call out as soon as I push in the code my grandmother had me memorize and open the front door. I slip off my sandals and take off my backpack before rushing upstairs to shuck off my bloody clothes. I toss them to the back of my closet and pull on a sundress. Then I rush to the back deck.

"We started dinner without you," Grandpa tells me as I join them outside.

"Sorry," I say, slipping into my seat at the table, my good-girl mask in place. "It got dark fast."

My grandmother has her lips pressed together in disapproval, but she can't get too angry. The last dregs of light don't disappear until after I've served myself some salad, so

I *did* make it back before dark. I can tell she's anxious and feeling a bit out of control. Being asked for advice always makes them both feel like they're in charge of the situation, and luckily I do have something I could ask them.

I don't want to let anyone else down today.

"I need a bicycle," I say. "Any tips about where to buy one?"

"I'll take you down to the Outdoor Shop tomorrow," Grandpa promises.

The Outdoor Shop is an equipment store for outdoor enthusiasts of all kinds—hiking, kayaking, rock climbing, and mountain biking, among other things. It's in the center of town, and Taylor works there. I don't mention that I know all about the Outdoor Shop and don't need him to take me there to pick out a bicycle. Best to just let Grandpa feel like he's helping.

I also decide not to tell my grandparents that I need the bike to get to and from the shelter to help Maria with stock-taking of the inventory—at least not right away. I have to ease them into it. They'll probably object to me being there more. As it is, my grandmother has already asked me a dozen times if three days a week isn't too much responsibility. Morning bike rides shouldn't be an issue, though. She'll probably tell me that they're calming or something. She's always worried about my stress level.

The thing about having a nervous breakdown is that no one ever trusts you to keep your shit together afterward.

July 25

MY GRANDPA AND I GO TO THE OUTDOOR SHOP FIRST THING in the morning.

Taylor is there, and he greets me like we've been friends for years. I can see my grandpa is torn between being happy that I have friends and feeling silly that I don't really need his help. As Taylor leads us down the row of different types of mountain bikes, I make sure to keep asking my grandpa for his opinion so he feels useful—and so that he doesn't feel like I was working him by asking him to come with me in the first place. Which I totally was, but it's better for everyone if he never catches on about that.

While we're at the register paying with one of the credit cards my father gave me, Taylor asks how I like working at the shelter.

"I like it," I tell him. But I have to make light of it so he doesn't sense that what I really mean is that I love it. "And if I ever want to get a job chopping onions in a restaurant, I'll have experience."

"Yeah, Mila mentioned they're keeping you back in the kitchen," Taylor replies. His wincing smile tells me that the kitchen job is probably considered the worst one, so I roll my eyes and throw up my hands.

"I'm the new girl. They're supposed to haze me," I say breezily.

"Yeah, but you gotta get out front to get to know the right girls," he says, like I know what he's talking about. I have no clue what girls are the *right* ones, and the confused look I give Taylor makes him switch gears.

"Do you want me to help you hitch that bike up to your car?" Taylor asks a little too brightly.

I look at my grandfather. "I think I'm going to take her out on her maiden voyage," I tell him.

"All right then," Grandpa says. "See you at lunch."

"I have to get back on the floor," Taylor tells me.

"See ya," I say half-heartedly. To be honest, I'm a little disappointed in him. I never pegged Taylor as someone who classified people as right or wrong. But who am I to judge him? The majority of my life has been about classifying people.

Taylor gives me an awkward one-armed hug, then goes

to accost some tourists who don't need a tent but will probably buy one from him anyway because he's such a charming bastard. My grandpa heads home.

It's still early, so I go back into town to check out the public library. I realize I'm pulling the "girl in a dress on a bike riding through town fetchingly" routine, but I don't care. All I can think about is that I'm going to see Bo tomorrow, and I want to make sure I have something to talk about with him. I'm no longer allowed to use the internet without adult supervision, and I'm okay with that. My phone is locked, and here at the edge of utter wilderness, internet access is spotty at best. It's a relief in many ways. I know I can't ruin any more lives with a few keystrokes and a click. But it does impede my access to information. So if I want to keep the existence of my "druggie" boyfriend hidden from my grandparents, I'm going to have to look things up the old-fashioned way.

Not surprisingly, there is a whole section in the public library dedicated to outdoor living in the Pacific Northwest and to bushcraft in general. It's overwhelming.

I decide to start with the basics. Shelter, fire, water, that sort of thing. I want to be able to ask Bo questions, not stare at him with my mouth hanging open.

This is how I know I really like him. It's not because my joints turn to goo when he kisses me. It's because I want to understand everything about him.

"Planning a hike?"

I turn to find the librarian standing behind me with a mild look on her face. She's a matronly woman, middle-aged, pudgy.

"Not exactly," I say. "Just curious about the outdoors and"—I gesture to the books on the shelf right next to us—"survival."

"If you have any questions, I'd be happy to help," she offers.

So I take her up on her offer. I ask her what books I would need in order to understand what it is to live in the wild with as little contact with society as possible. She gives me a blank look, and then starts pulling books from the shelf. I take three and follow her to the circulation desk. I fill out a library card and take my books home before Mila arrives to pick me up for our shift at the shelter.

When we pick up Aura-Blue, she's as chatty and upbeat as usual, but by the time we're done for the day, I get the feeling that something happened between her and Mila while they worked out front.

At the end of the shift, I'm last out to the car, as usual. Normally the two of them would have the radio on and they'd be talking and texting and sorting out plans for what they were doing later, but today they're just sitting there. The tension between them is painfully obvious.

"Ah...what happened?" I ask as I climb into the back seat, although I don't really want to know.

"Not sure. Maybe you can explain it to her, AB?" Mila looks over at Aura-Blue, but Aura-Blue refuses to turn her head. Mila glances over her shoulder at me and shrugs. "I guess nothing," she says, and then she starts the car and pulls out faster than is necessary, so I know whatever happened is probably Mila's fault.

After we drop off Aura-Blue, I move to the front seat. A strained silence follows until I feel I have to say something about it.

"She seemed upset," I say lightly.

Mila gives me a roguish half smile. "Aura-Blue is a good girl," she says. "Sometimes I'm not. She doesn't like it when I"—she searches for the right word—"stray."

"Oh," I say.

I guess Mila is cheating on Liam. I've kissed him, so I don't blame her. Something like that can really screw with group dynamics, so I can see why Aura-Blue is upset. Still, it's none of her business.

"She'll get over it," I say, shrugging. "It's not really up to her, is it? It's your body."

Mila pulls up to my grandparents' house, stops the car, and turns to me. "I just need a little something *extra* every now and again."

I nod. "I get it." She gives me a disbelieving look, and I smile. "I am no one to judge anyone else about needing extra," I say, thinking about Rob and Bo.

I almost tell Mila all about him. I actually take a breath and open my mouth. I look at her. But she's so much like Jinka. And I feel this deep longing and a bottomlessness that I've never felt from a break-up with a guy. I shut my mouth. I can't go through that again.

"Look, it's summertime," I say. "I've never heard anyone say, 'I should have partied less this summer.' Have you?"

Mila leans her head back on the headrest and runs her palms lightly over the steering wheel. It's a sensual thing—her breathing in, feeling the lowering sun on her face through the windshield.

"No," she says, her eyes still closed. "I've never heard anyone say that." She opens her eyes and looks at me. "I wish you went out with us more."

"I'd only slow you down," I say. I think about Bo, and I know I'm done looking for extra. "I just can't hang anymore."

She nods sagely and doesn't push. "I'm glad you're back in town anyway. Even if you never come out with us."

"Me too," I say.

She gives me hug. I feel her ribs under my hand. "Maybe stay in a night or two, though?" I say hesitantly when we break apart. "You still need to eat and sleep."

She grins at me. "Awesomeness is all the fuel I need." I roll my eyes and grin back at her. The sun glows behind her hair, twice as bright, as if it loves her more than other people. She looks wistful as she leans closer to me. "You're so beautiful," she says.

And then she kisses me. It's a fluttering, barely there kiss. Her skin is warm, but her mouth is cool. I think of a kiss given to me long ago by someone so much like her, I almost call her by the wrong name again. She moves closer, but I stop her.

"I can't."

She shakes herself, like she's as surprised as I am that she kissed me. "I'm sorry," she says, embarrassed.

"No, don't be," I tell her. "But I'm with someone, and I can't do this to him."

She laughs and covers her face. "I don't know what got into me." She scrubs her blushing cheeks and looks over at me. "Just forget I did that."

I pop open my door. "Mila. I sincerely doubt anyone who's kissed you will ever forget it."

She smacks my thigh with the back of her hand. "Get out of my car, you tease," she says, still blushing and grinning.

I laugh and go inside, worried that despite my best efforts, I might be starting to think of Mila as a true friend.

July 26
Morning

IF SOMEONE HAD TOLD ME NINE MONTHS AGO THAT I would be running to and from the middle of the forest every other day looking to hook up with some homeschooled tree hugger who'd never been kissed before me, I would have asked for some of whatever they were smoking.

Because to look at me then, in my up-and-coming-designer-only wardrobe, carrying my "It" bag, and wearing the shoes that you'll need as soon as you see them, you would know that anyone who would guess that in a few short months I'd be making out with a Marxist Mowgli would have to be smoking some pretty powerful shit.

And yet here I am. Literally running to throw myself into Bo's arms. It's pathetic. I've never been this happy before.

I wade through the river. I shuck off my backpack. I'm

hot. I'm cold. I'm effervescing out of my skin. I can't remember feeling anything this sharply before. Not even regret. It's remarkable, considering the current chemical composition of my blood. No, more than that. It's simply remarkable to feel this. Period.

He catches me easily and swings me around, and I wrap my legs around his waist, like we've done this a million times before.

"You're good at catching hurtling bodies," I notice.

"I've had lots of practice," he replies.

I jerk back. "With who?" I demand. I'm jealous—wildly, insanely jealous in an instant. Probably because I feel so guilty about killing some poor animal and I haven't told him. Yet. I'll tell him eventually.

Bo laughs, but his look is cautious when he sees I'm not kidding. "I have five little brothers and sisters," he reminds me. "I can't walk ten feet without one of them jumping on me."

"Oh," I say sheepishly.

"Moth, my littlest sister, thinks it's a game. She jumps out of trees to see if she can surprise me. It's like she's trying to make me drop her."

I imagine a little four-year-old girl tossing herself at Bo, and I soften. "Have you ever?"

"Dropped her? Of course not," he says, like that's a weird thing to ask. And maybe it is. Bo doesn't let people down.

He kisses me. I feel him smiling inside the kiss. The smile builds into a laugh.

"You got jealous," he comments, grinning against my lips.

"Of course I got jealous," I say defensively. "You told me you'd never had a girlfriend before."

"I haven't," he says. And then his eyes slide down. "Is that what you are? My girlfriend."

"Ah...*yeah*," I say. I gesture at my legs, still wrapped around his waist. "This is not the way I greet buddies."

He laughs, and I love the way his laugh feels when I have my legs wrapped around him.

"Good," he says.

He kisses me and lowers us gently down to the ground. He's so strong. Like, gorilla strong, but he keeps it all in check. He slows himself, steadies himself, forces his hands to be gentler. I feel precious under him.

He suddenly pulls back. "What?" I ask.

"Have you had boyfriends?" he asks with a frown.

I know this is going to hurt him, but it's better we just get this over with. In this, at least, I'm going to be honest from the start. So many things I'm withholding already. But this I will tell him. No matter what.

"Tons," I admit.

Words catch in his throat. "How many?" he finally asks.

"I honestly don't remember, but pretty much a different

boyfriend every month or so. Sometimes if he didn't bother me too much, I'd date him for longer, but they always started to bother me. I've never dated a guy longer than three months. I started dating five years ago, so..." I calculate fast. "I'd say I've dated about twenty guys. And I've kissed a couple of girls. My friend Mila kissed me just yesterday, but I stopped her before it got real."

Bo sits up. He's chalk white, and it looks like he's going to be sick.

"Okay. Ask me," I say.

"Ask you what?"

I sit up. "Ask me if I ever gave a shit about any of the boys I've dated."

He looks confused and overwhelmed. "Did you ever—"

"No." He's looking better, but still unwell.

"Ask me if I ever had sex with any of them."

He roils with discomfort, shifting this way and that with no idea which way to look.

"No," I say, answering the question he can't bring himself to ask. "I barely let any of them touch me because I've never wanted anyone to touch me before I met you." I mean, I touched *them*—of course. Something physical has to happen or you aren't really dating, but Bo doesn't ever need to know that. It doesn't matter anyway because it's not like I ever even registered it. The truth is, no guy before Bo has ever touched *me*, inside or out. "So think of it this way," I continue, "there are twenty guys out there who never saw me make an ass of myself running through a freezing cold river to jump into their arms."

He looks down, flattered, but still troubled. "But why did you date them if you didn't want them?" he asks.

"Politics." I laugh at the dumbstruck look on his face. "Not politics like you know them," I amend, thinking of his radical, leftist family. "High school politics."

"I have no idea what that means," he tells me.

I lean forward until my face is barely an inch from his. "I know," I say. And I kiss him. I push him on to his back and climb on top of him.

After a very long time, Bo mumbles, "My mother," around my lips.

I prop myself up over him. "Just a tip. Mentioning your mother while you're making out with someone is never a good idea."

He smiles up at me, holding my hair back with his hands. "I was supposed to bring you home with me today. My mother is expecting us for dinner."

I look up at the canopy, but with no sun and only filtered light to go by, of course I can't tell what time it is. "Can we still make it?" I ask him, because I know he can tell what time it is.

"Yeah," he replies. An anxious look crosses his face. "If you still want to go."

I stand up. “Definitely,” I say.

And then I start to feel worried, too. I mean, really, what do they eat? I’m imagining deer jerky and possum soup. Bo hasn’t really told me much about how his family lives out here. What if it’s disgusting?

“So, what’s your mom making for dinner tonight?” I ask as nonchalantly as I can.

“It depends on her mood.” Bo is quiet while I put on my backpack. When I face him, he says, “You know what? Maybe we should do this another day.”

“Why?” I say. My voice is too high. I sound phony and forced.

“This is a bad idea.” He starts to pull away from me, and it’s like hooks are dragging me with him.

I grab his hand. “I’m an idiot,” I say, pulling him back to me. “I freaked out because you started freaking out, but I don’t care if your mom puts a bowl full of live grub in front of me. I want to know where you come from. I want to know everything about you.”

He looks down while he considers it. “You say that now, but…” He blows out a deep breath and shakes his head.

“But what?” I ask.

He won’t look at me while he speaks. “When the novelty wears off, you’ll just think I’m strange.”

“That’s not going to happen,” I say. He shakes his head,

but I keep talking. "Because I already know you're strange. The good news is, so am I."

He still looks uncertain, so I smile at him and move closer. "Come on." I tilt my face under his so he has no choice but to look at me. "I'm just going to follow you home anyway."

He breaks a smile, at least. "You'd never keep up with me."

"Very true. I'd probably get lost and wander around the forest, starving and..."

He suddenly wraps his arms around me and holds me.

"Don't joke about that," he says, frightened. "People have died out here."

I think about that woman who wasn't killed by a bear and realize that my joke was really tasteless. She might have gotten lost and just...died. It happens here.

"Sorry," I say, still crushed against him. "You'll have to teach me how to hike better. I really should know how to navigate and stuff."

Bo pulls back and looks me over. "Okay," he decides, but only after giving me some serious consideration. "I'll teach you."

"That was a pretty long time you took thinking it over. You were the one who said I was a good student," I remind him.

"Yeah, but this is different from the bow and arrow."

He frowns and looks past me, almost like he's remembering something. "It's hard work."

I'm a little offended that he thinks I don't know what hard work is, but I don't say anything because, if I'm being objective about my life, he's probably right.

True to his word, Bo starts to teach me some basics as we walk mostly uphill to his campsite.

"Okay, let's start with what's in your pack," he says.

"Well, apart from books and my picnic blanket, I have water, energy bars, and a hat," I say.

"That's a good start," he says encouragingly. "But there are a few more things that you should always have with you, no matter what." He ticks the items off on his fingers. "A knife, a way to make fire, a very loud whistle, and a sheet of plastic large enough for you to stay dry under."

In typical Pacific Northwest style, it starts to drizzle at the mention of staying dry. Bo makes me memorize his list and tells me I should always carry it, even if I'm just going into the woods for a few hours.

"But you're not carrying all that stuff," I say.

Bo smiles and says softly, "All I need is flint and a steel knife."

I'm just about to tease him for being the big, tough survival guy, but I think better of it. Bo isn't trying to impress me. He's the furthest thing from macho I can imagine, but he is also a genuine badass. He could probably build a hut, start a fire, kill a wild boar, and whittle a miniature wooden masterpiece with just a piece of flint and that giant knife he has strapped to his thigh.

I feel something touch my arm, and I startle before I realize that Bo is just trying to hold my hand. He shies away, but I reach out and take his hand. We walk like that, hand in hand and silent for a while, before Bo starts the lesson again.

"What direction do you think we're going in?" he asks.

"Up?" I say, hazarding a guess. Bo laughs.

"I meant compass direction, but *up* is right." He looks over at me, and his face turns serious. "If you get confused, remember that town is down."

"Town is down," I repeat.

"There are rises in between, but in general, if you're heading down the mountain, you're headed back home."

"Town is down," I say again, trying to seal it in my leaky memory. "If the zombie apocalypse happens, I'm with you," I tell him.

He gives me a strange look. "Okay," he says, even though it's clear he has no context for my pop-culture reference. He gets quiet and uncomfortable, focusing on the disconnect between us again now that I've gone and underlined it in red.

"That was a dumb joke," I say.

He smiles at me to indicate that he's letting it go, but I can tell it sticks with him.

I look down. "It's a bad habit of mine. When I feel like someone might be better than me, I try to be funny to prove I'm clever."

"I'm not better than you," he says. "And I don't know if that joke was funny or not, but I think you're clever."

"I used to think so, too."

My lie worked too well.

I used to think there was no such thing. How can "too well" mean awful instead of great? But it can.

For three months, our Cultural Outreach Club did exactly what we needed it to. We had an ironclad reason to get out of any meeting or social function that we knew would bore the crap out us. The Five of us did whatever we wanted and we still looked like saints.

If we got "caught" by someone who saw us at one party when we were supposed to be at another, all we said was that the goat-blood ceremony or whatever it was ended early because, duh, they didn't actually kill a goat any more in modern voodoo.

Or whatever. We could seriously make up the most outlandish circumstance and say, "That's how they do it in the Amazon jungle," and nobody would blink an eye. Or we'd say something like, "We stayed until they insisted we drink our own pee to prove our purity. I mean, I support anyone's right to their own culture, but I'm not drinking my own pee."

And everyone bought it—all of our outlier friends, all of our teachers, our parents, everyone. At the center of it all was Ali Bhatti, our alibi. She was the invisible sixth member of our group and the ultimate Get Out of Jail Free card.

"Dad, I'm sorry, but it's Maha Shivaratri. I have to go to Ali's and stay up all night to celebrate the god Shiva."

"Mom, I can't. They're trying to marry Ali off to this savage. We're staying with her all weekend and barricading her in her room so her parents can't do it."

We got hounded by other students who followed my Cultural Outreach blog and wanted to join. We were barraged with emails from kids in other schools who wanted to set up satellite clubs. But that's not when the trouble started. In fact, that's when the real fun began. We were the most popular girls pretty much ever, and we had more power over the student body than the Dean.

I got creative with the blog. I did research into oppressed cultures and wrote scathing posts about fear and genocide and the importance of celebrating our differences. I "learned" some deep moral truth every week from some fake refugee I had "met." Shit, I used to make Jinka cry with some of the horrific backstories I fabricated. My un-journal was a hit.

All that praise made me bold. I wrote a five-part series

following one imaginary immigrant boy from Guatemala up through Mexico and into Texas. Jinka was hooked on that story. She had me print out hard copies of it so she could put her head in my lap as she read. She devoured the heartbreaking finale with the lights low and a bottle of pilfered wine split between us. That night, the line that separates friends from more than friends blurred a little. The next day, it was forgotten. Most girls experiment eventually, we told ourselves, and nothing really happened anyway.

Then our club was nominated for a humanitarian award. An actual adult humanitarian award that some people spend a lifetime trying to win. So we did the only thing we could. We stuck together and went along with it.

This is how I know I'm a sick person: Even though I was exploiting every culture I could read about on Wikipedia and telling lie after lie to glorify myself, from my rich, white, privileged point of view, I was convinced I was doing good because I was "raising awareness."

I actually believed I deserved to win that award.

July 26
Afternoon

WE ARRIVE AT BO'S HOME AFTER A VERY LONG HIKE ALMOST completely uphill. I'm exhausted. This is, hands down, the most effort I've ever put into a guy.

The woods turn into something like a trail, which suddenly crests and opens into a bowl-shaped clearing. I look around the open space. The ground is kept free of brush, and a large firepit dominates the center. There are seven canvas teepees set around the firepit in a circle. Where the most light is piercing through the canopy above, there is a fifteen-foot-long greenhouse that arches over the ground in a half cylinder of plastic and metal ribbing.

"We make our medicines in there," Bo says, gesturing to the teepees. "But we live up there." Bo points up into the trees. I follow his gesture.

"Oh my God. You live in a tree house," I say, staring up. There are several structures spanning across the largest trees that ring the outside of the clearing. Wooden-slatted rope bridges connect the different structures, and more ropes hang down to the ground, weighted on one end by rocks. I swear I saw something almost exactly like this in the Kevin Costner version of *Robin Hood*, so I know that those ropes with rocks at one end are a kind of pulley system to help raise and lower heavy objects to the ground with less effort.

"Wow," I say, because that's the first thing I think. The second thing I think is, *Where do they go to the bathroom?* but I don't want to ask yet, even if I really need to use the bathroom.

I notice that Bo has gone silent while I'm staring, so I look over at him and see him watching me nervously. "This is the coolest thing I've seen outside of a movie theater," I say honestly, and his face breaks with relief.

We're interrupted before we can speak any further.

"I don't care whose turn it is," a shrill boy's voice screams. "I made it; it's mine!"

Two mostly naked, dirty bodies erupt from one of the teepees and tumble across the ground in a tangle of skinny arms and boney knees. Nearest I can tell, two boys—both of them about ten—are fighting desperately over something clasped in the slightly larger boy's right hand.

A woman (inference tells me this is Bo's mom) bursts

out of the greenhouse and sprints at an enviable pace to the brawling boys. And it's a good thing, too. These two aren't pulling their punches. They both know how to fight, close-fisted, grown-man-style fighting, and they are truly beating the snot out of each other.

Their fleet-footed mom is a lean, graying woman with long limbs and a deep alto voice. From her first words, I know this isn't the kind of woman you screw around with.

"Karl! Drop it now!" she orders. She doesn't raise her voice—not in the way most women do when they get angry. Her pitch lowers, actually, and it takes on this rumbling quality that isn't loud but can't be unheard.

The bigger one—Karl, I'm assuming—lets go of whatever he's holding in his right hand, and the smaller one snatches it up tearfully.

"Aspen. Give it to me," their mother says.

Aspen shuffles from foot to foot in the same way Bo does when he's feeling tortured and rubs at his streaked face. One look at his mother's dark, piercing eyes and he knows he's not going to win this. He gives her whatever it is he fought so hard for.

She balls it into her hand and puts both fists on her hips. "Go upstairs. Both of you," she says in a quiet, almost tender voice.

They run away in step, and their mother calls after them, "Not together! One of you go to Ariel, and the other to Roost." They both pause. Then, reluctantly, they split up, and one of them goes to a structure on one end of the circle. It has a sign painted in red over the door that says *Ariel*. The other boy goes to a tree house structure that is as far away from it as possible. Above this door in purple is painted the name *Roost*. A quick glance around, and I see that all of the dormitories have different names painted above them, each in a different color of the rainbow.

Bo's mother faces me. And I almost pee a little. "You're late," she informs me.

"I am," I agree. "I'm slower than Bo." Honesty is best, I figure.

She gives me a little smile. "Most people are." She turns away from me. "Raven, make sure you shut the greenhouse before the crows get in there again," she calls calmly to a sullen-looking girl, who scurries to shut the door. There are some cock-headed crows hopping in their sidling way to the unguarded treasure trove of food. Raven scatters them with a few well-placed kicks as Bo's mom turns back to face me.

"Do you like vegetable stir-fry?" she asks.

"Love it," I reply.

"Good." She turns away from me again, making something of a show of how little attention she needs to afford me, but I know she's already studied me closely. She's seen my hiking sandals, and they're the best. She's ticked her eyes over my designer jean shorts and artfully distressed

T-shirt and knows how much they must have cost. Sizing someone up on the sly is an art. I've been given the once-over by a master.

And then it hits me. She used to have money. Probably a lot.

"You can help me cook it, then," she says. "Come with me."

Bo gives me a panicked look, but I smile at him and say quietly, "I'll be fine," as I move to follow her. He's reluctant to let me go with his mom, but I'm not. I've been hazed by the best of them, and I know it's better if she and I get this out of the way in private.

She takes me into the greenhouse, and I see right away that this is a bold move. Half of the growing things are edible—tomatoes, beans, cucumbers, carrots, potatoes, peppers, and the like. The other half of the growing things are cannabis plants.

"Hydroponic," I say absently, admiring the setup. The rows of tables are actually tanks with water circulating in a pump system. I can faintly hear the generator, but it's very quiet.

"Solar-powered," she says, nodding. "The panels are dispersed across the different dormitories. That's why we live in the trees in a circular pattern. To give the panels a little light every day, every season."

I admire the rich growth. "My grandmother would kill

for this kind of yield," I mumble, touching the swollen bellies on a vine of cherry tomatoes. I see something at the bottom of the tank flash pale and then disappear. "Are those fish?" I ask.

"Uh-huh. Catfish," she says. "They're bottom feeders. They clean the water. They were Rain's idea. He caught a few wild, raised them, and proved that they could create their own ecosystem. And now we eat fish once a week without having to work for it."

I turn and look at her. "Who's Rain?" I ask. Bo never mentioned a Rain. "Bo's dad?"

His mom gives me a strange look. "Bo. He never told you his full name is Rainbow?"

I turn away from her and gesture to the cannabis. "Bo told me you make herbal remedies," I say, purposely using the version of his name I have known, without answering her question.

"The cannabis is used in several salves. It's a powerful analgesic."

She looks at me, waiting for a comment. I don't fall for it. There aren't enough plants in here for them to be real drug dealers. And honestly? So what if they sell a little pot on the side? I'm not the purity police.

"I've heard it has many medicinal uses," I say casually.

"You've *heard*?"

"Yeah. But I've only ever smoked it to get high."

She laughs, and I feel like I'm getting somewhere with her. She respects honesty, and she can smell bullshit from a mile away. Good. She hands me a basket and tells me to pick the vegetables I like to eat. But she's a pro. Now that I'm relaxed because I think she's relaxed, she drops the bomb on me.

"What are you doing with my son, rich girl?" she asks.

What *am* I doing with her son? I pause and really think about it.

"Well," I say. "I guess I'd have to tell you about me, or it wouldn't make any sense."

"I'm listening," she says. And she really is.

"It isn't pretty," I warn.

"Okay," she says, and there's no judgment in her eyes. She wipes her hands, leans up against the potting table and crosses her arms, waiting. "You'd better start at the beginning."

Do I want to do this? I look her in the eye, and I already know two things. The first is I'm here because she wanted me here. The second is if I don't come clean to her right here, right now, I'll never see Bo again. She'll make sure of it.

So I tell her. Like a reporter, I tell her everything. I tell her about the Five of us. I tell her about Ali Bhatti. I tell her about the Cultural Outreach Club and how far it went. Without feeling, I tell her about how it all fell apart—Rachel's bat mitzvah—and how my friends turned on me. I tell her about my breakdown, the hospital, and the drugs they put me on. I even tell her some of the things I did while I was at the hospital. Didn't think I was going to do that, but I do. I haven't even said Rachel's name in my own head since it happened.

It helps that I stick to the facts. I'm not actually going through it again. I'm not reliving it, or faking feelings about it that I don't feel yet. I'm just giving her the facts.

She never flinches. Never backs away from me in horror. Never grimaces with disgust, though what I'm saying is disgusting, and the way I'm saying it is so unfeeling and inhuman. She just looks at me with patience and a little bit of sadness. So I keep going, because a part of me is scared that if I don't recount everything, I might forget it.

I don't want to forget it. I don't deserve to forget it.

I tell her the whole truth. It's too much to dump on someone, and too soon to do it. I know that. But here's the thing. By the time I am ready to tell her this stuff, it will be too late. That's always the way it works. You wait until you trust someone to reveal your darkest bullshit, but by then that person feels betrayed that you didn't come clean right from the start.

If she's going to hate me and forbid me to see Bo again, I want her to do it now, not when I've grown to trust her. Because by then, it would hurt too much. Like it's going to hurt when I tell Bo. I just want a little bit longer with him. And then I'll tell him.

When I'm finally done talking, she stares at me for a long time.

"Stop taking the clozapine. It can cause thrombocytopenia—fatal blood loss, from even a minor wound," she tells me.

"Among other things," I reply, nodding. "Every two weeks I have to get my blood tested."

"It's excessive," she says, shaking her head as if she can't understand it. "I mean—*clozapine*."

Clozapine is the nuclear option when it comes to antipsychotics, and I'm on the highest dosage my doctors at the hospital were willing to risk. A paper cut wouldn't make me bleed to death, though the cleanup might require a mop. It is dangerous for a dozen different reasons, but it works.

"You had a true response to a traumatic situation, and no one helped you. Not the doctors at the hospital. Not your *parents*," she says, like parents would be the last to abandon a child. Which they would, I suppose, if they weren't mine.

"They were too embarrassed," I say. Schizophrenia runs like wildfire in my family. It's the dirty little secret creeping stealthily up the ladder of our otherwise pristine DNA. "My parents can't even look at each other anymore, let alone me. I can't really blame them. I did a lot of shit that's just wrong." I look off, shaking my head. "I don't know why, really. I guess I was angry."

She nods gravely. "You did plenty of wrong things. But

did anyone ever take the time to teach you how to do the right thing with your anger?"

I smile ruefully. "In my family? We don't feel ugly emotions like anger. We drink Long Island Iced Teas and pop pills instead."

Her brow creases in sympathy and she hugs me. She smells like Bo, but in a softer way. I melt into her. I'm not crying. I still can't feel deeply enough to cry with the piles of Prozac gurgling away in my stomach, but the melting feels good.

We pick and chop vegetables and talk some more about how I'm going to move forward with my life.

"I'm not going to lie to you," she says. "If you go off these drugs, it's going to feel like you got hit by a bus. But it's *your* bus, you know?"

"Yeah," I say, nodding. "I've been waiting to feel something. When I'm not around Bo, that is." I laugh at myself. "So, to answer your original question—the reason I'm with your son is because he's the only person who makes me feel. It isn't always good, especially when I'm waiting for him, and I don't know if he's going to show or not. But I feel. He's managed to switch on a corpse. He's gotta be magic."

"Oh, he is," she says softly. Our eyes meet, and I realize we will always be able to agree on one thing: her son.

We're going to get along really well, I think.

At first I wondered why anyone would have so many

kids. Somewhere in the back of my head, I assumed she'd have to be some kind of Earth Mother hippie person, but that's not it. She just has a lot of love and a lot of patience, and the good sense to give both to as many children as she can. It dawns on me I don't know her name, so I ask for it.

"Maeve," she replies. "Maeve Jacobson." She holds out her hand, and I shake it a little self-consciously. In her way, I know she's telling me that from this point on she's going to be treating me like an adult. And she doesn't disappoint. "You are beautiful," she says regretfully. "I hope you're on birth control."

I'd be embarrassed, but—you know—clozapine, Ativan and Prozac, just to name a few. Puny emotions like humiliation don't stand a chance. Instead I give a little rueful smile.

"My mother's idea of being maternal was to put me on the pill as soon as I had my first period." I try to laugh, but it's not funny. "She didn't even ask me if I liked boys."

Maeve is quiet for a while. She frowns at her hands as they pick zucchini. "Mothers try to do what wasn't done for them but should have been. We think we're correcting some horrible wrong, but sometimes we're just inflicting a different kind of wound." She looks up at me and glances around at the general state of her present life with a fair dose of self-doubt in her eyes. "Ask yourself why she did that. And then ask her."

"If she ever speaks to me again, I will," I promise. And

I promise myself to ask Maeve the same question someday. But not yet.

I don't have to tell Maeve not to tell any of this to Bo. She knows telling him is my responsibility. And now that I've told her, the clock is ticking. Maybe that's another reason I told Maeve. Her knowing will force me to be honest with Bo sooner rather than later.

When we finally come out of the greenhouse, everyone is casually/not-so-casually hanging around the firepit. Bo is standing next to a man he resembles so strongly, there's no need to wonder if it's his father.

Bo's father is one of those people whose brain processes so much information so quickly that they blink their eyes really hard and fast when those inner gears start turning. Almost like a twitch. A kid in my elementary school did it, and he got transferred to genius school in the third grade. Even through the genius twitch, I can tell Bo's father isn't happy to have me here.

"Hi," I say, forcing a smile. He shuffles his feet and screws his face up at the ground in lieu of a smile, his eyes blinking rapidly.

"That's Ray, my husband," Maeve tells me. *It's okay*, she mouths silently. Like that's going to make me feel better about the fact that Ray definitely does not want me here.

I move to Bo's side while everyone else stares. On my way, I have to brush past the oldest girl. She's fifteen, maybe sixteen.

"Raven?" I guess. I smile at her, but she doesn't smile back or answer me.

She's dark-haired and dark-eyed and obviously has some opinions about my expensive clothes. They are not charitable opinions, but if memory serves, when you're fifteen very few thoughts you have are charitable ones. She's wearing a hand-sewn patch dress made out of what looks to be several different T-shirts. It's cool, actually, but it's too soon to compliment her. My hiking sandals have caught her eye, despite the fact she's decided to loathe me as a decadent capitalist.

Hovering close in her shadow, and obviously taking her cues from Raven, is another, much younger girl. She looks about six or seven, I guess. I smile at her and give a little wave.

"That's Sol," Bo tells me. Sol's holding the youngest and hikes her up a little higher and tighter as a way to look over and check with Raven if it's okay if she smiles back at me. It isn't, so she doesn't.

"And that's Moth," Bo says, his fondness for the youngest apparent in the way his voice softens.

Moth smiles at me from her sister's hip, with a grubby finger stuck in between her baby teeth. Cutest kid ever. She's practically edible. Rosy cheeks, big pouty red lips like Bo's, and the same blonde hair that runs on the father's side. She's only wearing cotton shorts and a handmade necklace of shells and twine, like some ocean sprite.

The two boys who were fighting earlier blush and smile, then frown, and generally don't know how to act in front of me. Both of them are trying really hard not to look at my legs. The bigger one, Karl, has a blue bruise forming under his right eye. I guess Aspen is a leftie like Bo. They're both dark like their mother, and I don't know if it's because my first sighting of them was when they were tangled up together or not, but I'll probably always confuse the two of them unless I see them standing right next to each other.

Before the silence gets overwhelming, Maeve steps in and gives everyone a task. Bo pulls me aside, his eyes wide and anxious.

"You okay?" he asks.

"Of course," I reply, facing him, grabbing both his hands, and leaning toward him. I need to fill up on him. "Your mom is amazing." His face breaks into a huge grin.

"What did you talk about?"

"Later," I say. And I will tell him everything I told his mother, and then some. Just not right now. "Are you okay?"

He nods, but his eyes shoot over to his father and Raven, who are both watching us with narrowed eyes.

Maeve saves us all from another long, awkward silence by doling out more chores for everyone, and in moments the freshly stir-fried veggies are divvied up into little wooden bowls with rice and some kind of spicy sauce that is just divine. We all take mismatched chopsticks and sit cross-legged on the ground together. Maeve starts asking her children questions about their day and lets me sink a bit into the background. I stay close to Bo's big body, sharing his silhouette.

The younger kids get swept up in their own stories and forget I'm there, tucked into Bo's shadow. Soon I'm listening to an exciting recounting of Karl and Aspen's hunt at dawn this morning, and how they came across a mountain lion that was tracking the same herd of deer as them. They're good storytellers, and the rest of the family listens completely. No one is waiting for a text message or thinking about something that might be more interesting than this. They're just listening.

A part of me is aware of the danger that Karl and Aspen were in this morning, but since no one else reacts with alarm, I don't say anything. What do I know about mountain lions? Maybe they're more scared of people than we are of them.

As Sol takes over recounting her day, Moth makes her way over to Bo and scoots herself into his lap. He makes room for her, holding her absently against him, like his lap is her personal story nook.

Dinner flies by, and before I know it I'm standing over a tin washbasin doing the dishes. I choose to wash, and Bo dries. Flush with calories, Sol and Aspen are running around, tickling Moth and howling like wild animals. Under cover of the din, Bo and I stand as close to each other as we can, our arms touching. His lips are set in a small smile, and his eyes are soft. It's gorgeous torture, just standing here.

When we're done, Maeve asks Bo to get more firewood from the pile before he walks me home. As soon as Bo is gone, Ray approaches me, and I realize Bo and I have been strategically split up for something. Maeve is *good*.

"Do you have any food allergies? Eggs, nuts, milk, shellfish?" Ray asks.

"N-no," I stammer.

"This will help with the withdrawals," he says gruffly. He places something in my hand. I look down and see it's a small leather pouch. "Take one in the morning instead of that poison they're forcing on you. Let it dissolve under your tongue," he tells me. His stony expression gives way to caring for a brief moment. I see Bo written all over him. "Ativan is highly addictive. Quitting won't be easy."

I open the pouch and see a pile of tiny white pills that look like beads. "Thank you," I say, still not sure if I'm going to use them or not.

A part of me wants to know what it would be like to feel again. Another, louder part of me is screaming that going off my meds without a doctor's supervision is about the stupidest thing anyone can do. People can *die* doing that.

But Bo's father is a doctor. While I don't think he'd advise me to do something that could kill me, he and his family do have outlier views on Western medicine that I don't agree with completely. I respect his and Maeve's holistic approach, but I've got problems that can't be fixed with some essential oil and a better diet.

Bo joins us cautiously. Ray turns to him and says, "You should be getting her back now," and he walks away.

Bo takes my hand and starts to lead me away. I stop him for a moment so I can say goodbye to Maeve. She gives me a hug.

"We'll be seeing you soon," she says with a knowing smile.

"Definitely," I reply, although she seems to be the only one inviting me back. My eyes flick over to Ray and Raven, just to make sure they are as disappointed by Maeve's invitation as I think they'll be. Disappointment doesn't cover it, though. They look downright dismayed. If I weren't on so many drugs, it would hurt.

Everyone pauses to watch Bo and me go, and then, after we've crested the rise that obscures Bo's camp from any approaching view, piping voices rise up in question and are hushed before I can understand what's being asked.

"Was that okay?" Bo asks me after a while of walking in silence.

"Yeah, except for one thing." I wait for him to turn toward me anxiously as we walk to say, "You never told me your full name was Rainbow."

I'm about to tell him my full name, but his face darkens.

"Someone told me once it was a girl's name. A *stupid* girl's name was what he said, actually."

"Who told you that?" I ask, but Bo shakes his head.

"I had a friend from town once," he says quietly. "I thought he was a friend, but I guess I wasn't cool enough for him."

"What happened?" I ask.

"We always did everything together. Fishing, tracking, hunting," Bo says. "Then when we were thirteen, it changed. He didn't want to be friends anymore."

I see Bo's face flush red with humiliation. He's so easy to read. It's like his face is a beach, and everything swirling around in that ocean inside of him washes up there eventually. So, this is why he thinks I'll find out he's strange and cut him off.

"What happened?" I repeat, louder. I'm angry now because I can see it all like a sad little movie in my head. Two young boys meet out in the woods. They become best friends. And then, one day, the city boy starts caring about clothes and who sits with whom in school, and all the bullshit that was my bread and butter not too long ago, and Bo is nothing to him anymore. And some dickhead breaks the biggest heart I've ever stumbled upon in my ridiculous excuse for a life. "Who was he?" I ask.

Bo looks over at me, suppressing a smile. "I'm sorry I brought it up," he says gently. "It's okay."

"It's not okay," I snap. I realize I'm yelling. "Just tell me his name and *he'll* be the sorry one," I promise.

Bo looks troubled. "I believe you," he says. "That's why I'm not going to tell you."

Then he's kissing me, and I can't be angry anymore because my thighs are on fire. How does he do it? I mean, *really*. I'm on the same dosage they give PTSD war vets. I'm supposed to be emotionally bulletproof.

But I can feel Bo. He's so real. So present. Every sound I make, it's the first time he's ever heard anything like it. Every place he touches me, it's the first time he's ever felt that. Our clothes come off easily. Clothes used to be so important to me. Now I see them as nothing but layers of bullshit that separate me from him, and I can't wait to be free of them.

It'd be so easy to slip into symbiosis, just one body instead of two. It would be the most natural thing in the world. Like coral—half animal, half plant. Me, red in tooth and claw, and Bo, green and open to the wide sky. The line between us is already blurred in every way but the physical. He and I were always meant to share a body, I think.

Still, I stop him.

"Wait," I whisper, pushing his hips away from mine. "I've never done this before."

He's flushed and pale and shivering and sweating and coiled tight and loose as melted wax and vulnerable and powerful and pretty much the whole world and everything in it to me right now.

"I'm sorry," he whispers, pulling back. "Did I hurt you?"

"No." I roll my eyes a little. He could kick me down a mountain, and it wouldn't hurt me. I'm frigging Teflon. "I just think, maybe not here, right now," I say, looking pointedly at the leaf litter we've stirred up around us and the sticks poking us pretty much everywhere we've managed to shimmy out of our clothes.

Bo laughs sheepishly as he sits up and pulls on his shirt. The getting-mostly-naked bit happened fast. Like, really fast. I think it scared him. And now I'm worried. I don't want anything about him to change, especially not the way he throws himself at me with a boldness that can only come from utter innocence. I love the way he's shy-not-shy.

"Look, Bo, it's not that I don't want to," I begin, but his head suddenly spins around and his entire body tenses.

"Shh," he hisses, and goes still. He listens intently for a moment, his eyes scanning, and one of his hands stretched out to me.

Moments pass. His tension dissipates but doesn't disappear.

"Come on," he says hastily. He helps me up to my feet, and we hurry on our way.

I know enough to stay quiet until we're nearly back to *there*.

"What was it?" I ask. "That noise you heard."

Bo shakes his head. "Not sure." He shrugs and lets out a long breath. "Maybe nothing." He looks up at the canopy. "It's almost sunset."

"I'll have to run," I say, finally noticing a shift in the light after so many days out here. "You should get back, too. I don't want you stumbling around after dark."

Bo opens his mouth to argue, but he can't. It simply isn't safe to go hiking at night with no flashlight. Even with a flashlight, it's extremely dangerous.

"Bye," I say, but Bo catches my wrist and pulls me back toward him.

"I know you want to," he says. It takes me a moment to recall that he's addressing what I said before we were interrupted.

"Oh, you *know*, do you?" I say huffily.

His smile is almost cocky, but it isn't. It's confident. The difference is ego. Bo has none.

"I'll go as slow or as fast as you want," he tells me. "You're in charge."

Well, now I can't be mad at him. Especially since he remembered what I'd said long after I'd even forgotten about it. Bo listens. He's a better listener than anyone I've ever met.

We kiss for longer than we should. By the time we make plans to meet back here the day after tomorrow, even this long summer day has had it.

"Be careful," he tells me sternly. "If you see or hear anyone on the way back, get off the path and go around them. No one out here after dark is out here for a good reason."

I'm about to crack a joke about him and me being out here after dark, but I can tell he's in no mood for that. I nod and plunge through the icy river, already sprinting by the time I reach the far bank.

July 27

SO HERE IT IS. MORNING. FIVE AMBER-COLORED BOTTLES with childproof caps sit in a neat row on the shelf in the medicine cabinet behind my bathroom mirror. And a leather pouch full of don't-know-what sits in my hand.

I'm already drowning, like every morning.

No, actually I think I'm burning. But it's not where I am right now that scares me. It's not that this, as uncomfortable as it is, is unbearable. It's the thought that it might become unbearable that makes me think I should take my meds. I am an ant under a beam of light that will only grow brighter and hotter.

But taking my meds is what I did yesterday. And the day before. And I'm not better. I still haven't paid for what I've done.

So here it is. Decision time.

Okay. This is a terrible idea. No one in the history of the world has ever had something *good* happen to them when they either started or stopped taking prescription medication without a doctor's supervision. But maybe Ray, the radical hippie genius in the woods, knows more than those quacks I had at the hospital. The doctors at the hospital didn't really want to help me. They just wanted me to obey them. One of the possible side effects of clozapine is sudden death, and those doctors put me on it. On the other hand, Ray seems like a zealot when it comes to holistic healing. His beliefs could be clouding his judgment.

Stopping my meds could kill me. Continuing on my meds could kill me. I have no idea who to trust anymore. Well, fuck it. I'm just going to be chopping onions and scrubbing pots at the shelter. I don't need to be anything but what I really am today. Tomorrow I might choose something else, but today—just today—I'm going to take the Gandalf pills from Bo's renegade genius doctor father, and if my heart stops, I'm pretty sure they'll have a kit at the shelter to revive me. In fact, a drug rehab shelter is probably the best place for me to be while I come down off my meds.

I try to think about nothing while I let the little white bead dissolve under my tongue, but the truth is I'm thinking about Bo. I'm wondering if I'm doing this for me or for him.

The answer will determine my success, but I honestly

can't tell right now, with Bo looming so large in my mind. I hope it's for me, but I'm pretty sure it's because I want to be the real me *for* him. That might still count as a good thing, though. This is the first time I've wanted to be the real me for any reason in a long, long time. Maybe ever.

I go downstairs to have breakfast with my grandparents. Is the sun always this bright?

I drink a cup of coffee and try to follow along with the conversation, but it's like I'm only catching one in three words. The rest of the time, I'm fighting the urge to simply leave. They are ridiculous. How is it we've never talked about my time in the hospital? Worse—we've never spoken about why I was there to begin with. We just talk about the crap other people are saying about each other. And the weather.

They aren't evil. They are pleasant people. We always have pleasant conversations. They were even pleasant when they agreed to let me stay with them, even though they knew it was because I had made myself into a pariah.

Here's the problem with always acting like everything is pleasant: zero accountability. My mother may be schizophrenic, but that's not why she's such a disaster. She grew up in a place where anything less than pleasant was hushed up and locked away, rather than dealt with openly.

My dad is the exact same way—when he's around. He doesn't do complicated or hard. If things get messy, he leaves. I think my mom chose him because that's what she was used to. Or at least, that's what she was used to manipulating. Not that it's been better for her in the long run. My mother never became a fully functioning human being because she never learned to itemize her bullshit and call it her own.

And neither did I. Until I found myself in boiling hot water for the first time, and it was sink or swim. Of course I drowned. Or burned. Still haven't decided which metaphor I'm going for on this one.

"I've really got to get going," I say, standing suddenly.

My grandparents look at me, shocked. I have no idea what I just interrupted, but it's totally awkward. They were saying something about the sheriff and the investigation? And then something about "those druggies out there in the woods," I think. Wait. Did they say something about *another* body found in the woods?

"Did I mention that I'm doing inventory now at the shelter?" I add as an excuse for my hasty departure.

"Yes," Grandma replies. "Several times." Her eyes widen anxiously.

"I'm kidding," I say, nudging her shoulder. "I know I've told you; I'm just reminding you how awesome I am at chopping onions." I smile, but she still looks hesitant. "I'll see you guys later," I say breezily as I hurry out to the shed to get my bike.

It's rather a long bike ride to the shelter from where I live with my grandparents, but I've never minded it. I didn't get many chances to ride bikes in New York City, so I've always seen it as a leisurely activity. Something you do in Central Park on a carefree day when you're feeling extra whimsical.

Today the wind on my face is soothing. The exertion keeps my mind in one place instead of scattered across a million different narratives. I press down on the pedals and feel my breath go in and out, and that is enough to keep me focused for now.

When I get to the shelter, I take a quick look at the delivery receipts on the spike in Maria's office and check to see that everything was logged on the clipboard that hangs just outside the walk-in. Then I go inside and count boxes.

You'd think no one would steal asparagus, but it happened just the other day. Junkies will literally steal anything. The woman who did it couldn't even sell the asparagus and ended up bringing it back. Maria fed her one last time and told her she couldn't come to the shelter anymore. I could tell Maria felt bad about it as she watched the woman weep uncontrollably. Then Maria said, "Rock, meet bottom," and walked away.

The woman stopped crying immediately. Like a spigot turned off. It was impressive, but I've seen better.

Jinka could talk and cry at the same time. Sobs sighed in and out of her effortlessly, and her nose didn't even run. Water flowed only from her eyes and slid off her sculpted jawbone like one of those miraculous statues that weep in everlasting perfection. And, while weeping, she'd tell her version of the story with such eloquence, how could it be anything but the truth?

"She was starting to scare me. She was scaring all of us. She took it so seriously, like it was real, and then it just kept getting worse and worse, and we all wanted out. But she wouldn't let us. It was like she believed it all," Jinka said as she wept.

And they had proof, in a way. It was in my notebook, written in my handwriting. I did all the posts online, even though the rest of the Five stood over my shoulder while I wrote. They told me how good my stories were. How amazing it was that I could come up with all of this in my head.

Jinka even called me a genius.

"Are you okay?"

I spin around and find Maria behind me. "Sure. Yeah. Just counting," I say.

Maria raises an eyebrow. She takes the clipboard and sees that the box count is completed, and her expression changes. "Sorry," she says, "but you were standing so still. I thought you'd fallen asleep on your feet."

I smile and scoot past her on my way to the chopping station. I'm not okay. Every second my body filters out more and more of the drugs. Soon, I'll be me. Or what's left of me.

"Hey," Maria says, calling me back. "Why haven't you ever asked to work out front?"

I shake my head and look at my feet. "I like where I am." When I look up at Maria, she's searching me for something.

"You're really just here to help. Or *for* help," she says. It isn't a question—but it is, too. She's making a statement, but she doesn't know if it's right or wrong.

"I'm here to work," I say.

Maria gives me another one of her penetrating looks. "I won't say no," she finally says, "but come with me to the circle first. You don't have to talk. Just come."

I shrug and follow her. The rest of the back-of-house staff are waiting for Maria to start.

I'm wedged between two of the beefy Latina cooks. They grab my hands automatically, like I'm just another chicken they have to butcher. That makes me feel oddly welcome. I am here, like them. No better, no worse, no different. I hang on to them because I know they're real. I can trust that. As soon as my antipsychotics wear off, I don't know if I'll be able to trust much else.

The meeting begins. Everyone communes with his or her higher power, asking to be granted the serenity to make it through another day sober.

"We got some sad news last night," Maria announces. "The police found more human remains that didn't fit with the out-of-state hunter. There's no easy way to say this. It turns out it was Sandy."

I did hear right. My grandparents *were* talking about another body.

I hear mumbling of all kinds from the circle. Things like, "*The program is life or death.*" And, "*But for the grace of God, go I.*"

"How'd she die?" one of the cooks asks.

"No word on that yet," Maria replies, looking down. Everyone is silent for a while.

"Do they know when she died?" the other cook asks.

"I asked, and they were shady on the details. Within the last few days, was all they said. So if anyone has anything to say to the police, speak up. Sandy had family, and they deserve answers. Even if it is just another OD," Maria says.

Everyone nods at the floor sadly, but it's obvious no one here has any information. I remember my first day here, two of the cooks talking about Sandy going missing, and how she was still able to trick. I steal a glance at them on either side of me now, but I can't tell what they're thinking.

Maria asks if anyone wants to share, but no one does. They're looking at me, but not in a judgmental way. They're all just waiting to see if I'm going to say something. When I don't, the meeting ends with the usual *Keep Coming* chant that I've heard a bunch of times, and then we all break off to get to work.

Aura-Blue finds me in the back before she starts her shift. She gives me one of her coconut-scented hugs and tells me she has so much to tell me, and how did I like riding my bike all this way? And then she realizes she's got to get started on her side-work because Mila was late picking her up again because she was up all night.

There's a lot hanging in that statement, and I'm assuming it has something to do with the new guy Mila's fooling around with, but my brain is flashing with so many lights, and everything seems so loud, that I can't manage to squeeze out anything more than an, "Okay, see you later."

Aura-Blue grabs me and hugs me one more time before she says, "You're still coming out with us after to get ice cream? Right?"

"Of course," I squeak, and I go back to my station.

I see my hands shaking and rub perspiration off my upper lip. I think I'm having a panic attack. I breathe in and out and start arranging my vegetables. Carrots, celery, kale, the dreaded onions, and potatoes should keep me occupied and calm.

Nothing to freak out about. I'm just going to chop.

The beam of light on me gets brighter and hotter. I tear up the kale. Sweat beads between my breasts. I peel the potatoes and then cut them into neat little cubes. My teeth grind. Time for the goggles and the onions. My leg bounces uncontrollably under the table, and my head pounds. I remember what they said in the circle about taking it one day at a time, but right now I'm only taking it one vegetable at a time.

I'm not going to think. I'm not going to remember. I'm not going to take myself apart sin by sin or give in to the whispers in my head. I'm just going to chop these onions, and then I'm going to do the carrots. That's all I have to do right now. Right now is all I can handle.

I go to the pots without being told. I get there before there are any pots for me to scrub, and so I start scrubbing the sink. I feel a hand on my shoulder and startle.

"This too shall pass," Maria whispers in my ears. I meet her eyes. She gives me a nod and walks away.

I repeat that phrase in my head over and over. And it helps. I manage to keep it together until I think of Rachel and the bat mitzvah I couldn't be bothered to go to and barf all over the pots I'm scrubbing. The first thing I think is, *there goes another half hour of drugs*. I don't know if I'm happy or sad about that.

I feel warm, rough hands and solid arms guiding me to sit on an overturned crate.

"Cold turkey?" one of the cooks asks me. I don't know her name, but I should. One of her painted-on eyebrows is raised in an even higher arch.

I nod. Her face softens with…no, not pity—with, "*Been there, done that, and it sucks.*"

"What's your name?" I ask.

"Gina," she answers. "Drink a lot of water. It'll give you something to throw up."

She hands me a glass of water and leaves me to get back to her station. No one here is going to hold my hair and stay with me, pressing a cool washcloth to my fevered brow while I puke. But no one will think less of me for puking, either. I down the water and stand up. Back to work.

I clean up my barf and then start in on the huge pile of pots I've allowed to accumulate. I'm in the weeds, and I have to hack my way out of them. Good. This is why I like this place. This is why I'm here. Honest, straightforward, backbreaking work. Work that serves someone other than me.

I'm not done when Mila comes into the kitchen with a hand on her hip and a surprised look on her face.

"Do you want us to wait for you?" she asks, and not in a snide way. I get the feeling if I told her to wait, she would.

"You guys are still here?" I say, like I have any frigging clue what time it is. "I'm so sorry. I got behind today. But you go on ahead."

"You sure?" she asks. "Do you want me to help?"

She actually walks all the way into the back and looks around for a rubber apron, but there isn't another. "Go," I say. "I'll see you the day after tomorrow."

"Okay," she says, genuinely disappointed. "But then we hang out for sure." She points at me with raised eyebrows until I smile and promise.

"For sure," I say, giving her a one-armed hug so I don't get her smeared with greasy water from my apron. As she leaves I wonder why she likes me so much. After she's fully gone, I hear Gina speak close to my ear.

"Don't do it," she warns. "That one just looking to party. She'll drag you in again 'cause she need pretty friends to take to the parties and get that shit for free. You feel me?"

I don't know Gina, but I know that AA has strict rules about never drinking again if you get sober. My problem was never partying. I was never into illegal drugs or got drunk that much, not even when the bartenders and the DJs were throwing all kinds of substances at the Five of us just to get us to stay and keep their club hot. I'm sweating out an addiction that was forced on me. But I can't say that to Gina or anyone else here.

"Getting sober" won't fix what's wrong with me, and if even the most on-point Manhattan nightclubs couldn't lure me into a world of alcohol and drug abuse, I doubt going to a keg party with Mila, where the strongest things offered are Jell-O shots, is going to make me a fiend for meds I never wanted to take in the first place.

I nod and pretend I'm taking Gina's advice to heart, because at least she cares enough to say something. That's more than most. More than my parents. They haven't even called me since we made the arrangements for me to come here and live with Grandma and Grandpa.

I go back to my grandparents' house just as the sun is going down. I'm riding west, so a big fat sun, sinking into orange gorgeousness somewhere behind the exhaling trees, is my compass. And that will have to be enough. A little bit of beauty to kick my ass across the finish line of today. It's more than I deserve.

My cheeks are wet with tears, and I ride faster and faster to dry them, or to outrun them. I was waiting to feel something, anything, and here it is. I asked for this, so no complaining.

I pull myself together before I get home. I run the grandparent gauntlet and text about nothing important with Rob for a few minutes before I'm allowed the privacy I need to unravel.

Somewhere out in the woods, there is a perfect boy named Bo. Someday I'm going to be good enough to deserve him.

But first, this.

July 28

BO SEES ME ACROSS THE RIVER, AND, FIRST, I WATCH THE same rush that's filling me filling him. Then he sees me better, and his expression changes. He meets me halfway to help me through the river.

"What happened? Are you sick?" he asks as he sweeps his eyes over my face and body.

I rub at the clammy paste of oily comedown sweat that's forming on my face and look away. My pores are oozing toxins. I've never felt this disgusting in my life, but at least I'm not hallucinating. My ghosts chased me all the way out here, but now that I'm with Bo they've vanished.

"No. Well, yes," I admit sheepishly.

"My dad can help," Bo begins, but I cut him off.

"Your dad's already given me something, and they're

helping. I think," I say. I watch his face go from confused to wary.

"When?" he asks me. "Am I missing something here?"

I nod and gesture for Bo to sit. "Let's spread out my blanket first. I have a lot to tell you."

He sits with wide, rabbit eyes—so round and open, and only just now realizing that the well-spoken stranger across from him is, and always has been, a fox.

"Your dad gave me pills to help wean me off the weapons-grade prescription meds I was taking right up until yesterday morning." I take a deep breath. Bo waits. I continue. "Until three weeks ago, I was in a psychiatric hospital for a total nervous collapse that left me catatonic. I was hospitalized for nine months."

I watch the fear in him melt into concern. But he's too quick to feel compassion. I wave off his reaching hands and tell him why I went catatonic.

Bo freezes. I sigh and smile because it feels so good to tell him. To finally say what a monster I am. Once I start, I can't stop. I tell him everything about the Cultural Outreach Club.

The more saddened he looks, the more honest I become about my own inner monologue. I tell him not just what I did, but what I was thinking while I did it—which was usually along the lines of how I could make it benefit me, even as it stole from others. I open him up and twist him inside out. I am now to him what I have been to myself for a long time.

A murderer.

I tell him about Rachel, and what happened.

Jinka pulled away from me suddenly.

One moment I was her hero, the cleverest girl in the world, her best friend. The next day, I felt her detach, like the Space Shuttle jettisoning a used rocket booster. She floated, and I fell.

She must have checked the website early that morning before school. She must have seen what Rachel posted.

That morning, I felt Jinka distancing herself. Then she turned me in. She went to the principal and wept out a self-absolving confession, which they filmed and later showed me. Trying to get me to confess, I suppose.

I went to the principal's office with no idea what waited for me. As soon as I walked in, it was like invisible hands wrapped around my face. Everything was muffled.

Teachers, parents, counselors, even a uniformed police officer was there to inform me that a body had been found. Fraud was the least of my worries. They all wanted someone to blame for the death of a thirteen-year-old girl.

When the officer started asking me questions about Rachel, I honestly had no idea who he was talking about. He had to read my online conversation with Rachel aloud, and even still it didn't ring a bell.

The officer had to explain to me that Rachel had written a five-page plea for my club to come to her bat mitzvah.

The plea began with the words, "I'm thinking of having a bat mitzvah, but I don't have any friends, so I don't think anyone will come. Do you think I should have one?"

After that, the message trailed off into ellipses. I would have had to click on those three little dots to read further, and—honestly?—I couldn't be bothered. I had close to fifty messages in my inbox that day. I wrote back a quick "Go ahead" and went on to the next message.

Had I read the rest of the message—which I didn't, which no one wanted to believe because they so desperately wanted to turn this story into another headline about the consequences of online bullying—I would have learned that Rachel went on to promise to kill herself if we didn't come.

No one went to Rachel's bat mitzvah. Rachel literally had no friends.

She filmed the nearly empty hall. She filmed all four members of her small family sitting at one table, and then table after table of empty seats. She filmed the vacant dance floor.

Then Rachel went into the bathroom and filmed herself slashing her wrists. She filmed herself bleeding out. With her dying breath, she posted it on my website—the website for the Cultural Outreach Club. Right under my comment that said, simply, "Go ahead."

Because I couldn't be bothered to click on three little dots. When I realized what I had done, inadvertently or not, the invisible hands wrapped around my body and closed me off.

Nothing could come in or go out.

I stayed in that cocoon for months.

When I told Maeve, I wasn't really feeling it. I was just reporting it to her, like it happened to someone else. But now, telling Bo, I feel it for the first time, and it hurts.

And I'm crying. But, finally, I feel clean again. I pull my sandals back on and stand up.

"So, that's it," I say.

Bo stares up at me with an empty look that I could never have imagined on his face without seeing it first. And I realize, that's *it*. He and I are over.

"Thank you for listening. I'm sorry," I say.

I pick up my backpack and stoop to gather the blanket, but Bo hasn't moved.

"Where do you think you're going?" he asks.

"Uh. Home?" I hazard.

"I don't get to ask any questions? I don't get a say?" he asks. The sharp ridges of his cheekbones flush red with anger.

I sit back down on the edge of the blanket, giving him as much space as I can. "Sure," I say, nodding. "Ask me anything."

"Are you okay?"

"Not really," I admit. Then I take a deep breath and sigh. "But I feel like something is thawing inside me, and maybe that's a start."

His jaw clenches. "Are you still in touch with her?"

"Jinka?" I ask. When he nods, I say, "No."

"Good. She manipulated you, and then betrayed you," he says angrily. "Are you still in love with her?" he asks. It comes out strangled and concerned, but not for himself.

How did he see that when no one else did? I've had my head shrunk by the best of them, but they all missed that. I missed that. Jinka was the reason I did it, and I did it to impress her. To win her. In a twisted way, I guess I was in love with her.

I stare at him. Smart. Sensitive. But most of all, he listens. It's amazing what you can pick up on when you really listen. I couldn't be more in awe of him, and I've just lost him. I threw him away so I could tell the truth. "No," I whisper. "I'm not in love in with her anymore."

I think it through carefully before I continue speaking. "I don't hate her. I don't love her. I don't miss her. But I'm still trying to find who I am without her."

I jump—literally gain air between my butt and the blanket—when he puts his arms around me.

"You're *Lena*," he whispers in my ear. "You don't need anyone to tell you who you are." I feel his laugh breathe across my neck. "Not even me."

The irony of this is so staggering, I don't know where

to start. But then, I don't have to. Because he kisses me, and everything goes out the window.

I have to stop him. To warn him. "Bo," I say, thinking about the hospital and what I did there. "I'm not well."

"I can see that," he says. His eyes are sad, but smiling, as he pushes my matted hair away from my face. "But you'll get better," he whispers. "It's not your fault Rachel killed herself," he says. I can't look at him, though.

It's not my fault, but I am to blame.

Bo lies down on his back. I sprawl across him with my leg wrapped over his hips and my head on his chest.

"I'm sorry I didn't tell you sooner," I say.

I feel him take a deep breath as he relaxes. "No, this was the right time," he replies musingly. "I knew you were hiding something or...I don't know...dealing with something big and dark."

I lift my head to look at him. "Then why'd you keep seeing me?"

He rolls his eyes and grins. "I couldn't stay away from you. I still can't. Even if it means..." He breaks off suddenly and his eyes turn inward.

"What?"

"Even if it means I'm fighting with my father night and day about it," he admits.

I was expecting this, but it still stings. "Night and day? Really?"

Bo nods. "It's dangerous for him. For my whole family."

I sit up. "I'm *not* going tell anyone you guys grow pot." This is so ridiculous, I almost laugh. "It's legal to grow in small amounts anyway, you know."

Bo sits up, too. "This isn't about the cannabis."

He can't look at me, so I know it's huge. "What?" I ask. "Bo. Why is your family hiding out here in the woods? And don't tell me it's just because you want to live close to nature."

He swallows hard and shakes his head, his mouth set. "I can't."

"Seriously?" I nearly shriek. "You're not going to tell me after I told you what I did?"

"The police aren't after you because you didn't commit a convictable crime. They're after my dad because he...he did," he says. His eyes are wide and rabbit-like again.

"What did he do?"

"I can't tell you," he repeats.

I stand up. "I can't believe you."

I grab the edge of the blanket, seeing red. I emptied myself out for this guy, and he still doesn't trust me?

"Get up," I order. He doesn't move. "Get up or I'm going to yank it out from under you."

He stands up slowly.

"Move," I say when he lingers. His feet are still on the blanket.

"Lena," he says.

"No," I say, cutting him off. "I trusted you and your parents. Do you know that you and your mom are the only people I've talked to about this? I never even spoke about it at the hospital. But if you can't trust me back, then what's the point?"

I roll up the blanket in a twisted jumble and try to cram it into my backpack, which is nearly impossible if it isn't folded right. I'm so angry and hurt, and feeling...I don't know—rejected, I guess, that I can't bear to be near him.

I turn to cross the river, and Bo grabs me. Hard. He holds me in a way that I know I could never break. He's so strong. He knows how to catch a deer with his bare hands—what chance do I have of getting away? I stop struggling and look up at him, furious. He's not angry. He's desperate.

"If I tell you and we get caught, they will charge you with aiding and abetting, obstruction of justice, and anything else they can think of. This is much bigger than whether or not I trust you." He lets me go and stands back. "I'm trying to protect *you*, Lena. Not him."

I look down. "What did he say to you?"

"He threatened to move us to one of the other sites we use. He actually started packing." Bo laughs and puts his hands on his hips like he's tired. "He said I could stay here alone if you meant that much to me."

I shift uncomfortably. "What did you say to him?"

Bo smiles. "I'm here, aren't I?"

"You mean they *left* you?"

He shakes his head. "My mom got between my dad and me." His face falls suddenly, remembering the conflict. "I'm going eventually. For college. My mom won't let me stay in the woods forever, but she's not ready for me to go just yet because she knows she'll never see me again."

"Wait. Never? I mean, you could come visit or..." I break off.

He shakes his head, his eyes far away. "No. As soon as I register at one of the colleges I've been accepted to, the FBI will be watching me. I can't see my parents again."

The words hang there, and I swear the whole forest goes silent.

"And your brothers and sisters?"

"Well, we've had time to plan," he says quietly. "They'll each come out to live with me when they're ready. But it will be years in between. Could be twelve or thirteen years before I see Moth again. And if one of them doesn't show, I'll never know if they decided to stay with Mom and Dad, or if they're...if something happened to them."

I sit down on the ground. "That's horrible," I whisper. Bo crouches down in front of me, his eyes intense. He brushes a lock of my hair behind my ear.

"I don't care anymore. I mean, I *do*," he amends quickly, "but my whole life has been about my family.

About my dad. And now I need it to be about something else."

I put my arms around him. That's all I can do, really.

Too soon, Bo pulls back and stands. "Come on," he says.

"Where're we going?" I reply, standing up and reaching for my things.

"I promised to teach you how to survive out here." He looks at the air between the sunbeams and shadows, judging the light, or the probability of rain, or the migration of gnats, for all I know. I really have no idea. "We'd better get going," he says, like the air told him something.

He takes me out into the brush, well beyond any human trail. He's in control out here, and I think he does it more to take a moment and slow down the physical side of things between us after what I told him, rather than to teach me anything. But I learn plenty anyway. He stops and stoops down, pointing out a small white flower. "Queen's cup," he tells me. "The leaves are edible." He picks a few of the leaves that grow around each flower, never stripping any of the flowers bare. He gives me a handful, and I put one in my mouth and chew. It's sweet.

I smile at Bo, and he smiles back, chewing on a leaf of his own.

We move on, chewing and scanning the ground. He shows me the yellow-flowered wood sorrel and makes a face.

"Sour," he says, gathering them anyway and putting the flowers and the leaves in the pockets of his worn cargo pants. "They're better cooked."

We go on like this for hours. Barely talking but looking and listening and finding. I take notes in my journal. I try to draw the flowers and the leaves.

"Do you know where we are?" he asks.

I look around. "Are we…?" I spin around. I hear running water and go toward it. We're back to *there*.

"You'll get better at it," he tells me when he sees the devastated look on my face.

"I had no idea we were heading back this way until I heard the water," I say, frustrated.

Bo nods. "But you heard the water and went toward it. Why is that good?" I shrug and roll my eyes. "Because water flows downhill," he says, answering his question for me. "And what's down?"

"Town is down," I say, finally getting it. "If I come across a stream, I follow it down the mountain."

"Right," Bo says, nodding. He's standing too far away from me. I step toward him, but he smiles and shakes his head, evading my touch. "It's too late. It will be dark soon."

He's aching to touch me. I can see it. I love how transparent Bo is. He really is a rainbow. Every color, every shade, and still so easy to see through him.

"The day after tomorrow?" I ask. "Tomorrow I have to be at the shelter in the morning for some deliveries."

He shifts anxiously. "Would you like to come home with me again?" he asks. "My mom was asking for you."

"Yes," I reply. "I really like your mom." Although I don't know why she keeps inviting me when my presence so obviously endangers her husband.

"Good. The day after tomorrow," he says, and moves away before I can come up with a way to ask him about that.

He drifts back into the gloaming, and I lose sight of him.

July 29

THE DRUGS ARE COMPLETELY OUT OF MY SYSTEM, SO IT'S with me all the time now. The image of Rachel's dead body. All the blood.

I can't tell if I'm nauseous because I went off my meds, or if I'm nauseous because I keep hallucinating Rachel's dead body everywhere *because* I've gone off my meds. It's a subtle point, but one I can't seem to get straight. The sweating has stopped and so have the tremors, thanks to Ray's little white pills, but the nausea is still there. I wonder if I'm going to have to spend the rest of my life seeing corpses and being sick to my stomach. It wouldn't be half the punishment I deserve; I know that. It would be inconvenient though, walking around always seeing the people I've killed.

First, always first, is Rachel. I see her at the foot of my

bed when I wake up in the morning, then stretched out under my grandparents' breakfast table when I go downstairs. I see her passing me in a car while I ride my bike to the shelter. I see her hanging from one of the hooks in the walk-in freezer. Her black tongue is pushed out between her blue lips.

But, wait. That wasn't Rachel. Rachel wasn't the one who hanged herself, I tell myself. I can't even keep all my ghosts straight anymore. And I need to keep them straight. I owe them that, at the very least.

"Miss?" says a man's voice.

I whirl around, my high-pitched bark of a scream cut off as soon as I see who's behind me.

"Oh, Officer," I say when I register the blue uniform. "You startled me."

The young policeman smiles at me. "I didn't mean to sneak up on you," he says, amused.

Why do men love scaring women so much? Nearly every boyfriend I ever had thought it would be a great idea to pull some prank on me to make me scream. What do they get out of that? It's never made any sense to me.

"Is Maria here?" the officer asks, all business now that it's clear I am not amused.

"No. Some mornings I do the inventory for her. Did you have an appointment?" I ask, stepping toward him and forcing him to move back so I can exit the walk-in. I'm not being rude. I smile to make sure he knows that. I'm just making it clear that I belong here, he doesn't, and I don't like to be cornered. Or frightened out of my skin so he can have a little chuckle.

"No. I..." He breaks off, cowed now that I've come right at him. He musters up his big-man voice. "I spoke with her the other day about a missing girl who used to stay at this facility."

I nod and look down sadly. "Sandy."

"You knew her?" he asks.

"No. She left before I got here," I reply. "But Maria told the staff that you found her remains."

"You're new here?" the officer guesses.

"I'm a summer volunteer. Officer...?"

"Langmire," he says, supplying his name. "What's yours?" he asks, pulling out a notepad and a pencil.

I give it, and now I regret standing up to him. But maybe if I play docile for the rest of this interview—and I see now that's what this is—I can seem innocuous enough so that he won't look too deeply into my past.

It's not like anything is on my permanent record. I'm not technically a criminal. No red flags are going to pop up if he enters my name into a computer.

But. He won't have to dig too far to find several newspaper articles about a major humanitarian prize and a high school hoax that have my name all over them. That's small potatoes, though. Embarrassing, but not criminal.

At least my involvement in Rachel's death never made the papers. After I was hospitalized, I was legally exonerated due to "extenuating medical circumstances."

But. There's a paper trail about how I was questioned by the police in New York City, although the details—including the fact that my interrogation was temporarily under the umbrella of a possible murder investigation—have all been expunged.

But. My state-mandated stay in a mental hospital would be easy for him to find, even if he did have to dig deep to connect my need for a state-mandated stay at a mental institution to a potential murder investigation.

Fear is a gymnast somersaulting up and down my bones.

My only chance to avoid further questioning from the police—and I've been down that road, so I know I don't want to go down it again—is to make this young officer not want to look into me at all, and hope I get lucky.

"I'm staying with my grandparents for the summer," I tell him, like I have nothing to hide. I give details about their address and how long they've had a summer home here without him needing to ask.

"I've been meaning to come and spend time with them forever but, see, I'm from the East Coast? Manhattan?" I make it a question, as if he's never heard of New York City, and put a hand on my hip and wave the other in the air. "And I have friends who always have amazing stuff—I mean, like, *amazing* stuff—to do all summer, and so I've been really, really bad about my grandparents, you know? They're not going to be around *forever*"—I duck my head down as if even mentioning death is somehow impolite—"and finally I realized what was important in my life, you know? Because, for *me*, my family is way more important than going to the Hamptons. In the long run, anyway. Although you do meet the *best* people there—not that this isn't great, too, but the Hamptons are on a different level, you know?"

I see him deflate after I turn stupid and chatty, like the thrill is gone now that I'm no longer a challenge. I keep going, telling him about how Aura-Blue and Mila invited me to join them volunteering at the shelter, and of course I was excited for the opportunity to help people less fortunate. Oh, and by the way, did the young officer know Aura-Blue? Her grandfather was the local sheriff for years. No? What a shame.

By the time I'm done with Officer Langmire, he can't wait to disentangle himself from the self-important asshole who obviously couldn't be hiding anything because she didn't stop talking about her meaningless life for a solid fifteen minutes.

"I really hope you find out what happened to Sandy," I say as Officer Langmire tries for a third time to break away from me. I lower my voice like Grandma does when she's talking about druggies. "Was it an overdose?"

"There's no indication of that as of right now," the officer replies, desperate to get the hell out of there.

"Really?" My voice solidifies from the breathy, girly tone I've adopted, as I'm momentarily shocked back into my real self. "Then how did she die?"

Langmire closes off. "We're still looking into it," he replies.

"Is there a connection between Sandy and the woman from out of state?"

His face freezes. I rock back on my heels, his answer implicit, and the officer realizes his mistake.

"There's no official connection between the deaths of Sandy Crosby and Chelsea Oliver at this time," he says curtly.

So, yeah, there definitely is.

"Let Maria know I stopped by and that I'll be back to speak to the rest of the staff."

"Oh, certainly, Officer. Maria will be here tomorrow morning," I say in that chirping, girly voice again.

After Officer Langmire leaves, Gina seems to magically appear out of thin air.

"You're good," she tells me. "Talking a whole lotta nothing."

I smile at Gina with narrowed eyes. "Hiding in the office?" I ask in return. Gina's completely plucked and redrawn-in eyebrows make her look permanently surprised. People without their real eyebrows are harder to read, I realize.

"I don't talk to police," she tells me. She looks away,

and I feel the sadness in her more than hear it or see it. "But I do hope they find whoever murdered Sandy."

"He never said mur—" I start to say, but Gina's eye-roll stops me.

"Be careful out in those woods," she warns. "Some heartless bastards out there."

I sputter for a moment, surprised.

"Like who?" I call after her.

"Like Dr. Goodnight," she says over her shoulder. The way she says it makes me laugh nervously.

She's joking. Is she joking? Dr. Goodnight sounds like a mattress store. Or a Stephen King novel. I think it *is* a Stephen King novel—no, wait, that's *Doctor Sleep*. Whatever. She's definitely trying to get me to bite, saying "Dr. Goodnight" in a low, ominous voice. I shake my head in frustration and go to my station to start work.

Rachel's there. Waiting for me. She's stretched out over my chopping block, dripping blood. I shut my eyes tight, and when I open them again, she's gone, but a girl in a hospital gown lies on the floor. *I never saw Zlata's body*, I think in an offhand way. It's not that my ghosts are coming for me. They never left. I knew they were there, but the drugs made it so I couldn't see them. Couldn't deal with them. Now I don't have much of a choice.

But Zlata is dead, and I know what I see is not really her. Since this is not the right time or place, I banish the image, pick up my knife, and start slicing peppers long and thin for fajitas.

Maria arrives and calls us all to the circle. At the end of Serenity Prayer, Gina decides to share something.

"The police stopped by. Found out Sandy was killed. It wasn't no OD," Gina says out of the side of her mouth. A low rumble goes around the circle. Breaths puff in and out of Gina, and her voice comes out strangled so she doesn't shout.

"Another dead girl?" she asks, incredulous. "How many girls I know gotta get killed?" A chorus of *uh-huh*s answers. "Hearing that? It made me want to use." She pauses. Collects herself. "But not today. Not today. I'd just end up another body like her."

I feel the hands holding mine tighten. The circle draws in, gathering strength.

"I hope they find him," Gina says. "Just once, I want someone who deserves to go down to get what's his."

A guttural "Hell, yeah" is said by all. Like they're saying *amen*. I'm the only one who doesn't raise her voice. See, I'm not a victim. Never have been. I'm one of the ones who deserve to go down.

We start work. Rachel's everywhere today. She's in my vegetables, and my pots and pans. I scrub and rinse and scrub some more. My fingers whiten, pucker, and split. I sweat buckets into the steamy air, and it sweats back on me. Still, Rachel's there, drifting in the mist.

At the end of my shift, there are two girls who expect me to eat ice cream and talk about clothes and parties and boys. I take off my rubber apron and put on my smile.

"Don't stretch your lips like that or they'll crack," Maria tells me. She hands me some udder cream. "For your hands," she tells me.

"Thanks," I reply, scooping out some of the balm and rubbing it on my ruined cuticles. I have so many splits, it looks like my hands have been shoved through razor wire. How did I get this hacked up? I'm bruised, too. It has to be the blood-thinning meds.

Mila is calling my name from out front, begging me to hurry. I hand the jar back to Maria.

"This was so much easier when I was on drugs," I say wryly.

"Drugs make everything easier," she replies with a grin. "Until they make everything impossible."

I nod and go to join Mila, who hugs me, and squeals, and insists she has so much to tell me.

"Where's Aura-Blue?" I ask. Mila purses her lips and flips her hair over her shoulder.

"Her grandfather made her quit."

"Quit?" I parrot back.

"Come on," Mila says, taking my hand and dragging me outside. "I'll tell you on the way."

"My bike," I say.

"I'll drop you back here after we eat. Now come on! I'm starving."

I am, too. Working in food service is like being a becalmed sailor, dying of thirst surrounded by an ocean. Cooks don't eat.

I close the passenger-side door of Mila's Mini and say, "So I'm guessing Aura-Blue quit because of Sandy's death."

"Murder," Mila corrects. "She didn't just die."

"You heard?"

Mila nods and cranks the engine. She swings out of her parking space with her usual disregard for the fragility of the human skeleton.

"Her grandfather doesn't want her hanging out in a 'high-risk' area," she says.

I can't tell how she feels about that. She's watching the road intently like she should, which is odd for her.

"But you're still coming?" I half ask, half state. "Don't you think it's too risky?"

Mila shrugs a shoulder and licks her lips. "I'm not like Sandy," she says. Again, I can't quite tell what she's thinking.

"OK. Back up," I say. "Why is it high risk to work at the shelter?" A thought occurs to me. "Do they think someone at the shelter did it?"

Mila looks at me out of the corner of her eyes. "Everyone who stays at the shelter is a drug addict. Drug addicts tend to do illegal things, like kill people."

"No. That's not it." I look out the window shaking my head. "Chelsea Oliver wasn't at the shelter."

"Who?" Mila asks. She pulls into the Snack Shack and stops.

"The out-of-state hunter who *wasn't* mauled by a bear. She never stayed at the shelter. There's no reason to think she was an addict," I say. "And the cops think the murders are connected."

I tell her about my interview with the rookie cop.

Mila throws back her head and laughs.

"What an idiot! He told you all that?" she says as she gets out of the car.

"Yeah," I say, coming around the car and walking next to her into the Snack Shack. "But what do I know? Maybe the connection between Sandy and Chelsea is drugs. Just because Chelsea didn't stay at the shelter doesn't mean she wasn't an addict."

"And she came from hundreds of miles away to camp out in the woods in camouflage gear to score drugs?" Mila asks doubtfully.

We get in line for a scoop. "I don't know," I mumble. "But I've heard there's more than deer out in those woods." I should shut up. I should just let it go, and get my ice cream, and ask Mila about her social life. But I don't.

"Have you ever heard of Dr. Goodnight?" I ask on a whim.

Mila's face doesn't move. She doesn't look at me. She stays calm and keeps her eyes trained on the people in front of us.

"Shut up," she says in a forced neutral voice that betrays how anxious she is.

She tosses her lovely hair over her shoulder, but only so she can look at the people lining up behind us to check and see if they're listening. When she finally makes her way back around to look at me, she gives me the bored smile of someone waiting impatiently for ice cream.

"We'll talk after we sit," she says, like she's telling me what flavor she's going to order.

I get my usual butterscotch sundae. Mila orders a chocolate brownie frappé. She's out of money again, so I pay. We look for a booth but have to settle for a spot outside so we can be alone.

"So who is he?" I ask.

Mila pulls her ice-cream-sleeved straw out of the glass and wraps her tongue around it, stripping off the sweet coating. She rubs the ice cream around her mouth, thinking.

"I first heard about him through Aura-Blue, actually," she says. "Her grandfather has been chasing him for years, but it's been so long now, no one really knows if he exists or not."

"Oh, right. Serial killers are his hobby, or something like that," I say. I shiver. The wind off the water is cold.

"Why was her grandfather after him?" I ask, recalling that Aura-Blue's grandfather was the sheriff here.

"Because he's the biggest supplier of drugs for a hundred miles, supposedly," she says quietly.

"Why do they call him..." Her eyes flash at me in warning, so I drop my voice and lean across the table toward her. I have to know. "Why do they call him Dr. Goodnight?" I whisper.

She shifts and looks around. "Because he's a genius. He can make any kind of drug you want from used refrigerator coolant and tree bark. And it's good shit, too. It's, like, medical-grade meth and fentanyl. Everyone says he used to be a doctor."

Her figure telescopes away from me as I sink. It can't be.

I've heard about how our National Parks are so underfunded that many illegal drug growers have set up shop in remote places that park rangers just don't have the resources to manage. I mean, I'm not a troglodyte. I listen to true-crime podcasts like everyone else. But how many geniuses with deep knowledge of medicine and/or herbal drug making could possibly be running around the same few miles of national forest?

But no. I just can't accept that Bo's father is Dr. Goodnight. I can't accept that he's got a meth lab hidden in one of the tree-house dormitories where his philosophy-professor wife and six hippie children live. It goes against everything Bo has told me about his father. And himself.

Except for the fact that Bo admitted his dad *did* commit a crime. A big one. If the FBI is after him, it's probably one of four things: terrorism, kidnapping, tax evasion, or murder. I shake my head, barely stopping myself from yelling at Mila. As if she were personally indicting Bo and his whole family.

"But why the Goodnight part?" I ask, digging for some incongruous information, some detail that would make it impossible for Bo's father to be tied up in this mess.

Mila's voice drops so low I can barely hear her. "Because he enjoys putting people to sleep. Most of the time, he just spikes the heroin with too much fentanyl, killing randomly just to kill people, but sometimes he likes to watch. He needs to watch. He's a psychopath."

I sit back in my chair and study her. Hoping that any second now, she's going to look up, laugh, and tear into me for falling for something so melodramatic. But she doesn't. In fact, she looks terrified.

"You think he's real," I say.

Mila nods. Then she rolls a shoulder. "Is it so hard to believe?" she asks. "Our shelter is over capacity, but how many people live in this area year-round?" She shakes her head and leans back in her chair. "Such a high percentage of addicts doesn't happen for no reason. And people have been going missing in those woods for years."

"The woods are dangerous," I say, but she shakes her

head and stops me from listing the many ways a vacationer can get herself killed.

"I've hiked my whole life. Camping, fishing—I've been doing it all since I was born. I love it."

She smiles softly, and I see another level to Mila I hadn't seen before, but I'd sensed. Mila is a not a party girl. Not in the center of her. Deep down, she's a forest thing, like Bo.

"I know the woods are dangerous," she says in a measured, rational way. "But this is something else. Too many people have died here. It's been going on for years. Even Aura-Blue's grandfather believes he's real, and he used to be the sheriff."

I sit back, momentarily silenced. But something still isn't right about all this. "Sandy and that hunter weren't put to sleep," I say. "They were cut up."

"Yeah. Cut up," she stresses. "That's no accident."

I resist the urge to nod. Obviously, there's more going on than just the occasional hunting or hiking accident, but I refuse to accept anything Mila is saying right now. Besides, it doesn't even line up. Cutting people up and putting them to sleep are two totally different things. She's got to be imagining a connection.

She has to be. Because if I start accepting any of it, this would be the moment I would have to open my mouth and say, "*Actually, I've met a genius doctor who lives in the woods and makes all kinds of drugs. Oh, and he's wanted by the FBI for a crime my boyfriend won't tell me about because he's trying to protect me from the police with plausible deniability.*"

Or, I say nothing and live with more blood on my hands.

So. What am I going to do? Nothing.

I'm not going to do anything because Bo's father is not Dr. Goodnight. Dr. Goodnight does not exist. There's an undeniably large drug problem in this town, and that explains the deaths.

I don't know anything about the drug trade, but I've seen network television. Where there are drugs, there is violence and a lot of dead bodies, and not just from overdosing. If this were New Orleans, the bodies would get dumped in the swamp, but here those bodies get dumped in the woods. It's Occam's razor: the simplest explanation is usually the correct one. And there is very rarely one diabolical genius masterminding a web of dastardly deeds in order to fulfill his bloodlust.

"You don't believe me," Mila says. Her eyes are sad, but her mouth is turned up in an endearing smile. I smile back and shake my head.

"I'm sorry." I stop to laugh, and then collect myself. "Look, it's not that I don't think there's something scary going on—that's obvious. People are dying, and the FBI is here investigating something that is not a bear attack or a drug overdose. So it's a big deal." I can't help but grin.

"But the whole Dr. Goodnight thing is a little..." I trail off. I see Mila's eyes blaze and all humor drops from my tone. "I'm sorry. You knew Sandy, and it's wrong of me to laugh. Nothing about this is funny."

"You don't believe me," she repeats.

I shake my head regretfully. "I don't believe in the bogeyman, either."

I look out across the water so I don't see Rachel bleeding out between our untouched ice creams, but instead I see a woman free-falling through the air to her death. *That was Brooklyn*, I remind myself sternly. *Brooklyn is on the other side of the continent. That isn't real.* I blink until the image is gone.

"I do believe that desperate people make bad choices, and there are a lot of desperate people around here. It's not as romantic as what you're suggesting. But the truth rarely is."

Her face hardens. "Do I look like a romantic to you?" she asks.

Again, I get a glimpse of something in Mila that goes against the grain of her perfect-girl persona. Something in her has shifted.

"No. You don't. And you're certain he's real," I say. She doesn't answer. "Why are you so certain?" I ask. She looks down. "Have you met him?"

Her eyes shift to a faraway place. She looks back at me, smiles, and says, "Yeah. He lives under my bed. Right next to the bogeyman."

She changes the subject, and I feel her take a giant step back from me.

We force down a few more bites of our ruined desserts, but the sweetness is too much, and our ice cream is too warm, and both of us just want to go. She takes me back to the shelter to get my bike in silence.

This is the first time I've left Mila feeling further from her at the end of the afternoon than I did at the start of it.

This, too, has happened to me before. Right before I lost everything.

July 30
Morning

I HAVEN'T FORGOTTEN ABOUT THE ANIMAL I SHOT. QUITE the opposite. I think about it all the time.

I've decided it had to have been a fawn hiding in the ferns. Too young and weak to follow its mother, the baby deer hid, waiting for its mother to return. I picture her coming back to the carnage I left behind.

Bo asked if I wanted to go back to his camp and visit with his mother while he hunted, but I said I'd rather spend time with him today.

So he's taking me with him. This would be the perfect time to tell him about the fawn. I could describe it in such a way that he got the whole picture. He would understand. Accidents happen, and I really looked for the poor thing, but…

"If you're not up to this, you don't have to come with

me," he says, eyes searching mine. "But I have to hunt today. We need meat."

"No," I say, shaking my head. "I can go with you. I want to go with you."

He gives me an uncertain look. "Okay. We probably won't find anything anyway," he says as we leave our spot and head out into the rich undergrowth.

"We're going to find something," I say quietly. I know because that's how things are with me. We're going to find something, and I'm going to help kill yet another unsuspecting creature.

"I don't know. We've pretty much exhausted this area of bucks."

"They have to be bucks?" I ask.

"Of course," Bo says, nodding. "The bigger the buck, the better for the environment. They take the most resources over the winter, and it's better for the species to leave the foraging for the does and fawns."

Here's the moment. This is when I should tell him. I take a breath to speak.

"My parents say we'll have to move soon," he says, before I get the chance.

"To where?" I ask, suddenly thrown.

"Not too far. Just enough to hunt different game trails." He smiles at me shyly. "Don't worry. We'll still be able to see each other."

We walk in silence for a while. "Would you rather just come back to my camp with me?" he asks tentatively. "I can tell my parents we'll fish instead."

"No," I say, a little too abruptly. The thought of possibly running into his father is just too jarring right now.

Dr. Goodnight does not exist, and Bo's family does not cook meth. I just have to keep telling myself that, and I'll be fine. Even though Bo just reminded me that they had more than one camp, and if one were going to have a family and cook meth in the middle of the woods, it would make sense to keep the two apart.

Christ, what's wrong with me? Ray is *not* Dr. Goodnight.

"I wish you'd tell me what's bothering you," Bo says. He huffs out a frustrated breath. "It's very quiet out here. I can practically hear you screaming in your head, you know."

He pauses, and I know I should laugh at his joke, but nothing's funny right now.

"Just talk to me, okay?" he pleads. "Did I do something wrong?"

"It's not you," I say, but he doesn't believe me.

Given the choice between telling Bo about the fawn or telling him what I suspect about his father, I don't really have a choice. I tell him about the fawn.

I make such a hash of it. I start blubbering in the middle and begging him not to hate me. I'm like a raw wound, now that I'm not drugged out of my mind. Once I start in on the fawn, I tell Bo about how I'm haunted. How I'm seeing Rachel everywhere. And how I deserve to be haunted because all I ever do is murder innocent things.

I'm wiping my nose on his shoulder when I realize that he's holding me. "It's okay," he murmurs against my cheek. "None of it's your fault."

I pull back, still sobbing. "How can you say that? It's all my fault!"

He shakes his head and smooths my hair. "You've done a lot of stupid shit, but it's not all about you, you know."

"What?" I say, utterly confused. "I'm having a fucking..."—I search for the right word and find it—"*epiphany* about how my self-absorption is the root of all the evil in my life. I know it's not all about me! That's my point!"

He smiles indulgently and nods. "Okay. So right about now, you should be realizing that you didn't actually kill anyone."

"Rachel killed herself because of me," I argue.

"She killed herself. Period. When someone wants to die, they will find a way to do it." His voice roughens with anger. "And they'll drag down anyone they can with them."

He turns sharply to the side, draws his bow, and looses an arrow into the ferns.

"Huh. Look at that. No baby deer this time." He retrieves the arrow and strides back to me. His cheeks are flushed, and his thick chest is swelling with skipping breaths. "Not everything in the world is set up to teach you a lesson." He laughs through his frustration. "And as powerful as you are—and I know you are a terrifying force of nature—you aren't powerful enough to be responsible for everything that happens around you. Sometimes things are completely out of your control. So, no. It's not your fault."

But he wasn't there. He doesn't understand. "I heard a noise in the undergrowth, and I shot at it," I say, shaking my head. "I knew something was there."

Faster than I can see, he raises his hand and snaps his fingers next to my ear. My head flicks toward the sound.

"Reflex," he says gently. "It's a prey response. Humans turn toward unexpected or threatening sounds and go into fight-or-flight mode. Our species used to be hunted by everything that was in the undergrowth." He smiles at me, watching my face as I think. "You let the arrow go on instinct. Self-defense is actually a better way of defining it. Some people freeze, and some people shoot. You're a shooter. It's not bad or good; it's how you're wired."

I feel something in me uncoil.

No. I can't let myself off the hook that easily. Bo wants to see a better person than is actually here in front of him, so he does.

But that's not really it. He's not making excuses for me. He knows I'm broken, but he also believes I'm getting better.

I don't know if that's true or not, but his faith in me is so strong, it makes me become that better person he sees.

It's not the same as it is with my grandparents or my father. They only see what they want to see. Bo sees all of me—good and bad. He's not insisting I'm something I'm not. He's not shutting his eyes or walking away from me when I force him to open them.

Bo sees the good person I could be if only I had someone who could accept the bad first. I couldn't love him more for that. And as soon as the words run through my head, I realize they're true.

"I love you," I say. And it isn't hard. It's not forced or awkward. I laugh, but it's a joyous laugh, not a bitter or sarcastic one. I laugh because I feel like sunshine inside. "I really love you," I say.

"I love you, too," he says, but his face is sad, and his eyes darken.

I take a step back from him. "That wasn't very convincing, Bo."

He captures one of my arms and pulls me toward him. "I know exactly what I'm feeling, and I know I'll never feel it again. And the summer is half over."

There are so many times I look at Bo and think of him as younger than me because he's less experienced in worldly things. But in this, in love, I know I'm less experienced than him. I don't know if I've ever fully loved anyone, including myself, and Bo has spent his whole life surrounded by it.

Benching, ghosting, breadcrumbing—I'm a master at all of these tactics, but I don't know shit about love. And here he is, out in the middle of the woods, trying to find food for his family because he loves them. And he'd sweat and struggle and even kill to feed them.

My mom once asked me to go ten blocks out of my way to Zabar's Deli to pick up some bagels, lox, and cream cheese way too early in the morning because she had a craving, and I did it. That's about the biggest favor I ever did for her. The biggest favor she ever did for me was to hire a really sweet nanny.

Okay, scratch that. I completely loved my nanny. I called her La-La because she was always singing, and I couldn't pronounce her name anyway. She was an angel to me, and my mom fired her out of jealousy. That's what I know of love.

"What happens at the end of summer?" I ask.

He looks like he's going to cry. "I have to go to college."

"Have to?" I ask. It's like I'm shrinking. My voice, my body, it's all raveling in.

He nods and swallows. "It's the deal. I leave the woods and go to college or my mom will turn herself in. She won't let me stay. I told you."

I feel my face twisting into a snarl, and then the anger

disappears. Of course Maeve would do that. She loves her son, and she won't let him ruin his life for anyone. Not for her, not for me. She's kicking him out of the nest in a month and a half. That's all I have left of Bo.

"Your mom's absolutely right," I say in a flat voice. "You're getting out of here. You're brilliant and beautiful, and you're going to add so much to the world."

He kisses me. Even if I won't have him for much longer, knowing him at all is the real miracle.

As he cradles the back of my head and lifts my weight to lay me down on the ground, I think of the girl he'll meet at his Ivy League school. How she'll marvel at her luck. If she's smart. If she's true. If she's everything that I'm not.

I'm not saying no, but Bo will only go so far. We're still learning each other. We're still learning ourselves. I don't have enough experience to know what I like yet, but it seems as if everything he does is what I would have asked for had I known anything about it. Nothing is uncomfortable or awkward with him. Nothing he does is something he saw on internet porn. It all flows, one thing into another. It's seamless and seemingly random but guided by an invisible force. Like leaves on the wind. It might not be intercourse, but it is definitely making love.

I'm a screamer. Didn't see that coming.

He falls asleep almost immediately afterward, which is half-infuriating, and half-gratifying. I'm either not interesting enough to stay awake for, or I'm so damn amazing, his brain needs to shut down for a while in order to process.

He doesn't snore.

I am awake. I am more awake than ever. I can hear everything. Moisture pattering through the leaves. Maybe it's a light rain, or maybe the leaves are just breathing out water. It's hard to tell when you're on the bottom level of a rain forest. I hear a birdcall. Time passes. I lie on my side in the crook of Bo's arm. The warm weight of him presses against my back. I'd rather yank out a tooth than give this up.

And then…

An enormous buck wafts out of the shadows from behind a great, mossy tree less than a hundred yards away. His thick antlers are only half-grown and still covered in summertime velvet, but his body is so large that the lack of sound he makes creates a disconnect in the mind. Like seeing a ghost.

The buck dips his head to graze.

We must be downwind, Bo and I. The buck has no idea we're here, our naked bodies obscured by ferns. This is just the kind of kill Bo and his family need. Without it, they might go hungry.

If I wake Bo, he might unintentionally startle the buck. I'm lying on my left side, so my left eye is partially obscured by the leaf litter and the ferns. Just beyond my hand is the bow and quiver. The bow slips easily into my right hand. I take a breath and let it out before I ease myself toward the quiver.

The buck keeps grazing.

I slip an arrow out and, staying low, I shift my weight oh-so-slowly until my knees are under my torso. In yoga they call it *child's pose*, but in my version I have a deadly weapon in my hands.

Drip, drip, drip is the only sound.

I rise up on to my knees and draw in one motion. The buck looks me in the eye as I loose my arrow.

He falls.

He doesn't bellow or screech. The only thing I can hear at this distance is the sound of his body crashing to the ground.

I jump up, and I feel Bo startle and jump up behind me. "What happened?" he yells.

I'm too dumbstruck to speak yet. I point toward the fallen buck with his bow. Facing the buck, we both hear another sound coming from directly behind us.

"No way!" yells a young woman's voice.

"Raven?" Bo says disbelievingly.

His sister strides out from the deep cover of the mottled forest gloom. She's moving fast, and as she passes us, I can see she's covered in mud to camouflage her outline and her scent.

"How did you do that?" she growls over her shoulder in my direction.

Bo looks at me, lost. I shrug back, and he and I pull on our clothes, then race to catch up with his sister, who is already crouching down next to the buck.

She inspects the fallen beauty. "Right through the eye," she whispers. "How?"

They're both looking at me. The buck's lungs heave out a death rattle in a wet rush of falling tissue and conquered life. The buck lies still. And that weight, or presence, or hum—whatever it is that separates the living now from the dead forever—it's gone.

Raven is still staring at me, waiting for some kind of explanation. Her distrust is mingled with curiosity and unwelcome respect. I don't want respect for this.

"I guess I'm good at killing things," I admit, ashamed, looking at the corpse at my feet.

I turn and try to walk away, but Bo catches my arm gently and leads me back to the buck. I look into his eyes as he places my hands on the buck's flank.

"Thank you, brother," he says, like he knew him. Like this was one of his pals. "We needed you, and you came to help us."

Bo looks at me, his honest eyes digging deep. I nod and look down at the warm, caramel-colored fur under my hands.

"Thank you," I whisper. "And I'm sorry," I add.

Raven puts a hand on the buck's hindquarters, bows her head, and murmurs her gratitude.

I can already feel his body cooling. I stare at him while Raven and Bo discuss the logistics of getting his huge carcass back to camp. Raven says that the rest of the family is scattered throughout the forest, each on a different game trail, so finding help would take too long.

"Yeah," Bo says, nodding and frowning, "the plan was to split up." A thought occurs to him. "You knew I'd be on the river trail. What are you doing here?"

The tone in his voice makes me look up from the deer and at them. Raven looks away uncomfortably, blushing and shifting. I laugh.

"She came here to watch us," I say flatly.

Raven glares at me, her face bright red. "I came to make sure my brother was hunting, and not..." She trails off and makes a vague gesture toward me.

Bo's face flushes red at the thought of his sister watching what we just did. And she was watching us for a while, I'd bet. Maybe for the whole thing.

I stand up. "So, rather than just being one hunter down, your family effectively loses two hunters today because you're tracking your brother instead of the deer. And why would you do that?" She shuts her mouth with a snap. "Your family needs meat, right? But proving you're better than Bo was more important than that?" I glance down at my kill. "Good thing I was here."

She keeps her mouth shut, and I nod. Good. Now she

knows what the pecking order is. I start to walk away, but Bo grabs my arm.

"Where are you going?" he asks.

"Back to your camp. We need help," I say, gesturing to the enormous dead deer.

"We'll butcher the buck right here so we can drag it back in sections," Bo says, shaking his head. "We can't wait for help. We have to work fast."

I'm already getting queasy at the thought of butchering an animal. I've never even carved a turkey.

"Why do we need to work fast?" I ask. A weak laugh escapes. "It's not like he's going anywhere."

"No, but the bears are. Every bear in a ten-mile radius is going to smell this kill," Raven says, but with less acid than she usually has when she addresses me. "We have to work fast because they're already headed this way. We'll take the best cuts of meat back to camp first. And later we'll come back with a rifle."

"*If* we come back. Might not be worth it," Bo says. He pulls out his knife. "Let's get to work."

What comes next is the most gruesome twenty minutes of my life. While we butcher the buck, I try not to gag. I turn my head to the side and hiss breath in and out through my bared teeth. Bo calmly teaches me what the most valuable cuts are. It's not just the meat, either. The liver is so nutritious that it's one of the first things Raven wraps in ferns and lays on top of the long sticks she's woven together with tree vines and…I don't know, frigging fairy magic, to make a crude sledge.

Bo's tone is soothing and steady as he instructs me and encourages me, but I can see the strain around his mouth. A bear could come at any time. Or a mountain lion. Or a wolf. The sheer number of carnivorous animals in this area dwarfs the human population.

After what seems like a purgatory of sawing and slicing and hacking, Bo is satisfied that we've harvested the best of the carcass that is in our ability to transport. He takes me down to the river to wash off the blood. We dunk and rinse in the frigid water and come up mostly clean, but there's still blood under my fingernails. I'd have to scrub my hands with steel wool to get it all out. If I was cold from the water, that ends as soon as I start to drag my sledge. While Bo and I were butchering my kill, Raven made another sledge for each of us, and in between managed to load the hundreds of pounds of meat and organs that we hacked away from the bones on to them.

We start out. Bo's camp is miles away, uphill. The hour-long trek is torturous.

I am one foot in front of the other. I am hands grown into wood. I am forward—one breath—one step. Then another. And another.

I drag my dead behind me up a mountain.

It's strange. I just realized that when I'm with Bo, I never see dead bodies. When I'm with him, my ghosts are gone.

"You can let go."

I blink.

"Let go," Bo tells me.

He unwinds my fingers from the sledge's crude handles, and I can feel them creaking on the inside, like twisting wet rope.

He leads me to a canvas folding chair and sits me in it while someone else deals with my sledge and its contents. The muscles in my forearms and calves twitch. Bo sees it and starts rubbing my overly taxed arms.

"That was amazing," he whispers.

"Amazing?" I repeat, lifting my mouth into a wry smile. I motion to him and Raven, who is already recounting a heavily edited version of the kill. "I'm practically falling over, and you two aren't even out of breath."

He smiles. "We've had more practice." And then he frowns suddenly, looking off as he rubs my twitching forearm. "I meant that shot. Right through the *middle* of his eye, straight into the brain. I've never seen anything like it."

"Beginner's luck," I say.

"No," he replies with immediate certainty. "You're a born hunter."

I nod, because I recognize now that this is completely true. Some people are born with perfect pitch, some people have eidetic memory, and I have this.

"I'm good at killing things," I say again, but Bo immediately shakes his head and pulls me closer.

"No, that's not it." His fingers run down my arms. "The best death a buck can hope for is a quick, clean one. You gave him that. You are a hunter."

I see something flash through his eyes—regret, maybe. Something he did wrong, or didn't do as well as I did. He's measuring himself against me, and he thinks he's coming up short. Even the notion is so stunningly off base that I fail to find a way to address it before we're interrupted.

"Rainbow, let her have a drink of water," his mother scolds laughingly. "She's about to faint from dehydration." I take the wooden bowl full of water offered to me and tip it into my mouth. She leaves a bucket of the cool, sweet water next to my feet and angles the ladle in my direction so I don't have to lean far to get it. She and Bo hustle off to orchestrate the unpacking of the meat.

Sitting helps a lot. The water helps even more. When I'm finished, and ready to stand, I try to find Maeve and ask her what she wants me to do. The rest of Bo's family notice that I'm done with my break and start to gather around me, waiting expectantly.

It dawns on me that they all want to hear me tell the

story, especially the little ones. Sol and Moth are crouched down in front of me. The interchangeable boys, Aspen and Karl, hover just behind my left elbow, trying not to look too eager.

"I'll take that," the smaller boy—Aspen—says as he gathers the empty bucket and bowl from my hands.

"Rain says he didn't see it, when you took down the buck?" Karl says, eyes narrowed and lips tilted in a challenging smirk. He doesn't believe I'm the one who made the kill.

I look at Bo, and he smiles at me, tipping his chin as if to say, "Go ahead."

"Well, Bo fell asleep," I say, feeling heat build low in my belly. I know he's remembering the same things I am.

"What?" Karl sputters, disbelievingly, interrupting our communion. "Rainbow *never* falls asleep on a hunt."

Bo is grinning now. "I did," he admits. "Keep going," he urges me. "I'd like to know what happened."

I give a moment-by-moment recounting of my kill. I leave out that we were naked, of course, but I tell them everything I can recall. The sounds, the smells, the exact positioning of the buck in relation to myself. It's fun, actually, being the TV instead of watching it. I can't stop myself from reenacting the grand finale for Moth. She gasps and covers her mouth when I pull my arms back, drawing an imaginary bow. When I get to the end of my story, everyone sits in silence for a while, just thinking it through.

Moth suddenly springs up and grabs what looks like a toy bow and arrow from the side of the firepit. She tries my move for herself, her tiny body straining to pull back the arrow. As small as that bow is, it's no toy. Sol watches her little sister as she practices the move on her training bow carefully and then tries it once herself.

"Wait. How did you generate enough force from your knees?" Sol asks, confused.

"Some women have a lot of strength in that position," says a male voice.

I spin around and see that Bo's father has joined us. I stare at him. He looks away from me, disconcerted, and finishes answering his daughter's question.

"You couldn't make it using just your arms, Sol. But most women have very powerful muscles in their thighs and pelvic floor, and enough flexibility in their lower backs to create the torque necessary. It'd be a tough shot, though."

Sol rocks up on to her knees, testing it out again, but this time trying to use her deepest belly muscles. She nods, as if to admit she could imagine it working.

I look down at my hands, remembering the shot, and realize my left forearm is injured. I have a series of red welts on the inside of my forearm that are quickly turning purple. I wasn't wearing an arm guard, and the bow-string skipped across my arm during release. I have no idea how I'm going to explain that to my grandparents. It looks like I was raked with claws or beaten with a cane. There is literally no scenario in my life that would explain these marks in a nonviolent way.

"Does that hurt?" Ray asks.

"A little," I lie. Now that I have a minute to think about it, it's quite painful.

"Come on," Ray says, walking away. "I've got something for it."

I stand up reluctantly. I look for Bo, but he's caught up in a serious conversation with Raven. I can't really wave him down without making it weird.

I follow Ray out of the circle of dormitories, past the greenhouse, and through some trees. As the foliage closes in behind me, I glance back over my shoulder, trying to judge the distance to the main camp. Could Bo still hear me if I yelled for him?

My feet slow and my breathing quickens when I see Ray is leading me toward a padlocked shed. There's an ax driven into a weathered stump right out front. Every rational part of my brain knows that Ray is not Dr. Goodnight, and he is not going to kill me with his family a few hundred yards away. But the rational parts of my brain are too busy freaking out to be effective right now. I keep my distance while Ray unlocks the shed, one foot planted in case I need to run. But run where? I realize with a jolt that I don't know my way back home. Not all the way. I know bits and pieces of the trail, but it's so easy to get lost out here. I glance back over my shoulder again in the direction of camp, wondering what Bo would do if I screamed.

And that unearths a thought I don't want to have. I bury it again.

"Are you allergic to penicillin?" Ray calls from inside the shed.

"Ah...no," I answer back.

He pokes his head out of the door of the shed. I peek around him and see that long, thick flaps of plastic separate the doorway from the outside. Beyond them I can just make out stainless-steel-topped lab tables, glass beakers, scales, and other equipment, and shelves of neatly arranged white bottles. Inside the shed, everything gleams with the futuristic look of a spaceship. It's like he's opened a door to another world. Even the chilled air leaking out between the flaps of plastic smells dried and scrubbed.

"Any history of blood clots?"

"No," I reply, still trying to see over his shoulder.

"I can't let you in here," he says, understandingly. "It's a clean room." That's when I notice he's put on gloves and some kind of backward smock that reminds me of surgeon scrubs.

He disappears back inside the plastic flaps for just a moment. Not long enough for me to make up my mind about whether or not I want to run. He comes back out, minus the scrubs and gloves, and gives me a small tub of goo and a small, rattling bottle of pills.

"The pills will bring the swelling down and help with the pain. The arnica salve will keep the bruising to a minimum," he says. His eyes drop and shift around.

"You were a doctor," I say mechanically. He nods.

"What kind?"

His voice is reluctant as he answers. "Anesthesiologist."

I have to know. I don't know why I have to know, because I don't really want to know, but I'm in this too deep to back out.

"What did you do?" I ask. "Why are you out here?"

He stares at me for a while, caught. Then he really looks at me and takes my measure. He seems to make up his mind about something.

"Assisted suicide," he replies. "I helped seven people end their lives."

He pushes past me, and a mangled half laugh huffs out of me while I watch him head back to the main camp.

"You put them to sleep," I say. But he's too far away to hear me.

I startle at Bo's voice. "Hey," he says. I don't know how long I've been standing here. He's right in front of me. Bo dips his head down to look directly into my eyes. "Are you okay?"

I shake my head. "I want to go home now," I say.

"Okay," he says, looking spooked.

He starts to lead me back to the main camp to say goodbye, but I just can't see Ray again or I'm going to lose it.

"Now," I say, almost shouting. "I want to go now."

He doesn't move right away, so I strike out on my own. I really don't care which way I'm going. I don't care if I'm wandering around the woods all damn night. I have to get out of here.

Bo catches up and runs backward in front of me as I march on. "You're going the wrong way," he says, putting his hands on my shoulders to stop me. "What happened? Did my dad say something to you?"

I look at him, and the thing my mind unearthed earlier rises again like the undead. Which is: if Ray is Dr. Goodnight, then Bo has to know. There's no way Bo can't know. He's not blind or stupid or too young to get it. If his father were a kingpin drug lord and a psychopathic murderer to boot, Bo would know.

I shake my head, but I'm not sure at what. I think I'm just saying no to my own inner voice. I cannot accept that Bo could be a part of anything like that. I don't care how bad it all looks. There has to be another explanation.

"Please tell me what's going on," Bo whispers. His mouth is still a little swollen from kissing me.

I give up and lean against him. I'm too tired to talk or think, and I just want to be close to him. I want him to hold me, and I can't help but think that if I truly thought that he was the willing accomplice of a brutal psychopath, I *couldn't* want that.

Unless I am fully insane.

July 30
Afternoon

BO WALKS ME BACK TO OUR SPOT, BUT I INSIST HE TURN back, rather than walk me all the way home.

"There's still plenty of light," he says, glancing down shyly. He turns to face me, holding both my hands in his. "I want to meet your grandparents."

"That's a terrible idea," I groan.

"No it isn't," he says, smiling. His face suddenly falls. "Unless you're embarrassed by me."

I give him a warning look. "We're past that."

"We are?" he asks uncertainly.

I roll my eyes. "I'm in love with an idiot," I grumble. He laughs, and I know we're okay. "I'm not bringing you home to meet my grandparents because they're going to ask all kinds of questions you can't answer, and you're not good at lying, Bo. If my grandparents even think that you live on public land, they'll report you. One of the first things my grandmother did when I got here was warn me about the druggies in the woods."

"We're not druggies," he says, confused either by the word or the notion that anyone would define his family in that way.

"To them you are. My grandmother would love to turn you in. It would make her year. She'd probably put the fact that she got a whole family arrested in her Christmas cards."

He mentally stumbles for a moment over the Christmas card thing, clearly not understanding that most people give yearly updates to acquaintances that way. In fact, I sort of wonder if Bo knows what a Christmas card even is. He shakes off his confusion quickly in lieu of frustration. He's frustrated because he knows I'm right.

"You said once that you wanted to come home with me because you wanted to know everything about me," he says. "I feel the same about you."

"You're not going to learn anything about me from my grandparents," I say, shaking my head and smiling. "They're cardboard cutouts. They're not real, because real people are messy, God forbid. And when I'm around them, I'm not real. I live in their house, and I'm grateful they've taken me in, but in order to stay, I have to be the granddaughter they want or they'll kick me out. And I don't have anywhere else to go," I admit. "My parents made that clear. I can't live with either of them in New York anymore."

I look down, a little ashamed of it all. The compromises I've made since I got here, the fact that my grandparents really would tell me to move out if I bothered them too much, and that my parents are done with me and each other *because* of me—I burned all of those bridges.

"Besides," I say, breathing a tired laugh and looking back up at him, "you don't need to meet my grandparents to understand me. You already understand me better than I understand myself."

Bo shakes his head slowly and moves a lock of my hair behind my shoulder. He stares at me for a long time before he kisses me.

Why did I never like the idea of sex before? This is the second time in one day I'm practically tearing Bo's clothes off and begging him. He pulls back and shakes himself.

"Not like this," he says, more to himself than me. "Not on the ground. I mean, I want to." He sits back and rubs his forehead. "I *really* want to." He laughs at himself and looks up at me longingly. "But you're tired, and your arm probably hurts, and we don't even have a blanket."

I laugh and nod. "My arm does hurt," I admit, looking at the welts the bow left.

"Did my dad give you something for it?" Bo asks.

"Yeah," I whisper, staring at his worried, precious face.

I dig out the salve and pills from opposite pockets in my shorts.

Bo hands me his canteen, discarded in the mad rush to get out of our clothes, and shakes out a pill for me. I swig it down while he rubs my arm with the salve.

"This looks worse than it should. You bruise easily," he says, frowning. Then he narrows his eyes at me. "Do you have an iron deficiency?"

"No, it's probably the lithium," I say, staring at the inky map under my skin. When the silence becomes too heavy, I notice and look up at Bo. "They put me on lithium for a while. It does weird shit to you for years afterward."

He nods, but his face twists like he's going to cry. "It's okay," I say, moving closer.

"No, it's not," he says, and he pulls me to him, wrapping me up in a full-body hug. I'm warm everywhere. I'm warm down deep in the frozen parts of me. "Why did your parents do that to you?"

"Because I turned them into the horrible parents of a girl who encouraged a thirteen-year-old to kill herself on social media." I breathe out. It's not a laugh, but it feels good like a laugh does. To let it out. "Everyone blames them for raising such a monster. When I lost it, they didn't try to help me. My mom put me in a room, and they pumped me full of drugs, and she promised me I'd never really come out of it." I look at him. "I'm never getting out of that room, Bo. Even here, in the middle of the woods, I'm still there."

He shakes his head. He won't accept it.

"Come with me," he whispers. "When I leave for college, come with me. Live in *my* room."

He can't be serious. "Bo. You'll be starting over. Meeting new people," I say.

He shakes his head. "I won't go without you."

"But you *have* to go," I say, frowning. "Your mom..."

"I don't care." He laughs in a rough, pushed way. "My whole life has been about my parents' choices. Even college." He rolls me under him and holds my face between his hands. "You're my choice. I want you with me. Come with me when I leave."

He's hovering over me, waiting for an answer. A part of me is screaming *yes*. I could get a job in a kitchen somewhere near his school. Maria would write me a recommendation. Bo could sneak me into his dorm room until I found us an apartment. I could figure this out, even without touching a dime of my enormous trust fund. I could do what I've always wanted to do but never had the guts to try. I don't have any reason to stay here once Bo leaves, anyway.

I shake my head.

"This is insane," I say, trying to sit up, but he won't let me. "What about your parents?" I ask.

"Are you kidding? After my mom met you, she told

me you were perfect for me," he replies, smiling. "She'll be thrilled."

I'm confused. Why would Maeve think I was perfect for anyone? I'd just told her I was a liar. A fraud. A conniving, vindictive... Oh. Now I get it.

Maeve is *good*. Who better to protect her painfully naive son from a world full of social situations he has no clue how to navigate?

I'm angry with Maeve for maneuvering me (again) for about a microsecond, because the thought of Bo going to one of those exclusive universities full of teenagers who are used to either being the smartest in their class or the richest in their town turns my stomach. They'll eat him alive. Unless I'm there to eat them first.

And I would. If anyone ever tries to hurt Bo I will destroy them. Maeve knew that, the moment she looked me up and down. I have to go with him.

"Okay," I say, deadly serious.

"Really?" Bo says, surprised.

"I've got nothing to stay here for." I smile up at him like I'm doing this solely for me. "I'll go with you wherever you go."

"Yes!"

He's giddy and boyish. He laughs and squeezes me and makes promises about how great it's going to be. He even asks me to help him choose a school. He's narrowed down his choices to the West Coast, to stay close to his family, but he'll go to whichever of those I like best. It's all the same to me, but I appreciate how hard he's trying to give me some kind of power. But that's Bo. Always giving, even when he's getting.

"I think I'm going to like California," I say.

"The redwoods," Bo says, picturing a colossal forest to rival his own.

"The freeways," I say, picturing a sprawling city to rival my own.

Bo laughs. "Figures you'd be romantic about freeways." I roll toward him, laughing.

"Of course, I'll have to learn how to drive, first. And then I'll spend all day changing lanes and taking exit ramps."

"Just like Joan Didion," he says, touching my face.

I shake my head. "I'm not a writer," I say with finality.

I roll on to my back again.

That's another bridge I burned. Who would ever believe anything I wrote after my completely falsified blog for the Cultural Outreach Club?

Which is a relief, actually.

Because, in my hand, a pen is a sword.

There was a ceiling fan in my room.

The ceilings in the dormitories at the hospital were high, so it was maybe twelve or thirteen feet up. From that distance, it made a faint woop-woop noise that I could only hear when all else was silent, which was surprisingly often.

Before the room, I had pictured insane asylums as noisy places. You know, Bedlam. But that place was quiet because everyone was drugged. It was a good thing, being drugged. So much easier than being me.

My room wasn't padded, but there were no hard edges anywhere. Everything was soft. Everything was designed to soothe. The furniture, which was bolted in place, was done in pastel colors.

I didn't have a window. Forget about locks: a window is the real difference between a prisoner and a patient.

The only break in the monotony of my room was my daily therapy sessions. During the twice-a-day flashes of lucidity between one dose and the next, I was taken out of my room and brought to individual therapy in the morning, and then group therapy in the afternoon.

The first two months, I didn't speak. Catatonic people rarely do, although I have no memory of that time. The next two months, I didn't speak, either, although I was no longer catatonic and finally aware of my surroundings.

I remember trying to shape words in my mouth, trying to push air past my teeth to make sound, and nothing would come out. But there was stuff going on behind my eyes again, so I wrote.

I didn't write replies or questions the way someone with

laryngitis might. I still wasn't engaging with people directly. Instead I wrote narratives about what had happened, and what was happening around me, as if all of this had occurred not too long ago to someone else, somewhere else. I wrote in the third person. I wrote about the people who had hurt me, the people I had hurt, my doctors, and the people sitting in group therapy with me as if they were characters in a book. I wrote about myself as if I were a character in a book.

It was all one big story.

The team of analysts that handled my psych ward of deranged teenagers encouraged me to write. They felt it was a necessary part of my rehabilitation. I gave them my journal right before I went to sleep every night, and they read every page, of course. I got my journal back first thing in the morning while they had meetings about my writing. In my individual session, they made observations based on what I had written in an attempt to draw me out and start a dialogue.

Dr. Holt in particular tried to get me to talk. She usually led group therapy. She really cared about us, and although she was young and pretty and should have had a life of her own, she devoted all of her time to helping everyone in our group get better. Like Mary Poppins with those anemic English kids. She tried to coax me out of my cocoon, but I knew I needed to stay in there because I wanted to be a better person. In my cocoon, I was learning how to be honest, and everything I put into my journal was the truth as I saw it. No more un-journal. No more lying. I was going to burst out of my cocoon a beautiful, honest butterfly, and I'd never hurt anyone again.

But my truth turned out to be as toxic as my lies.

Bo and I spend too long lying on the ground, looking up at the sky.

We don't fall asleep exactly, but I wouldn't say either of us is fully awake, either. California dreaming.

I hear a noise and bolt upright. "What is it?" Bo asks.

I hold my breath while I try to pinpoint what I thought I heard. Footsteps. Clothes brushing against leaves. I don't hear it again, but I know it was a presence, not the random rustling and creaking of the forest. It was human.

"Someone's here," I say, so softly I'm basically mouthing the words.

Bo nods and rises soundlessly. "Which way?" he mouths. I point, and he shifts into the brush, joining its substance.

And then, nothing.

No sound, no motion, no hint that the situation is either good or bad. I'm thinking it's been too long when I hear Bo making his way back to me. He's moving fast, not trying to be quiet.

I stand before I see him and start gathering up our things. When he breaks through the brush, he nods his approval that I'm ready to go.

"I found tracks, but whoever left them doubled back and was able to throw me," he says, his voice low and rough.

"Raven?" I ask hopefully.

Bo shakes his head and pulls me along with him quickly. "No. She'll never shadow us again," he says with certainty. "And whoever it was weighed more than any of my brothers or sisters."

"Who, then?" I ask, once we're through the river.

Bo shrugs and hurries me along. We don't talk. He glides over and through the brush, showing me where to step. He brings me most of the way through the forest and almost to town, but I stop him as the light shifts from the golden of late afternoon into the blue hue of evening.

"Go," I say. "I'll see you the day after tomorrow."

He nods, his eyes still sharp and scanning for danger, and kisses me hard. "Be careful," he pleads. Then he turns and breaks into a run for home.

I do the same. I arrive at my grandparents' at a sprint. Exhaustion has taken on a hallucinogenic quality at this point.

I see too many cars parked out front. I'm stumbling, and the light is nearly gone. I push my way inside with no thought about the parked cars or anything else, because I think I might literally faint, and I just need to get to the end of this marathon day of exertion and fear and love so I can sleep and wake and remember the way Bo feels and tastes and how he sounds when he breathes my name.

July 30
Night

LIAM, TAYLOR, AND AURA-BLUE ARE IN MY LIVING ROOM.

I can't see them, but I hear their voices, chatting with my grandparents as I stumble inside. They are making polite conversation, a specialty of my family's, but even for pros like Grandma and Grandpa, I can tell this is strained.

I hear my grandmother calling me.

My arm looks like I've been in a car crash, and my clothes are stained with deer blood. I don't have a choice. I run upstairs.

"I have to go to the bathroom so bad!" I yell, forcing laughter into my voice so they think this is just a pee emergency.

I tear my clothes as I pull them off my sweaty limbs and throw them into the back of my closet. I run into the bathroom, step into the tub, and rinse off as best as I can. I smell like Bo—leaves, and rain, and that half-feminine, half-masculine smell of lavender and sage that always clings to him.

I choose a lightweight but long-sleeved shirtdress, swipe on some lipstick, and add a squirt of the perfume in the neon bottle to cover Bo's scent before I run back downstairs.

"You guys," I'm saying, grinning as I swoop into the room. "We didn't make any plans..." I break off as soon as I see their faces.

Liam, Taylor, and Aura-Blue are standing. They all look pale and wide-eyed. I hear the ice cubes in my grand- father's glass clink as he finishes off his gin and tonic.

"Have you seen Mila today?" Aura-Blue asks.

"No," I reply.

Liam swallows before he speaks. "Did you leave work yesterday with her?" he asks. His voice is shaking.

"Yeah," I breathe, blindsided. I look at Aura-Blue. "What happened?"

"Did you go out after? Did you go to a party, maybe?"

"No," I say immediately, then shake my head and scroll back, trying to remember. "Wait. We went for ice cream, but we didn't stay long. Then she took me back to the shelter to get my bike. I got home..." I stop and look at my grandmother. "When did I get home?" I ask her.

"Before four," she says anxiously.

They all share a look before Liam says, "You didn't go out with her later?" He glances at my grandmother apologetically. "You didn't sneak out, maybe, and go hiking?"

"Hiking at night?" I laugh I'm so surprised. They aren't joking. I change my tone to something more serious. "I didn't go to a party, and I don't go hiking at night," I say clearly. "What happened?"

"Mila's missing," Aura-Blue says in a tremulous voice. "It's too soon for the police to get involved, but we know something's wrong. No one's seen her."

"Mila hasn't spent a day by herself ever," Liam adds, and I nod. Just like Jinka, Mila was never alone.

"She's not answering her phone—and she *always* answers her phone," Aura-Blue says. She grimaces. "Even when she shouldn't."

"We were hoping she was with you," Taylor says.

I shake my head. And that's as far as I can stretch my strength. I have to sit down. I take a step to get to the couch, and my knees buckle. I feel Liam and Taylor catch me. My bruised arm complains, but the pain is a good thing. It keeps me here. They guide me around the sofa and help me sit.

"She was fine when she dropped me off," I say. "Maybe she drove off the road on her way home? Have you checked?"

"Her car is parked at her house, and some of her hiking gear is missing," Taylor says as he and Liam take seats on either side of me.

Aura-Blue stands in front of us, wringing her hands. "Did you see her out there on your hike today, or did she mention where she might have gone when you talked after work?" she asks.

"No," I say. Something doesn't sit right. "If she took her hiking gear, why did you ask me if we went to a party?" I ask.

Another look passes between Liam, Taylor, and Aura-Blue.

"What?" I snap, annoyed now. "What aren't you telling me?"

"I told you guys, she really doesn't know," Taylor says, laughing despite the situation.

"Tay," Liam says sharply, silencing Taylor.

I look at Aura-Blue. "Tell me."

She shifts uncomfortably from foot to foot, glancing back at my stock-still grandparents.

"Because you know the drugs come out of the woods, right?" she says timidly.

"Yeah, I know. In fact, Mila and I were talking about people making meth and fentanyl in the woods when we went for ice cream yesterday. But she was terrified of all that," I say.

Mila would never go out looking for Dr. Goodnight just to prove to me he existed...would she?

"You guys, she *really* doesn't know," Taylor says, enunciating clearly so they actually listen to him. "She has no idea what working at the shelter means, AB."

"What does it mean?" I ask slowly.

Aura-Blue takes a breath and just says it. "Some girls who volunteer at the shelter do it so they can buy drugs off the guests."

My grandparents gasp, and Aura-Blue looks mortified to have to say this in front of them.

"You can only score if you work out front. Back of the house is for the hard-core rehab people," she mumbles in their direction, even though they have no idea what that means. She looks back at me. "But you never tried to get moved out front. You never asked us to buy for you. You never went out with us, even though you were this big Manhattan socialite. Rob showed us your Instagram from a year or so back. You knew legit celebrities."

She sounds so impressed. It makes my skin crawl.

"At first we thought we were too D-list for you, and that's why you always went home," she continues with a self-deprecating smirk. "Then later we realized you just didn't party. We figured you had quit."

"What does that have to do with Mila?" I snap, frustrated. "She wasn't doing drugs."

A look passes between the three of them. Aura-Blue shakes her head, confused.

"Wait. Mila said she talked with you about how much she was using, and you told her not to worry."

I couldn't be more shocked if she'd slapped me. "We never talked about that," I say.

"When she and I got into that fight that day," Aura-Blue explains. "After work at the shelter, when you came out to the car, and there was all that drama? Do you remember that?"

"Yeah...no," I sputter defensively as Aura-Blue pushes on.

"I was trying to get her to quit with me. She told me later that the two of you talked about it, and that you said it was just a summer thing, and she shouldn't worry. She figured you'd know because you used to be a big party girl and you were able to quit."

Liam stands up stiffly and has to walk around.

"No. That conversation was about..." I gesture to Liam, and my hand drops. "She used the word 'stray.' Then she said sometimes she needed something extra. I thought she was talking about guys... Oh my God." I drop my head in my hands. "I swear she never said anything about drugs."

"She'd never say it," Liam growls from the other side of the room. "Mila never really says what she means. That would be too ordinary."

I just sit there, overwhelmed.

"She kept promising she would quit before school started. It was just a summer thing. Like you said," Aura-Blue adds quietly. "Then she ran out of money and started going out with guests from the shelter. She was going to parties with the dealers. She tried to get me to come, but I wouldn't because I know what that means."

I nod, still taking it in. I remember Gina in the kitchen, warning me off Mila. Saying Mila needed to bring pretty girls to parties. It was because Mila needed fresh meat for the dealers to get free drugs now that she was out of cash. She kept borrowing money and stopped wearing jewelry, probably because she'd pawned it all. She'd lost weight and she looked like she wasn't sleeping. I noticed all this stuff, but I never put it together. I can't believe I didn't see the truth.

"That's why we think she went hiking last night," Taylor says. "She must have run out, and we think she went looking for the source."

"No," I say, shaking my head. "She was too scared."

"You don't know what she would have done to get more," Liam says darkly.

Aura-Blue sniffs, and I realize she's crying. "It feels like it happened overnight. One day she was just buying Oxy for the weekend, and the next..." She trails off.

If I had stopped to think about it—actually think about Mila—it would have been blindingly obvious. The way she ran her hands over the steering wheel sensually and tilted her face into the light. The fact that she *kissed* me. She was so high. I noticed the details, but I didn't want to look harder at the whole picture. I didn't bother to ask her what the fight with Aura-Blue was really about because I didn't want to get dragged into it.

I didn't want to read past those three little dots.

And that day in Mila's Mini, after Aura-Blue had tried to get her to stop, I told Mila to have fun. Of course she listened to me, not her best friend Aura-Blue, because I used to party with legit celebrities. Look at my Instagram. I'm an expert at this shit.

I told Mila to do more this summer. I told her, *Go ahead.*

"This can't be happening again," I say, shaking my head. I think I stand up. "It can't."

I'm drowning. I need to get out. Death goes everywhere I do. I should be as far away from people as possible.

I see the stars and feel my lungs fill with night air for a brief moment before I feel hands catching me, trying to get me to sit or stay or stop.

I see my grandparents' faces and hear them scolding. Someone's yelling something about how they shouldn't upset me. That I have suffered tragic losses. That I came here to get away from it all, and why can't they just leave me alone?

The hands don't let me go. I see Taylor's worried face as he carries me upstairs and lays me on my bed. He tucks the covers around me. He's a sweet guy.

"It's okay," he whispers. "It's not your fault." Sweet, but so very wrong.

When your room is silent and still, the single object that creates noise and motion becomes a point of fixation.

The fan went woop-woop, and it filled many hours of my day. It was the whirring pinwheel around which I rotated between therapy sessions. I was always spinning, even lying down.

One day, after group therapy, they shuffled us into the common room, ostensibly for our daily allotment of supervised socialization, but really it was to give us our second dose of medication. Before mine kicked in, I noticed something. I noticed that one of the boys in my group was looking out the window. He was smiling.

David was his name. OCD. Manic depression. He'd lost his marbles when his girlfriend dumped him, and he'd tried to kill himself.

I'd like to say I knew him well, seeing as how every day I listened to him spill his guts, but the truth is, when you're sunk so deep that you're in a hospital, other people glance off you like rocks skimming the top of a pond.

I could give you a list of all David's triggers. I could tell you everything about his family and about his friends on the volleyball team. But I never knew him. I never interacted with him. I never invested myself enough to decide if I even liked him or not. I watched him and wrote down the details. Just the details. Never the whole picture.

I'd written about him before, but this particular day was different. I needed to describe the way he was looking out the window because I couldn't figure it out. Seeing his smile was like a seeing a sheep walking down Fifth Avenue. It didn't belong there.

I took my journal out of the pocket of my robe and wrote about David's smile. He was looking out the window and thinking something magical. I realized that it was the wistful, longing look of someone who was in love. Not that I'd ever been in love. But I'd seen movies, and David was definitely in love.

It was so enchanting to see it there in the hospital. That anyone could feel anything so deeply that wasn't paranoia, anxiety, or desperation struck me as otherworldly.

I wrote about the sun coming through the window, hitting his sharp, pale features and lighting up his extraordinarily long and thin body. David was an exceptionally tall, skinny guy with a Byronic air. He even had the romantic curls of a poet, now that his hair had grown back in after they'd shaved it.

I formed an opinion about David in that moment. And it was that I liked him. But I kind of wanted to kick him, too. I wanted to tell him to tuck his heart back in. It's sloppy to leave it hanging out like that.

Even then I knew I was watching something deeply private. Embarrassed by his earnestness, I started writing about the floors and the walls and the texture of the paper under my fingers. I wrote about the nurses and the clocks and the feel of the medication seeping into my veins, turning my blood to chalk.

I never stopped to think that I had been writing in group therapy just moments before. I had written about how he kept complimenting Dr. Holt. How he laughed at every joke and hung on her every word. The other doctors, watching the video surveillance cameras of the session, would only see David engaged and responding to treatment in a positive way. But my journal was not a camera hanging in a high corner. My journal was on the ground in the thick of it. Moment to moment. It caught and recorded more than the bird's-eye view. I never stopped to think that an outside set of eyes reading my observations about the therapy session, followed so closely by my heavily detailed description of David's burgeoning attachment, would see the whole picture through me, which I still couldn't, trapped in the absolute truth of the details as I was. The whole picture was that David had fallen in love with Dr. Holt. Given David's history, falling in love was the first step toward his self-destructive impulses. It became imperative that something be done about it.

Unfortunately, the wrong "something" was done.

The effect my journal had on others, be it an un-journal full of lies or the hyper-truth of moment-by-moment life, was still beyond me, although it was the reason I was in that hospital to begin with.

I wrote until the drugs made me still again. The red light on the surveillance camera blinked on, telling me that night had come, and it was time to sleep. Then I stared at the fan, rotating way above me in the never-darkness of my hospital room. I thought about how tall David was, and the distance to that fan. I thought about it, but still in my cocoon, I couldn't say anything. So I just stared.

Woop-woop.

July 31

I WAKE UP ACHING, LIKE A FIST CLENCHED FOR TOO LONG.

I open my mouth wide, and my jaw cracks. It's a satisfying sound and feeling. I unwind myself from the blankets Taylor wrapped around me.

I sit up and see that my phone is vibrating. I know who it is before I check the caller.

When I don't answer, Rob sends me a text.

Are you okay?

Yes, I text back, *just a little shaky.* ***Did you talk to Liam or Taylor?***

Both. Aura-Blue, too. I'm coming back early.

The thought is actually a comfort, even though I'm going to have to break up with him as soon as he's settled. ***Is your mom okay with that?*** I text. He's told me bits and pieces about her. She's very attached to Rob, and she's jealous of any time he spends away from her.

Don't care. I'm so worried about you. Taylor told me you took the news hard.

No other way to take it. I'm glad you're coming back.

There's a pause before he writes, ***I miss you.***

See you soon.

He doesn't try to continue the conversation. I've been keeping our exchanges brief for the past week. I won't lie to Rob, so I haven't been able to say much at all. I still want to break up with him in person, and I'm sure he knows something like that is coming.

I'm probably overthinking the whole thing. I should just text him and tell him that I've met someone else.

But I actually care about Rob, and I want to do this as respectfully as possible.

So instead, I guess I'm stringing him along.

Jesus. Is there ever a right way to break things off with someone? I never cared before, so I never gave it much thought, and now I'm pretty sure I'm making a mess of it. I swing my legs out of bed even though they're screaming at me. Everything hurts. I'm still wearing the shirtdress I put on after getting back from the forest, and I consider whether or not I can get away with just staying in it. But no. I've got to get to the shelter, so I drag myself into the bathroom to get ready.

What the hell am I going to do about my arm? I take a pill, put on the salve, but it's still purple. It doesn't hurt as much, but it looks atrocious. I realize my hands are all scratched up, too. Must have happened while Bo and I were butchering the deer, or maybe when I was dragging the sledge, walking through some tougher brush. I'm covered in bruises. It's alarming. I'll have to wear a long-sleeved shirt and keep my hands out of sight.

I wash my face and stare in the mirror. I open the vanity. The orange bottles of pills are all lined up, just as I left them.

I waver. They would make this easier. I want easier.

But I don't really deserve it.

I shut the vanity and go downstairs. My grandparents aren't up yet. I make coffee for them, have a cup myself, and then get on my bike.

This is the way Mila came after she dropped me off at the shelter to get my bike. After we got ice cream. Right before she fell off the face of the earth.

She drove on the other side of the street. What doesn't make sense to me is how Mila went from being scared out of her mind about what was in the woods to going on a hike through them just minutes later.

Did she see something on this road that made her decide to go home, get her hiking gear, and go into the woods? It's kind of a busy road—if you can call any street in this sleepy pocket of the world busy. It runs through several towns going up the coast. Did she pass someone or something on the way that made her decide suddenly to embark on a dangerous night hike?

I slow down and look around. I see tire tracks as if someone went off the road. They look new. Excited, I pedal over to them to get a closer look, and as soon as I do, I recognize the ridiculousness of my actions. They're just tire tracks. I'm not a sleuth. Any clue short of a blinking neon arrow saying "She went that way!" would be lost on me.

I push on to the shelter, still thinking about Mila. I can't fathom why she would go into the woods at night. I don't buy that it was to find drugs. There are a dozen ways a beautiful young girl can score if she wants to. Ways that are far more certain that she will actually get drugs than wandering around the woods blindly.

Unless she knew where she was going and knew for certain that there were drugs there.

Unless she knew how to find Dr. Goodnight.

I don't know how I know I'm right. I just know I am. Mila wasn't telling me a ghost story at the Snack Shack. She was asking for help without asking, because that's her way. Speaking around the problem. Never naming the unnameable.

I remember the desperate way she looked at me. How she kept begging with her eyes. She was hoping that I'd be smart enough to figure it out, or at least that I was suspicious enough of her behavior at the Snack Shack to follow her out on a hike, say, that afternoon. She knows I can hike, and she knows that I'm fascinated with Dr. Goodnight, or I wouldn't have grilled her about him. She was practically daring me. She wanted me to follow her. Find him. And save her.

And I laughed in her face. "You coming in?"

I turn and find Gina standing next to me. I'm still at my bike, although I've already chained it up. I'm just standing here, stuck.

"You ever think you've already been the worst person you could possibly be, and that you're past all that, that you've grown, and then you wake up one morning and realize that you're an even bigger asshole than you ever were?" I ask her.

She looks me up and down, sucks her teeth, and says, "Girl, you need a meeting."

"Mila's missing," I say. I realize I'm twisting the bike chain in my hands. "No one's seen her. It's been almost forty-eight hours."

Gina sighs heavily, and all the tough-girl bluster goes out of her, and I swear I can see a teenaged girl inside this forty-year-old woman standing across from me, and she's hearing for the first time that her friend is gone. The police don't count someone missing until after forty-eight hours. But after forty-eight hours whatever is going to happen to a girl has already happened. We know that. We both know what forty-eight hours means.

"He has to pay," Gina says.

I nod. "Yes. He does." I keep nodding hectically, but my voice is calm. Because this is something I know I'm good at. I had a lot of practice making people pay while I was in the hospital. "I will make sure he does."

"Come on," she says. "You got family inside, and we'll get you through it." She locks up my bike for me and corrals me into the kitchen.

We go in the back, but before we can pass the walk-ins and go on to the kitchen, I stop Gina and pull her into one of the freezers.

"You know him," I say flatly. "Dr. Goodnight. You know him."

Gina bites her lip and shakes her head. "I haven't seen him in years," she mumbles. "Way back before he was Dr. Goodnight. Even before he had a kid and disappeared into the woods."

"A kid?" I say, my voice thin. "So…what, does he have, like…a family out in the woods?"

"How the hell should I know? I got clean," she says. "I know he had a son about seventeen, eighteen years ago, and so he had to be more careful. Then he disappeared. Twelve or thirteen years later, everyone's talking about Dr. Goodnight out in the woods." She looks down. "Same guy, though. He liked it when people would nod out and not wake up. He used to laugh."

All the air rushes out of me. In the sub-zero temperature, it looks like a ghost.

"I said nothing," Gina says, fierce now, pointing a finger at me.

"Where is he?" I say, grabbing her arm before she can walk away. "Gina. Who is he? What's his real name?"

"We're done," she says, shaking me off roughly and going for the door. But she's not angry. She's scared.

Gina pulls the door open and stops. She sighs and turns back round. "Come on. You don't need to talk in circle time, but you should listen."

When I don't immediately follow her, she comes back and puts an arm around me and brings me out with her. She holds my hand all the way through circle time.

Gina is a good person. And she thinks I'm a good person. That's why she's trying to protect me, and maybe herself a little, too, by not telling me his real name. She thinks I'm the type who'll go running to the police, get caught up in the witness thing, and end up dead. And she'd end up dead for telling me.

But I'm not a good person. And I'm not going to the police.

I'm going into the woods.

I knew something was wrong the next morning. They wouldn't give me my journal back.

The deal was I would give them my journal right before

I went to sleep, and it would be returned to me first thing at morning check-in.

But that morning, they gave me a new notebook and told me to keep writing. But I couldn't. I hadn't finished all the pages in my last one. You can't start a new book of your journal with a ton of blank pages left in your old book. You just can't.

I stood at the door of my room, dangling the foreign object out in front of me like it was a wet cat. I held it toward the door for I don't know how long, waiting for someone to come and take it away and give me my journal back.

I remember my arms aching, but in an offhand way. Finally, one of the doctors came and took it. He said that it was going to take a little bit longer for them to return my journal to me, and they didn't want to leave me with nothing to write in.

I still couldn't talk. I remember thinking that I should say something, that I should demand my journal, but nothing came out of my mouth. So I stood at the door. Again, I'm not sure how long I stood there.

Someone came to take me to my individual therapy session. I stood in the middle of the room, unable to sit. Three doctors came in and tried together to talk to me. Until now, I had shown no signs of disobedience. I ate, slept, peed, and walked when they told me to. The only thing I hadn't done when asked was speak. This was different.

I stood through the whole hour of my therapy session

with Dr. Jacobi. She sighed a lot. Frustrated with me, or my silence, or my sudden disobedience—I'm not sure which, really. Dr. Jacobi was an extremely astute psychiatrist, probably the smartest person in that hospital, but she didn't have a lot of compassion for the patients. Made me wonder why she did it at all.

When an orderly led me back to my room, I stood at the door of my room until it was time for group therapy.

It wasn't stubbornness. I wasn't making a statement. Without my journal, I couldn't write. I couldn't eat. I couldn't rest. Standing was, simply, the only thing I could do.

Someone brought me to group therapy. Dr. Holt wasn't sitting in the leader's chair. I stopped a few steps in the door, knowing this change had something to do with my journal somehow. I did not come in any further, even though the new doctor, Dr. Weinbach, waved, then coaxed, then urged, and then finally allowed me to stay where I was as if my standing was his idea.

Dr. Weinbach explained to all of us that he would be the new group leader and that Dr. Holt had been moved to another floor.

David demanded to know why. The doctor sidestepped this question. Then David wanted to know how long before Dr. Holt returned to our floor. When the doctor dodged this question as well, David started yelling and swearing, setting off the more easily agitated members of our group.

Everyone started hurling questions at the doctor. Insisting that we don't hold back in group. That none of us would ever tell him anything if he wasn't straight with us first.

Once we cobbled together all the half answers the doctor reluctantly gave us, it became clear that it was very likely none of us would ever see Dr. Holt again, due to an emotional dependence that had developed between her and a certain member of our group.

That's when David attacked Dr. Weinbach.

Gina spends the rest of the day hovering. She asks me what my plan is for after work. She invites me to hang out with her, which is totally awkward for both of us, but I appreciate it. She's worried about me.

At the end of my shift at the shelter, I go to the office to figure out my upcoming schedule with Maria. The door is shut. Which is unusual if someone is in there.

I hear voices inside, so I lean up against the wall and wait for the door to open rather than disturb what must be an important conversation. When the door swings open, Maria and her companion jump at the sight of me. Like I've caught them doing something wrong.

It's Officer Langmire.

"What are you doing out here?" he barks at me.

"Uh... I was just waiting for Maria," I stammer.

"Come in," she calls. "I'll be in touch, Officer," she says, dismissing Langmire, and then she waves me in impatiently.

I have to pass the officer on my way in. "Sorry I startled you," I tell him, barely able to suppress a payback smirk. He gets it just as I turn away.

"Shut the door," Maria tells me.

I do as she says. She stands behind her desk, and she doesn't invite me to sit opposite her.

"What did you hear?" she asks plainly.

"Un-muf-ner-rumm-sss-murf," I mumble incoherently. I pretend to think it through. "Yeah, I think I got that word for word."

Maria stares at me for a moment and then breaks up laughing. "Okay, sit. You want to talk schedule?" she says, still smiling and shaking her head. "You're funny, you know."

"It's my only redeeming quality," I say. I watch her pull out the schedule sheet. "But, just out of curiosity, what were you talking about?"

She looks up at me and narrows her eyes. "I don't want to upset you."

I meet her gaze. "Too late."

She studies me before answering. "Mila."

"What have you heard?" I ask, coming to the desk. "Do they have anything?"

Maria holds up her hands. "No, nothing. There's no

news yet. He just wanted to ask me some questions about her and her…habits." She looks away.

I nod. "He wanted to know if she was using."

Maria nods. "It changes where they look and how they look…"

"Or whether they look at all," I finish bitterly.

Maria sighs. "Yeah," she admits. Then she leans toward me earnestly. "What happened to Mila is bound to throw you, but don't let it throw you off the path. Don't let her bad choices choose for you."

I nod and get back to the schedule. I've already made my choice.

Aura-Blue answers her phone before the first ring ends. "Did you hear anything? Did they find her?" she asks breathlessly.

"No," I say, sighing so I don't start yelling. "They don't know shit."

I debate telling Aura-Blue about Officer Langmire coming to the shelter today, but I decide it's too much. She needs to think the police are doing something to help, even though I can tell from the way Maria looked at me that the police are ready to write Mila off as a runaway drug addict who doesn't want to be found.

Unless the FBI gets involved.

They're here for something, and I need to know specifics. Right now all I have are vague similarities. If I'm going to rat out Bo's family, I want it to be because I know for certain that Ray is Dr. Goodnight, not because he helped sick people end their own lives. Because if euthanasia is his crime, who the hell am I to judge? I've done far worse.

"Listen," I say, putting some hope in my voice. "I want to talk to your grandfather. He used to be sheriff, right?"

"I mean, of course you can meet him, but why do you want to talk to him?" she asks.

"Is he still in touch with the FBI?"

"Yeah," she says curiously. "What are you thinking?"

What *am* I thinking?

"I don't know," I admit, "but I'm not okay with leaving Mila's fate in the hands of Officer Quagmire," I say, purposely missaying his name. Aura-Blue bursts out laughing.

"And why's that?" she asks, still chuckling.

"It's just a feeling I have," I reply, "but I need to talk to someone who believes that Dr. Goodnight is real. For a bunch of different reasons."

There's a long pause before Aura-Blue replies. "Grandpa lives really close to your house, you know. We can go see him right now."

As we drive down the long driveway right along the edge of the forest, we pass a sign that reads WHISPERING PINES. My heart sinks.

"You didn't tell me your grandfather was in a nursing home," I say. I don't try to hide my disappointment.

"I know it looks bad," she says, pulling into the back lot where the guests park like she's done this a million times, "but that doesn't mean he doesn't know what he's talking about." I watch her profile as she carefully avoids my gaze and parks. "Most of him is still there," she insists. She turns off the engine and faces me. "If you don't want to talk to him..."

I open my car door and get out in answer. What a mess.

Grandpa is in the rec room. I spot the nurses, the orderlies, and the locked doors as I follow Aura-Blue back toward an old man who still looked quite strong and healthy, considering. He was reading a newspaper by the window.

The hospital was like this, although the clientele was significantly younger—just as addled, of course, and just as many drugs and rubber diapers, but far fewer wrinkles. I used to think that the elderly in nursing homes were sad, but I don't anymore. They lived a full life and now they get to forget all the mistakes they made. Sign me up.

"Grandpa?" Aura-Blue says, touching the surprisingly fit-looking man's shoulder. His hair is thick and solid white, like he's about to pitch a reverse mortgage commercial. He doesn't use glasses to read. There aren't that many older people that I know of who don't need glasses. I'm wondering why he's in a home at all, considering his vision is good, and he looks really fit for an old guy. He smiles up at Aura-Blue and stands to give her a big hug.

"Marcy, where you been?" he asks, squeezing her tight.

"Mom's not here," she tells him, casting a nervous glance my way. "It's just me, Grandpa. Aura-Blue."

"Oh," he says. Like now he gets the joke and he can't believe he missed it. "Every day you look more and more like her," he says, recovering winningly, though now I'm getting an idea as to why he's in a home. "That's a compliment, too," he informs me.

I smile and nod politely, but I've never met Aura-Blue's mother, so I have no idea.

"This is my friend," Aura-Blue says, introducing me. I shake Grandpa's hand as he looks me over approvingly. I know how to dress for a visit with my elders.

"Very nice to meet you," I say clearly, not too high and not too low, but dead center in my register so he can hear me without me having to raise my voice.

I don't know if he's hard of hearing, but it's best to start out neither shouting at an old man nor whispering. I've spent a lot of time reading to the elderly when my mother was still volunteering me for everything. You never know who's all there and who's stone deaf.

"Francis Tanis. What can I do for you?"

He gestures with his rolled-up newspaper for me to sit opposite him, and I see the sheriff in him still. He's obviously done this many times, and his hearing is all there.

I fold my skirt under me and sit with my knees pinned together and tilted to the side.

"I have some questions for you," I say.

"About your missing friend Mila," he replies. He leans back and adopts a small smile, meant to goad me into telling all. Good cops never give more information than they get, unlike Officer Langmire.

I tip my head to the side. "That depends."

"On what?" he asks, still smiling, sphinxlike.

"On whether or not her disappearance is related to Dr. Goodnight."

He leans forward suddenly and shoots a look at Aura-Blue.

I lean forward as well and press on before he can get clearance from her. "I'm here because I want to know everything you know about him."

"Most people would say that he doesn't exist," Grandpa says cautiously.

I lean away and echo his sphinx smile right back at him. "We're not most people."

A laugh lives and dies in his breath. "No. I guess not." He glances at Aura-Blue, and she shrugs. Given the semi go-ahead, he starts talking.

"He was always out in front of any drug. Always knew how to grow it and refine it if it was an organic or make and manufacture it simply and quickly if it was a chemical. And he did it before we even knew what the drug was. He made ecstasy before we knew what to call it. Meth. Molly. Fentanyl. Always out front. He's a genius."

Mr. Tanis goes on to tell me a story.

I know stories, and this one is about a detective who was no Sherlock, but who followed the footprints anyway. He stumbled over bodies and saw the same pattern over and over, but never laid eyes on his Professor Moriarty. After listening for half an hour, I see the patterns as clearly as he did. Dozens of women fell asleep and never woke up. All of them were addicts. All of them tried recovery, failed, and then disappeared.

"Why doesn't anyone believe you?" I ask and, a moment too late, realize how insulting that was. "Sorry," I say, cringing and looking down. "But someone must have seen him," I say, laughing to cover the fact that I know someone who had seen him. Gina. But she won't talk. "Someone must have come forward."

"Couldn't get one person to go on the record," he says sadly. "Too scared."

"What do you know about him? Any personal details at all?" I ask.

"He'd be late forties now. Caucasian. Fair. Quiet type.

Strange." The old sheriff shrugs. "He had a son who'd be about your age."

"That's it," I say, leaning forward. "If you know he had a son, then he must be on record somewhere. A birth certificate, at least. Who had his son? What was her name? What hospital?"

Mr. Tanis smiles at me. "You'd make a good cop," he tells me. He's wrong, of course, but I don't correct him. "It was a home water birth," he says. "The woman went by the name Aurora. She took the name from the sleeping princess in that Disney movie. We never found out who she really was, and we only knew about the boy because ten people overdosed in one night. The sole survivor told us it was a bonfire to celebrate a birth. Before she sobered up and conveniently forgot."

I sit back. I look out the window. Every detail makes it worse. A strange, genius dad and an Earth Mother woman have a baby in the woods just when Bo was born. It's too close, but I can't accept it.

"So you have people dying in droves in this area, but no one will believe you when you say it might be a serial killer?" I raise an eyebrow at him. "No one from one of the big agencies—the FBI or the DEA—would even hear you out?"

"Oh, they heard me. But they wrote us off as a town with a drug problem." His brow furrows as he thinks of how to explain. "Drug dealers get caught for a few reasons. Most of them have to do with money. The FBI follows the money, right?"

I half nod, half shrug. I really don't know.

"Well, they do. People make drugs to make money, and then they have to launder that money somehow, right?" He leans forward. The gleam in his eye gets an unstable edge to it. "The FBI came here before. They could never *find* the money. Never. No money, no drug dealer. Dr. Goodnight became a joke."

Mr. Tanis shifts in his seat and looks out the window. I look at Aura-Blue as his agitation builds. She leans in and touches his arm.

"Grandpa, it's okay," she says, trying to soothe him. That only makes it worse.

"Okay?" he scoffs. "Do you know how many people he's killed?"

Aura-Blue sits back, her lips a thin line. I glance over at the orderlies. They aren't making a move yet, but their radar is on. Mr. Tanis seems to know he's running out of time, or maybe he knows he's past the sweet spot in his meds when he's calm and charming, and he tells me the rest in a rush.

"The reason we could never find him is because he didn't make the drugs to make money. That's where the FBI went wrong. That's why they can't find him and why they don't believe he's real. It was never about the money. Not for Dr. Goodnight. It was about killing. But something's changed. Twenty years of sleep and now blood. He never chopped people up before!"

By this point, Mr. Tanis has jumped out of his chair and he's pacing. Two orderlies are coming toward us.

"Is that why the FBI are back?" I ask, standing and pacing with him so I don't miss a word before he disappears into anger. "Do they believe you now?"

"No!" he screams. "It's all wrong! They're still girls, and the killings happened on his turf, so it *has* to be him. But...the blood! He likes things *clean*."

He laughs as the orderlies grab him. He feigns weakness for a moment and then surges with strength and breaks free, charging at me again.

"They can ignore dead junkies who overdose, but those bodies...what he did to them. They can't ignore that." The orderlies grab him just before he can grab me, and Mr. Tanis struggles and screams at the ceiling as he's carried out.

The orderlies get him through the door and carry him off to the never-never land of his room.

August 1
Morning

I'VE BEEN WAITING FOR BO FOR OVER AN HOUR.

I got *there* early. I woke when it was still dark and set out barely past dawn. I brought my blanket this time and spread it out, but I didn't take anything else out of my pack.

I'm just sitting here. I still don't know what to say, but I can't pretend that Dr. Goodnight doesn't exist anymore. And I can't pretend that every new detail I learn doesn't point directly at Bo's father.

Mr. Tanis said Dr. Goodnight likes things *clean*. It's difficult to keep things clean in the middle of a temperate rain forest that's brimming with living things and seeping water.

But Bo's dad has a clean room, right here in the middle of the woods. It was miraculously spotless.

I need to be sure that Ray is Dr. Goodnight. If he is,

there's no way Bo doesn't know *something* about it. The only play I have is to get Bo to say something that he shouldn't know—like the fact that one of my friends is missing—and then I can go back home, march right into Officer Langmire's station and tell him that I can lead him and the nearest SWAT team to the killers.

But how? Bo and I have never spoken about Mila. Except that one time I told him that my friend Mila kissed me. Was saying her name enough for him to be able to find her? Was saying she kissed me enough for him to want to kill her? I know someone from his family takes a monthly trip into town for mail and news. I don't know if one of them took that trip yesterday and heard about Mila's disappearance, or if they would know Mila is missing because Ray has her tied up in that shed where he makes his drugs.

I don't know Bo.

But I don't know how much I don't know him, and that's why I'm just sitting here, combing through every conversation I've ever had with him. Searching for a way to either trap him or trust him. But I've got nothing. There's no web of lies I can entangle him in. No easy key that unlocks the box and lets the demons out.

I always thought I was smarter than everyone else. Well, I'm not. I still haven't figured out what changed. Why did Dr. Goodnight go from the clean death of sleep to the gory messes that he's been leaving lately?

Unless it's not the same killer.

That's a stretch. One killer is hard enough to buy into, but two killers occupying the same area of forest? If Dr. Goodnight is real, he wouldn't allow someone to come into his territory and start killing people in a way that would draw the attention of the FBI. That could bring *him* down. Unless Dr. Goodnight knows the killer, and either can't or won't stop the fledgling psychopath from poaching his prey.

Dr. Goodnight had a son. He had a fledgling.

"You're here early," I hear Bo say before I hear his footsteps.

He breaks through the brush, his cheeks flushed and his eyes sparkling. He's rushing toward me with all the certainty and warmth of the rising sun.

What the hell am I thinking? There's no darkness in Bo. No gruesome secret. I know liars. I know when I'm being manipulated. Bo is certainly not a murderer, and if Ray is Dr. Goodnight, then Bo doesn't know. Even the thought is ludicrous.

Bo stops at the edge of my blanket. "What's the matter?" he asks, his face mirroring my tortured expression.

"My friend is missing," I say, and I burst out crying. I cry over everything, now that I'm not on my meds. No, actually, that's not true. I only cry when Bo is with me.

He sits down next to me gingerly. He doesn't crowd me or try to hug me. "Was she out hiking?" he asks. I nod, and his face brightens. "How long? When did she go missing?"

"The day before yesterday, right after we worked together at the shelter," I answer while I sniff and wipe my face on the back of my hands. "We went out for ice cream, and then she must have gone home and got her hiking gear..."

Bo interrupts. "What time was that?" he asks urgently.

"After four."

"Did she bring a tent? Camping gear? Does she hike a regular path?" He's standing up now and helping me to my feet as he speaks. "Think, Lena! We could still find her. Show me where she started from, and I can track her."

I'm shaking my head. I don't know if it's because I don't dare get my hopes up or because I'm so surprised by his reaction. But I shouldn't be surprised. Bo is good through and through, and I can't believe I was such a fool to think what I did.

"Can you really track her?" I ask.

"You said she went missing after four, the day before yesterday. It hasn't rained since noon, the day before yesterday," he says. His voice is deep and sure. "I can find her. Just show me where she started from."

I start to gather up my things, but Bo stops me. He hefts my pack. "Too much weight," he says, and he starts emptying it out.

He removes everything that isn't survival gear, including my journal. I almost stop him, and then I don't. I don't need my journal. Not anymore.

"I'll show you where she lives," I say, shouldering my nearly weightless pack.

I knew. A few days had passed since David attacked the doctor, and he seemed to have settled into the new routine. Still, I knew.

I stood at my door. Mute, but screaming inside until someone came.

They all wondered how I knew, of course, but it's not that difficult to put it all together if you had watched him closely. And no one had watched him more closely than I had. I just needed to stand back and see the big picture, and finally, I did.

When Dr. Jacobi opened my door, she sighed—a martyred saint, bleeding to death for my raging stupidity.

"You need to verbalize what you've got locked up inside you," she told me, shaking her head sadly. "The only way you're going to get what you need in this world is if you ask for it."

I dodged and weaved on my bare feet. I pushed past her and pointed. She followed me a few steps, but then nodded at an orderly to grab me. I struggled, but let's face it, I'm not a wrestler, and the orderlies at the hospital were very good at restraining people.

I made my first sound in months. Or I tried to. It creaked out of my throat, barely intelligible.

"David..."

It surprised everyone just enough that I could slip away and run the few steps down the hallway to his door.

The furniture was bolted in place, and the ceilings were so high. No one thought it was possible, but David was exceptionally tall, and he'd played volleyball his whole life. He was an outside hitter—one of those guys who jump up so they can spike the ball down on to the opponent's court at an impossibly steep angle.

The details. That's where the devil lives.

I can never know for sure if it was what I wrote in my journal that made the doctors aware of David's feelings for Dr. Holt. And maybe if I'd said something about David's height and his ability to jump, they still wouldn't have listened to me. It was their job to keep him safe, not mine.

All those little details that I saw that they didn't. How silent he'd become since Dr. Holt was moved to another floor. How hopeless yet determined he'd seemed. And then, that night after dinner as both he and I shuffled to our rooms, how relieved he looked. Like it was all going to be over soon. All of these details were there, waiting in my inbox for me to read into them if I had just taken the time. If I'd clicked on David's three little dots.

As I climbed into bed that night, I knew what he was going to do, but I didn't fight off my drugged sleep. I didn't shout at the cameras. I stayed silent. It was not my fault, but I didn't stop it. I should have said something. I should have found a way to speak for David, but, as usual, I was too wrapped up in myself to give it a thought until it was too late.

The next morning, I could have just looked in the window, but I didn't. I threw the bolt on David's door and swung it wide open.

In that slim slice of time after morning check-in when they turn off the night surveillance cameras, but before they came to take him to breakfast, David had hanged himself from the ceiling fan.

Woop-woop.

I bring Bo back to Mila's house.

It's odd to see him like this, so close to pavement and pollution and GPS-led cars. We're standing on the edge of the forest, and her house is across the street. Bo is already looking around for her possible entrance site.

"Don't move," he orders softly.

I stand stock-still while he works his way around the area in loops. After about fifteen minutes, he calls out, "How much does Mila weigh?" He looks up at me.

"Hundred pounds, soaking wet," I reply.

He smiles. "This is her." He points down at the ground.

"Can I move?" I ask.

His smile turns into a grin. "Yes. Come here. I'll show you."

I go to him and look down. I see something pressed into the ground. *Maybe* it's the waffle print of a hiking boot.

"How did you see that?" I ask, shaking my head.

"Practice," he replies. "We're lucky it had just rained. She kicked up some mud with the edge of her boot. See right here?"

I look closer and see it. And it's like something unwinds in me. "We're going to find her," I say, just testing it out, really—the possibility that we could do this.

"We will," Bo says absently, looking up the trail. "Is this the girl that kissed you?"

I knew this was going to come up eventually. "Yeah," I admit, grimacing. "But I stopped her before she *really* kissed me. I definitely didn't kiss her back."

"Why not?" he asks. "You like girls, too, don't you?"

"Yes, but boy or girl doesn't matter. I don't want to kiss anyone but you," I say, like it's obvious. He looks up the trail, embarrassed, but pleased with my answer. Then his expression falls.

"This way," he says.

Bo slides into the underbrush, lithe and sure. I follow in his footsteps.

A million possibilities unwrap in my mind.

Mila could be hurt. Fallen. Broken leg or bleeding wound.

Or she could be secluding herself so she can detox—purposely out in the woods all by herself so she can sweat it out without temptation.

She could already be back home, and I just don't know it because I don't have my phone on me. There's no point taking it into the woods. The coverage is nonexistent where we're going.

Bo moves quickly. He sees Mila's tracks clearly, and he rarely has to pause to make sure. He points down at the ground and mumbles briefly about turned moss and scraped logs.

He's still trying to teach me, which is adorable. He tells me that her trail is easy to follow. It's purposeful. Straight. Like she knew exactly where she was going.

The most unlikely possibility is the one I entertain last. Mila could be leading me right to Dr. Goodnight.

August 1
Afternoon

Had it been a conscious choice, I would have felt more responsible. Guilty, even. But that's not how it happened. I didn't set out for revenge. I didn't make a plan and execute it—not at first.

I was angry, yes, and who wouldn't be? After David killed himself, I wanted out of the hospital. I would have done anything. And even though I was talking again, and apparently responding to therapy, I was no closer to getting out of there than I was the day I'd arrived.

The doctors had to want to let me go, and with my growing body count, they definitely didn't want to. I guess I made one choice, vague though it was when I began. I made the choice to use my journal as a tool. Or weapon, depending on your point of view. But after how horribly they'd handled David, they had it coming. Every single one of them.

The truth. I was going to give them nothing but the truth as I saw it and watch what happened.

I started with the new leader of our group therapy, Dr. Weinbach.

There were a dozen better ways to deliver the news about Dr. Holt being moved to another floor, but he wanted to impose his leadership over our group. He wanted to show everyone how amazing he was. He wasn't thinking about David when he told us Dr. Holt wasn't coming back. He was thinking about his career, about his promotion from the state cases downstairs up to our floor with the rich kids whose parents he could rope into expensive private therapy sessions when their kid got out. He was happy Dr. Holt was gone, and he wanted to keep it that way.

He went down first.

It's easy to create a character that readers hate. You don't even have to make it obvious. No mustache-twirling required. All you have to do is show a character make a very big mistake that they cover up with a bunch of excuses and finger-pointing so they can hold on to a potentially lucrative position.

And then you just let that character get away with it.

After several weeks of reading a story about a doctor who occasionally bullied his more suggestible patients into saying things they weren't ready to say so he could manufacture yet another "brilliant breakthrough," the hospital board took a second look at the video surveillance footage of how Dr. Weinbach broke the news to David.

Like meeting an actor who always plays the bad guy, they couldn't watch that footage of Dr. Weinbach glibly telling David that Dr. Holt wouldn't be returning and see it as anything but the reckless mismanagement of a tender soul by a man engaged in a pissing contest with his predecessor.

They fired Dr. Weinbach. We got Dr. Jacobi for group leader.

Which worked for me because she was next on my list.

Bo and I track Mila for hours.

We're moving fast, even though it's unbearably hot, and traveling deep into the forest far from any path. I'm glad I've had a few weeks to toughen up out here or I'd never be able to keep up with Bo. He's a machine.

Despite that, I'm keeping close tabs on where we're going. I'm still no tracker, but I have learned a few things about finding my way through the woods. We're going northeast. I've never been this way before. It's steep. It's dense. In places, it's nearly impassable.

The deeper we go, the more fear I sense in Bo, and the faster we move.

Something about this isn't right.

I reach out and grab his arm to stop him. I look up into his face, but his gaze scatters off, his eyes darting anxiously around us.

"What?" I ask, instinctively keeping my voice lowered. "What's wrong?"

"Everything. This is *all* wrong," he whispers, shaking his head.

"Why?" I ask. "What is it?"

"There's more than one set of tracks, but the first set is faint," he whispers. "That can mean two things. Either your friend was following someone who knows how to cover their tracks, or she's coincidentally going in the same direction as a really skilled hunter. But there are no game trails out here." He points up the incline, and even I can see that deer don't come this way. "There's no reason for a hunter—or anyone—to cover their tracks. Unless they thought they were being followed."

I stare at him, not sure what to make of that. And from the look on Bo's face, he doesn't know what to make of it, either.

He scans the ground, frowning. "Was Mila a good tracker?"

"She said that she grew up hunting out here, so probably?" I reply, shrugging.

"She could have been out here tracking someone who's really good?"

I shrug again, and his frustration turns back into anxiety as he looks around at the tangled brush.

"Something else is bothering you," I say, knowing this goes deeper than finding two sets of prints.

"It's this area," he snaps, and then immediately lowers his voice again. "My dad made it off limits years ago. There are dangerous people out here, Lena."

I look into Bo's dilated eyes.

"Like who?" I whisper. He doesn't answer me. "Like Dr. Goodnight?" I press.

Bo's face twists up comically as he pauses to think. "Dr. Goodnight? Isn't that a Stephen King novel?"

I stifle a bark of laughter, and not just because I thought the same thing once, but because I'm secretly relieved. There's no way anyone could fake Bo's response. He literally has no idea what I'm talking about. I've never been so happy to be so misunderstood.

"No, that's—" I start to say, and we both finish, "*Doctor Sleep*," at the same time.

He smiles, bemused. "Who's Dr. Goodnight?" he asks.

"Wow," I say, wondering how the hell I'm going to tell him. "Where do I start?" I say, cringing at my colossal foolishness.

I'm saved from having to explain for now as a few fat drops patter down through the canopy ominously. A cold wind gusts through the stifling heat.

"Oh shit," Bo mumbles. He looks skyward.

Thunder rolls. And just like that, a downpour begins. Bo looks at me, his face falling. "I'm so sorry," he says.

In moments, the ground is sopping wet, and all trace of Mila's trail is gone.

There was no malice in what I did. There was anger and a sense that justice hadn't been done yet, but I'm not Machiavelli, ruthlessly plotting to eviscerate my enemies. It wasn't like that. I had just been watching for a long time. Months. I had been paying attention to the inner workings of the hospital. Boring things. Strange things. Everything.

I saw stuff that was already there. Risky behaviors that, but for dumb luck, should have cost any one of them their jobs.

Take, for instance, Dr. Jacobi's near constant miscommunication with the nurses who administered our meds. At least twice a week, Dr. Jacobi would pull one of the nurses aside and grill her about why so-and-so was still on this dosage when the order had been put in hours ago for a change. Dr. Jacobi couldn't seem to understand that hospitals, like big ships, could not turn on a dime.

Nor did they want to. Not for her. It wasn't that the nurses couldn't understand Dr. Jacobi. It was that they couldn't stand her. Like many brilliant people, Dr. Jacobi's disdain for lesser mortals always seemed to bite her in the ass. Her impatience translated as condescension, and you should never, ever talk down to someone who can, in essence, spit in your soup.

There had been many near misses where the meds were concerned. The nurses always put Dr. Jacobi's changes in last because they had no desire to put them in sooner. Once, I even saw them put a change in so late that Dr. Jacobi went and got the dose from the locked room herself. Not knowing this, the next shift nurse prepared it a second time. It was only blind luck that Zlata was in the bathroom and that Dr. Jacobi happened to come back out front and see the second dose of phenobarbital waiting.

I watched Dr. Jacobi carefully in that moment. I wrote it down in my journal—the falling look of terror on her face. A second dose would have killed Zlata. Shit, a second dose would have killed a young hippo. Zlata's phenobarbital had been grandfathered in from Russia. She was skating the knife as it was.

Dr. Jacobi had a history of miscommunication, which is pretty unforgivable in a doctor. No matter how brilliant she was, or how much of her outside life she'd sacrificed to her job, she had done things that endangered patients. She deserved to get fired, and not just because I hated her.

That's what I told myself. That I was saving people from an eventual catastrophe.

All I had to do was wait for one of the biweekly power struggles at the nurses' station to make my move. Dr. Jacobi would swoop in and drag the nurse distributing the meds back to her office to scream at him or her, and a fill-in nurse would stand at the post.

Nothing I was on would kill me if I took twice as much of it. I would tell the fill-in nurse that I hadn't received my dose yet, even though I had. There was only ever a tiny chance that the fill-in nurse would believe me, but if she did, I'd get my second dose and go straight back to my room so I could drool and babble for the night surveillance cameras. I needed this on tape if I was to get Dr. Jacobi fired.

What I didn't know, had never dreamed, was that the fill-in nurse would assume that everyone on the roster after me had also not received their meds.

She double-dosed half the floor.

I didn't find out until I woke up two days later. My throat was raw from having my stomach pumped. Zlata had died. Two more patients were in comas, and they were both still in them by the time I left the hospital.

I told anyone who came within ten feet of me that it was my fault. I had done this on purpose to take down Dr. Jacobi. To expose her as the emotionally bankrupt egomaniac that she was. I insisted they put me in jail before I killed anyone else.

They had to put me in solitary for a few weeks and

pump me full of Zlata's phenobarbital because I was upsetting the other patients. But no matter how much I yelled that I was a murderer, I could not legally be considered culpable in any way.

It is the responsibility of the doctors and nurses to administer the drugs properly, no matter what a patient says to get more, or what that patient means to do with them once they're obtained. We're just mental patients.

Maybe the rest of the hospital could be considered that way—victims of their own minds—but I knew better about myself. I've never been a victim.

The entire nursing staff was fired. Dr. Jacobi was arrested for first-degree manslaughter, and it was clear from the onset that she would be convicted. After all, there was precedence for her malpractice. It was all recorded in my journal, which the police copied in less than an hour and returned to me.

But Dr. Jacobi didn't make it to trial. After posting bail, she jumped off the roof of her Brooklyn apartment.

I had settled down by then. I was talking, and not screaming anymore. I was allowed back into group therapy and into the common room, although no one ever came near me again. Not that they ever had before, but now instead of avoiding me because they simply mistrusted what I was writing in my journal, they genuinely feared me and my journal. They were right to be afraid. What I'd done was scary. It scared me, so I stopped. I wrote one last time, and then that was it. No more journal.

We got Dr. Holt back as group leader, which was nice. I liked her.

August 1 and 2

WE TRUDGE BACK TO OUR SPOT MUCH MORE SLOWLY THAN we set out.

We are silent the whole way. The rain stops as quickly as it started, the damage already done. When we get back, I see all the stuff Bo took from my pack lying scattered and wet on the ground. I have no idea what to do next.

I actually feel worse now. I'd only entertained the barest spark of hope for such a short amount time, it shouldn't affect me so to have it snuffed out again.

But still. Losing hope is harder than never having it at all.

"I should have left you at Mila's house and tracked her myself," Bo growls. He grabs his hair with his hands, like he's trying to pull all the bad thoughts out. "I could have gone twice as fast. I might have been able to make it before the rain started, and..."

I step toward him and put my hand on his chest to quiet him. "It was never going to end well. She's gone."

"You don't know that," he says, wrapping me against him. "Someone could still find her."

I shake my head. "The time when I could have helped her came and went. And I laughed at her. I'm going to have to live with that. Like I'm living with so many other mistakes."

Bo holds me, but I'm not crying.

"It's not your fault she ran away," he says.

"Bo. I'm so far past thc point where anyone can make excuses for me anymore," I say. "I should have helped her when she asked. That's what good people do. You wouldn't have avoided getting involved because you couldn't risk getting hurt by a friend again. You'd have just helped her. Like you did with me."

"I haven't been hurt by my friends as many times as you have," he says quietly. I touch his face, remembering that Bo had a friend once who had turned on him. I see the pain and humiliation in him again.

If I ever find that guy...

"No, don't get angry," he whispers, and he kisses me. This is what I need. To touch and to be touched. To live outside myself by letting someone else live inside of me. Finally, for the first time ever in my sewn-up little life, to open myself up fully and come out of the cocoon.

Bo insists on spreading out the blanket, on taking all of our clothes off first, on taking off his socks. It's his sweetness that makes me want to gulp him down whole. "Wait," Bo gasps, pulling back even as I'm pulling him into me. "Are you sure?"

Of course I am.

I regain consciousness in the river. "Are you okay?"

Bo is holding me draped across his arms and I'm floating on the roiling surface of the river. It's like flying. I see his pale face over mine, and I reach up to touch him.

"What happened?" I ask.

"I think you fainted," he says. He takes a deep breath and lets it out. "There was some blood, and I didn't know what else to do, so I brought you in here hoping the water would wake you—you really scared the shit out of me."

"Blood?" I say muzzily. I try to sit up.

"Easy," Bo says. "Let me get you to shore first. The water's too fast."

I can't take my eyes off him as he wades over to shore, still holding me. I know vaguely that I should be embarrassed—I fainted; who faints when they have sex? But I can't be anything but happy right now.

He puts me on the mossy bank and jumps out of the river to sit next to me.

"Does it hurt?" he asks bashfully.

"No," I say, grinning at him. I am sore, to be honest, but it's a good sore. I can't stop smiling. He smiles back at me, but he's shaking his head, too.

"You have no idea what you just put me through," he says, but now he's laughing, and I'm laughing, and our shoulders are touching. The laughter dies, and we just stare at each other. Speechless.

He shivers violently, and I realize how cold I am.

"Can you stand?" he asks.

I nod, and he helps me to my feet. I'm woozy, but he steadies me. I look at the blanket.

"That's probably more blood than normal," is all I can say.

"I *hope* so," Bo says. He looks at me, his eyebrows raised, and we both burst out laughing again.

"The clozapine makes you bleed more, even for something small, but I didn't even think about it for...this. I'm so sorry. I should have warned you," I say, and now I feel terrible for putting him through that.

"No—*I'm* sorry," he says, worried again. "You sure you're okay?"

I nod and move closer to him. "Better than okay."

We flip the stained blanket over and lie down together.

We intertwine our fingers and memorize every freckle, dimple, and scar. I never used to understand why people cry when they're happy. I get it now.

I don't know when we fell asleep. "Shit," Bo whispers.

I sit up and see dusk is falling. "I'll have to run it." I sigh.

"Can you?" he asks, worried about me again.

"I'll have to," I say, reaching for my clothes.

I really don't care about curfew right now, but I can't spend the night out in the woods and put my grandparents through that kind of worry. Not after Mila's disappearance.

Bo folds up the blanket while I stuff my things into my pack. We don't get to say any kind of goodbye before he's jogging along next to me, still concerned that I've lost too much blood.

"Go, Bo," I tell him, giving him a little shove. "I'll see you tomorrow."

"You sure?"

"Yes," I say, rolling my eyes. "You have farther to go than I do."

"I love you," he says, and then he breaks for home.

"I love you, too," I say, glancing back for him. *Poof.*

He's already gone.

I feel like I've barely fallen asleep when I hear my phone buzzing.

Normally—now, in this tech-free era of my life—I wouldn't bother answering it, but something reaches inside my dream of rushing water and blood and sex and whispers Mila's name.

I answer before I sit up. "Yes," I say.

There's nothing, and then a shaky, wet inhalation. "They found her," Aura-Blue gasps. "They found her in the river."

I'm standing. I'm moving. But I don't know where I'm going. So I stop.

"She's dead," I say, pointlessly.

All I hear is Aura-Blue's sobbing. I sit back down on my bed and I wait. "Tell me," I say when Aura-Blue has calmed down enough to speak.

"She was stabbed, I don't know, dozens of times," she says, sounding garbled. Probably because her mouth won't shape words while it's pulled into a grimace of grief. I wait for her to continue. "She must have fought him, because there were defensive wounds, and they say it took her a while to die."

"That's good," I say, too loudly. "If she fought him, there'll be some kind of evidence. DNA. Hair. Skin."

"No," Aura-Blue says, and stops to sniff. "He was careful."

I hear my grandparents wake up and call out to me, but I don't care.

"They'll look under her fingernails," I shout. My grandparents appear in my doorway with owlish, staring eyes.

"No, they won't," Aura-Blue says with finality. "Because they cut off her hands."

I sit on my bed for a long time after Aura-Blue hangs up.

I sit long after my grandparents have given up trying to tell me to pretend that it never happened. To get on with my life. I didn't openly reject their calm, rational bullshit, and so they took my passivity as compliance and finally left me alone. I'm not catatonic. I know that. I'm just waiting for dawn. Some glimmer through the gray. Just enough so I can slip into the forest and run to Bo.

My phone buzzes again, and I answer it without looking. It's Rob. He's crying.

I try really hard to listen to him. He knew Mila much longer than I did. He dated her, and I'm pretty sure she let him do far more than I ever entertained doing with him. I never used to equate sex with an emotional bond, but I do now. Rob is really hurting.

My eyes locked on the window, looking for daylight, I

uh-huh him and tell him there's nothing he could have done. That it wasn't his fault. He tells me he'll be back tomorrow—or is it today? Anyway, he's nearly back and he can't wait to see me. He needs to hold me, he says.

Dawn breaks. I tell Rob I have to go. I hang up. I stand up.

I understand that this is the end of something. I don't know what yet, but I know I'm leaving. Either I'm going to live in the woods with Bo for a few weeks until we go to college, or I'm going to find out that Ray is Dr. Goodnight and I'm going to kill him. Quietly, of course. Maybe out hunting? I don't know. I'll figure it out. And then I'm taking Bo away from all of this so he can go to school. So he can be brilliant and kind and generous and bring something beautiful to the world. Either way, we're leaving.

I'll have to change my name, and that's fine with me. I've never been tied to the name Magdalena. Everyone in town and back home calls me Magda, and I hate it. Reminds me of magpies. I've never liked that bird. They're too clever, but not clever like an animal. They're clever like humans in that they aren't trying to simply survive. They're trying to win. No one likes magpies.

I'll be Lena, because that's what Bo and his family call me. I'll take Bo's last name. What did Maeve say her last name was? Jacobson. I'll be Lena Jacobson. Maybe I'll even ask Bo to marry me to make it official.

I'm laughing as I throw a few things into my pack. This is stupid. Reckless. But it may be the most unselfish thing I've ever done. One way or another, I'm going to save Bo. I'm going to get him as far away from this place as I can. I'll carry him, kicking and screaming if I have to. Maeve will help me.

Wait. I can't find my journal.

I take everything out and lay it on the floor in a line. It's not here. I go into the closet where I threw the stained blanket from this afternoon, thinking maybe my journal got trapped in a corner of it while Bo was rolling it up.

I see the pile of hidden clothes just under the blanket and hesitate. How many times have I come out of the woods covered in gore?

I count shirts and shorts. Three times? That seems like a lot. I hold up a T-shirt and recognize it as the one I was wearing that day when I met Bo—when he and the doe fell on me, rather. Then there was the fawn that I shot in the bush without ever seeing it. Yes. These shorts were ruined while I was trying to track it. There was blood all over those leaves. And the freshest outfit to be destroyed was from when I shot and butchered the buck.

I don't have time for this. I open up the blanket, ignoring the rusty scent and deep wine stain of my blood. My journal isn't here. I must have left it in the woods. I can't believe I'd have done something like that, but I must have. Bo came and left empty-handed—I'm sure of that. I can still picture him leaving. He wasn't carrying anything. My journal has to be *there*.

I stuff everything with blood on it back in the closet and put everything I'm going to take with me back into my pack in a rush. I only take what I need, just like Bo taught me, but this time what I need has to last me forever. My ID, definitely, so I can burn it later, and lots of underwear and socks. I tie off no loose ends. I clean up no messes. I write no note.

Maybe they'll think I was another victim.

I'm sad about that for my grandparents' sake. They'll feel terrible for a while, but if there's one thing I'm sure of, it's their ability to move on. They moved on just fine after they committed my mother to the same institution she committed me to.

I set out while the dew is thick and the sky is barely blushing dawn.

I get to our spot far too early for Bo to have come, but I'm disappointed anyway.

I use the time to look for my journal. I scour the area.

I kick through leaf litter and overturn rocks. I look places I know it won't be.

I find a piece of paper under a rock with my writing on it. It takes me a second to put all the pieces together, to think back to when my memory was a porous thing, and

I remember. This was the note I left Bo when I thought I wasn't going to meet him, and he'd wait here for me until he gave up.

I can't tomorrow. The day after?

I see that he's written a reply on the other side.

AND THE DAY AFTER THAT, AND AFTER THAT, AND AFTER THAT...

I stare at his handwriting. Heavy and thick and a little smudged, like most lefties. I'm soft and smiling while I stuff it into a pocket of my jeans. I miss him so terribly, and it's only been a few hours. In the past, I'd feared other people's absences, wondering how my status in the group had changed, but I'd never missed anyone before.

It's exquisitely awful.

I sit down on the ground, hoping my journal just manifests itself. When that doesn't happen, I decide I can't stand being away from Bo any longer. I know the way to his camp. I'll head in that direction and hope we cross paths before I get there. I want us to be alone when I ask if I can live with him in the woods until we leave. Just in case he says no.

August 2 (Before) and August 3 (After)

THERE REALLY IS NO BETTER FEELING THAN KNOWING you're going to be with the person you love.

To be clear, nothing feels better than being with the person you love. That's not a feeling, though. It's a state of being; one that's apart from the real world. Like entering fairyland. That's when you become a we.

But on your way to see the person you love, you're still you. In fact, you're probably more you than you'll ever be again. The quintessence of you. You're the you who's been granted the love of the person you think the most highly of. You—exactly as you are—are worthy of the most precious thing in the world.

And there's no better feeling than that.

I should want to prolong this moment, but instead I'm

running the steep trail up to Bo's camp. Running feels good. It feels pure. I'm so much stronger now that it's a pleasure to push myself like this. To know that I can ask, and my body will say yes. Excitement makes me run, and running makes me more excited.

Thrill feeds thrill.

Until…

I'm just outside Bo's camp when I hear the screaming. I don't run toward it, but rather, I slow down. Legs numb, I recognize the voice of a girl. She's screaming, but not in pain or fear. She's screaming accusations. Like I screamed about myself once.

"You can lie as much as you want, but I know you're a murderer," she howls.

"Calm down! You're going to make yourself sick, Sol," Bo is yelling back. *His* voice I know, although now it sounds so harsh, it's nearly foreign to me.

"I saw it!"

"You don't know what the fuck you're talking about." His voice is low and dangerous.

I stay in the cover of the thick brush just outside their camp and peer in.

"You keep saying I don't understand, but I saw you kill her," Sol screams, pointing a finger at Bo. Her voice is hoarse, like they've been screaming at each other for hours. "You killed that druggie townie girl and dumped her body in the river! I saw you do it!"

"You don't know what you saw," he says, with a tired shrug. He turns to his father, who is standing just behind them.

"Dad," he says, fed up. "You should have explained this to her by now."

"Sol," Ray says, reaching out a tempering hand. "Try to understand."

"There's nothing to understand!" she rages. "I saw them struggling, but he didn't stop until she was dead! I heard her scream! I saw the blood! I saw her die! I saw him throw her in the river!"

Sol runs away, hysterical. She hurls herself up a ladder and into one of the dormitories, loudly slamming the door behind her.

Bo turns to his father, and they bend their heads together. Conspiring. There's a buddy-buddy feeling between them. I can't hear their words, but whatever it is, they're in it together.

And then it hits me. Twenty years of sleep, and now blood. Because there are *two* of them. I can't breathe. I can't miss a single word, a single gesture, but my eyes are blurring with tears, and my pulse is pounding in my ears. Bo stresses something important to his father, and Ray looks up at the dormitory that Sol has barricaded. Bo turns and stares up at it, too. They exchange a few more words, and then Ray claps Bo on the shoulder. Like everything is peachy keen. And then

Bo pulls his long knife out of a nearby stump, sheaths it in his thigh guard, and stalks off.

I stumble downhill for a while and then sit in the underbrush, leaves folding over me. The world is just paint, and now it's smeared.

There are two killers. One clean. One bloody. Ray and Bo. Dr. Goodnight and his son.

Rob stands over me. He's offering me his hand. I stare at it until he grabs me and hauls me to my feet.

We don't speak.

It's past sunset. I stand in the entrance of my grandparents' house. Rob is saying something quietly to my grandparents. Then he takes me upstairs to my bedroom.

"Sit here," he says, placing me on the edge of my bed. "Your grandparents said you take medication?"

I look up at him. He's so worried. I nod and gesture to my bathroom. I can't speak.

Rob disappears into my bathroom, and I hear him rummaging around in there. Opening doors and bumping around, not really knowing what he's looking for or where to look for it. I hear him shake out a few pills, pour some tap water into the glass I keep on the sink. He comes back out and puts a pile of pills in one of my hands and the glass of water in the other.

He stands in front of me. "Take them."

I gulp them down, not caring to look at what I'm swallowing.

"When did you stop taking your medication?" Rob asks quietly. "Before or after I left?"

I shake my head to clear it. I can't remember. I open my mouth to speak, and nothing comes out.

"It's okay," he says. "You don't have to say anything right now."

Rob goes back into the bathroom and returns with a wet washcloth. He kneels down in front of me and takes off my hiking sandals before cleaning my feet. A few more trips to the sink to rinse off the washcloth, and he cleans my face and hands as well. Then he pulls the covers back and tucks me in. He shuts off the light and sits down at my desk.

"I'll be right here," he says. Then I feel nothing.

I wake to low, orange light. Must be sunset.

So. This is what a broken heart feels like. It's unique. And now sunset is what a broken heart looks like to me, and it probably always will. Sunset is ruined.

My head hurts, and my body is impossibly heavy. I don't know if I've slept one day or two. Rob is sitting at my desk.

I sit up. I have to push myself with my arms to do it, but

I finally manage it. Rob is leaning forward with his forearms resting on his knees like he's just lifted his head out of his hands.

"You're still here," I say. The sound of my own voice surprises me. I was half expecting to be mute again, but I guess I'm done with that.

Rob nods and leans back, rubbing his eyes and then scrubbing his face with his hands. I notice my journal is open on the desk next to him.

"Where did you find that?" I ask, pointing at my journal.

Rob frowns. "Right here. It was on your desk," he says. "You didn't know that, though, did you?" He looks sad.

I cross my legs under the blanket and curl my hands in my lap. "Did you read it?" I ask. He nods. Sighs.

"I went into your closet to get a blanket last night. It got pretty cold," he says. His eyes are darting around everywhere, unable to land. "I saw the bloody clothes. The picnic blanket." He suddenly tilts forward and drops his head in his hands. "There are three pairs of shorts and three T-shirts that are covered in blood." He looks up at me, his eyes rimmed with tears. "Was it you?" he whispers.

I stare at him, dumbstruck.

He gestures to the journal. "I'm sorry I invaded your privacy, but after I found the clothes..." He trails off, and tears tip down his face. He gathers himself and continues. "Three sets of clothes, three women. I had to know."

"Had to know what?" I ask robotically.

Rob stands up, suddenly agitated, and starts pacing, talking more to himself than to me.

"You were off your medication. You thought you were hunting deer. But you're on your medication again now. You'll be okay." He faces me. "You won't hurt anyone else, right?"

I swing my legs out of my bed and stand. I'm wobbly, and Rob steadies me. "What the hell are you talking about?" I say, angry now. And, to be honest—afraid.

He narrows his eyes at me. "You really don't know, do you?"

I shake my head.

"Magda, do you know what you've been writing in your journal?" he asks calmly.

"I haven't been writing in my journal," I reply. "I haven't written in it in months."

He picks up my journal and shows it to me. It's almost completely full of my blocky, minuscule handwriting. My heart speeds up, and my skin tightens. I let the pages flop closed. I don't want to see.

I stopped writing in it. My journal is dangerous. I'm dangerous.

"The first time you said that to me, I thought you were kidding, because you had just been sitting right across from me moments before writing in your journal. Do you remember? We were at Taylor's?" He waits for me to answer. I guess

I know what he's talking about, but it's all so vague. I shrug, and he continues. "Then I realized that you really didn't know you were writing in it. Like someone who bites their nails and doesn't realize they're doing it."

I take a step back from him and hit the edge of the bed. He sits next to me and takes my hand.

"You don't know you made up a whole story about a family living in the woods, do you?"

My eyes unfocus. It's like falling. This is impossible. "What are you talking about?" I demand.

"That guy you call Wildboy in your journal, and his family. You made them up, and you think they're real."

"No," I say, shaking my head. "I couldn't have."

A pained look crosses Rob's face. "You've made up people before," he says quietly. "Ali Bhatti?"

"How did you…?"

"I've been getting all your posts since we were thirteen," he says, like it's obvious. "I know all about the Cultural Outreach Club, and about the mental hospital. Your New York friends did a long post on your blog after you were committed, and they were…not kind. I never believed their side of it, but I didn't want to push you and ask a lot of questions. I was waiting for you to talk to me about it when you were ready."

All I can do is stare at him.

"I didn't tell anyone here any of that stuff," he assures me.

I stand up. "I didn't make Wildboy up," I say. I start pacing. Thinking back. "You were there," I insist. "You came and got me in the woods. You must have seen his camp."

Rob's face falls with compassion, and it only makes me angrier.

"Last night!" I yell. "You came and found me right outside their camp and brought me back here and gave me my pills and sat down at my desk. You were there, in the woods!"

"Me? In the woods?" he asks carefully.

Rob hates the woods. He never goes in them. I sink back down on to the bed. I'm scared to breathe. Scared to move.

"I was here with your grandparents, waiting for you, as usual, when you came back. You couldn't speak. You looked traumatized, and your grandparents told me that schizophrenia runs in the family and that you take antipsychotics for it. I brought you upstairs to give you your medication. When I saw that the dates on the bottles were from over a month ago, but still almost full, I knew you hadn't been taking them."

"No. You found me," I say weakly. I look up at him.

He's shaking his head.

"I just appeared out of nowhere and found you in the middle of the woods?" he asks doubtfully. "How could I know where you were?"

"You followed me," I accuse, but we both know I'm grasping at straws.

"Magda? Have you ever seen things that weren't there?" he asks. "Have you ever seen people who weren't there?"

I freeze and nod slowly, thinking of Rachel. "Dead people. People who've died because of me."

He smiles at me, like this admission means I'm getting somewhere. "If you've seen that, then why is it so hard to accept that—off your medication—you've imagined seeing living people?"

I open my mouth to answer him, but I have no answer. There's only one answer. I never hallucinated dead bodies when I was with Bo. Because I was hallucinating *him*. I look down at my journal, and now I can really see it. It's filled up. I can remember writing in it now. I wrote in it every day. If I can repress that, what else have I done without knowing it?

"Oh my God," I breathe. "What did I do?"

I run to the closet and open it. My clothes are in a rumpled heap. So much blood. How could I have ever thought that was normal?

"But, it wasn't really you, right? It couldn't have been you," he says, his voice trailing off into a whisper. But he knows. I look over my shoulder at him.

"I don't remember," I whisper back. "I don't know."

Rob takes my hands and guides me back to the bed. He sits next to me and turns my hands over in his, noticing them. We both see the scratches and bruises peppering my forearms. Like I've been in a fight.

"There has to be another reason for all of these cuts, right?" he asks. He's begging me for some kind of explanation, but I don't have one.

"Hiking?" I say uncertainly. But I'm shaking my head because I know that doesn't explain this. Hiking doesn't explain the soreness in my back and arms.

Rob just looks at me.

"What did I do?" I say again, my voice sliding up. I'm becoming hysterical, I know it, but I can't seem to stop. I press my hands against my mouth, trying to stuff the shrill sound of my desperation back inside.

"Shh," Rob says, pulling me into a hug. He holds me for a long time, rocking me back and forth. "You would never hurt anyone."

Wrong. I've hurt lots of people. But murder? "I don't *remember.*" My voice gets high and thin again.

"It wasn't you," he whispers, easing me back into bed. "You need to rest. You'll have an explanation for all this after you rest. I know you will."

He goes into my bathroom and comes back a moment later with another handful of pills and a glass full of water.

"It'll be okay. I promise," he whispers. "You inherited a condition, and you went off your medication, but it won't happen again. You'll be okay."

I'm shaking my head at him. It won't be okay. Nothing will ever be okay.

"You'll feel calmer after you take these," he says, pouring the medication into my hand. "Take them, Magda. It'll be okay because you're not a bad person," he says, too firmly, like a part of him is still not convinced.

"Yes I am, Rob. I'm a very bad person."

"No, you're not. You just need your medication. We'll—get rid of the clothes." He frowns, looking down, as he realizes what he's committing himself to. But he doesn't back out. Instead he nods his head, his decision made. "We'll never tell anyone about this," he says firmly.

I take the pills and lay back, my stomach swooping like I'm sliding down a steep slope. I'm so tired.

"You should hate me," I say. "Why are you protecting me?"

Rob shakes his head, smiling sadly. "Oh, Magda. I'd do anything to protect you. I love you. I've always loved you."

I never got used to everyone being afraid of me.

Probably because it didn't make any sense. There were some seriously scary people in that hospital. There were the explosive kind who would lose their shit over anything, and the creepers who watched and waited and harbored filthy intentions. I was neither of those. Yet everyone at the hospital was terrified of me.

I never had anything against any of the other patients.

I genuinely wanted to get better. Well, okay, to be honest I always knew I wasn't like the other patients. I had a handle on things, and they didn't. But even though I knew there was no way for me to technically get better because I wasn't sick like them, I did want to change myself enough so that I felt better. That's nearly the same thing.

When Dr. Holt came back as group leader, I began to hope I might actually achieve that. She was the one doctor on that floor who was there for the patients and not for her career. She was still alive in that part of her heart that allowed her to connect with us as a human and not just as an authority figure who was going to "fix" us.

So when she pulled me aside and told me that she was going to recommend that I be released immediately, I was confused. I'd wanted out, but that was before. That was when fumble-fingered morons were in charge of me. I wanted to learn from Dr. Holt. I wanted to get better. She was going to heal me.

"But… I have so much work to do on myself," I said, shifting uncertainly.

She nodded hastily. "And you'll do it someplace else," she said, lips pinched, eyes reluctant to meet mine.

I remember laughing. The weak kind of laughter that people do when they're trying to convince themselves that they're not getting thrown away.

"They'll never let me out," I said. I was trying to

bargain with her. Make her see sense. But I already knew that even if I stayed, I wouldn't be working with her anymore.

Dr. Holt looked right at me.

"You're not staying here," she whispered. A look of anguish crossed her face. "In one year, three suicides have been directly connected to you. I've never even heard of that before. And Zlata is dead because of your revenge plot to bring down a doctor—which worked. What if someone else angers you? Letting you out is a crime, I know that, but I'm trying to save these kids," she said, gesturing to our group of neurotics, shuffling weakly toward the rec room and their second dose of synthetic stability. She shook her head, her eyes shut, fighting a battle inside herself. "Out there, you'll at least be dealing with people who can get away from you. In here, these kids are sitting ducks. You'll kill them all." Her eyes grew sad. "I can't stop you. I know that. I'm not clever enough to beat you, so I'm letting you go. God help me, I'm letting you go."

The next day, I was released with a plastic baggie chock-full of prescription drugs, a plane ticket to my grandparents' house, and a clean bill of health.

And my journal, of course.

August 4
Dawning

I WAKE IN THE MIDDLE OF THE NIGHT.

Hunger has given me the jolt of adrenaline I needed to pull myself out from under the weight of my chemical sleep. Suddenly lucid and full of energy, I feel that I'm not alone in my room. I sit up carefully and see Rob sleeping on a mattress at the end of my bed.

I regard him for a while, noticing small things, like the fact that he's changed his clothes and brought a small leather travel bag with him. It's Hermès. Bespoke. But there's no designer name stamped gaudily on the outside announcing its exclusive pedigree. I only recognize it because of the strap and distinctive hardware around the top.

I stare at the bag while, from the corner of my eye, I watch Rob's chest rise and fall with the oceanic sound of deep-sleep breathing. The drugs have brought me back to that impassive state that seems safer for everyone. In this detached way of being, I notice that the bag has captured my attention, but I don't know why because I feel nothing about it.

Maybe it's because I haven't seen such a raw display of status since I left New York. An overnight bag like that costs about twenty grand, but it's not about the exorbitant cost. It's the fact that you can't walk into a mall and buy that bag. You go on a list. You wait. It takes commitment as much as it takes money. But I know that about Rob already. When he wants something, he can be patient.

I slide out of bed and move silently to my desk. Even my skin is listening to Rob's breathing. I don't want to wake him. Some things are meant to be done in private, I guess.

My journal is waiting, pages open. I sit and read, really taking in the depth of my sickness. The first entry begins back in the hospital, when David was still alive. The last entry is from before Bo and I had sex, I'm assuming because it was lost.

But it wasn't actually lost. Rob said he found it right here. Some part of my fractured mind must have placed it on the center of my desk without informing either the part of me who wrote in my journal or the part of me who had no idea about the journal writing.

How many *me*s are there?

I skim through pages, checking the dates. Trying to pin

down exactly when I started writing behind my own back. I had thought I'd stopped writing after Dr. Jacobi killed herself, but I hadn't. After her suicide, my style of writing changed dramatically, though. It went from the third-person, past-tense voice that I used to tell the "story of me" like it was happening to someone else long ago, to close first-person present tense, where I am narrating my life as it happens.

And as if that isn't confusing enough, later, after I'd been out of the hospital and living with my grandparents for a week, a new voice appears. It's written in first person, past tense, and I seem to be looking back at what I've done. The first entry like that begins, "*I was not the most popular girl in school. That was Jinka Pritchett.*"

Now that I think back, I remember writing in my journal and telling myself this was the last time. When I left the hospital, I must have convinced myself that I'd kept that promise to myself and really stopped, but I hadn't.

It seems so odd. Now I can remember sitting here, at this desk, writing furiously every night before I went to bed. I can even remember spreading out my blanket in the woods and filling a few pages before Bo met me there.

Stop.

He's not real. I'm not allowed to mourn the loss of a fictional character. Anyway, deep down, part of me always knew he was too good to be true. I kept thinking it was all like a dream.

I need to figure out what I was doing all those hours I thought I was with him. That leaves a lot of hours. I couldn't have been writing all that time, or I'd have filled volumes. I could have been killing people. That almost seems like the most obvious possibility at this point.

But I need to remember.

First, I need to sort out how many personalities I have. There is the me who I was aware of all along, the me who wrote and who I remember now, and a third who is still hidden from me. She's the me who took my journal and left it sitting here on the desk. She's the me who did *something* while the other two *me*s believed we were with a boy who doesn't exist.

My eyes shift to the closet. The door is cracked open. There are three bloody outfits in there, and there have been three women found cut to pieces since I arrived in this small town. I have no memory of doing violence to anyone, not even now that I've been confronted with that possibility. As soon as I was forced to see my journal, I remembered writing in it. So I guess I need to force myself to remember killing them.

Rob simultaneously came to the conclusion that I'm the killer and excused me for it by reading my journal cover to cover and realizing that I believed I was killing deer. But is he right? Do the dates match up?

I was extremely faithful to my journal. I'm writing in

it right now. I wrote about everything, it seems—everything that happened to me at home, with my friends, at the shelter, with Bo and his family, my attempt to quit the drugs, and the subsequent hallucinations. In between these present-tense daily reports are the bursts of past-tense storytelling.

I page back through my journal, looking for the days I came back bloody. The first time I met Bo, I thought I fell asleep and woke to a boy and an injured deer falling on me. The next evening, I found out about Chelsea Oliver, the dead hunter, while playing mini golf.

Then, I thought I'd killed a fawn by accident and chased it through the brush, only to get covered in blood. A few days later, Sandy Crosby's body was found. And finally, Mila. She went missing the day I killed the buck and butchered it in the woods. I don't need to look that up. I remember coming back here to my grandparents' house. How everyone was waiting for me. I was the last person to see Mila alive. The police must not know that, or Officer Langmire would have questioned me. Or the FBI would have. Maybe my friends are protecting me.

They really shouldn't.

I close my eyes and try to edit the images in my mind. I force Mila's face and her body under my knife because I know if I make myself see it, then I'll remember what the third me did. I need to remember it.

And when I remember, I'll…what? What will I do? I

can't go back to the hospital, because if I really did do these atrocious things, and Dr. Holt let me out, she won't just lose her license. She'll go to jail for the rest of her life. So I can't turn myself in.

I know Dr. Holt hates me, but she has every reason to. Because of me and my journal, the other doctors at the hospital stepped in and had her moved to another floor when she was probably managing David's attachment just fine. I can almost picture Dr. Weinbach waving my journal around, insisting that Dr. Holt had lost her professional detachment and needed to be removed. Because he wanted her job.

Of course Dr. Holt blames me for David's death. If it weren't for me and my journal, she might have been allowed to help David work through his feelings when he was ready to. She's a good doctor. She cares. I won't ruin her life by going back to the hospital.

This time I'll do the right thing. Probably the thing I should have done as soon as I found out about Rachel.

But I don't remember. Not the way I remember writing in my journal. It won't come back to me, no matter how hard I push.

Something is still hidden from me. There's got to be a missing piece, something that will trigger the memory. I have to find it. I *have* to. Because there's also another thing I know for certain. Dr. Goodnight started killing people at least twenty years ago, and I definitely wasn't killing people before I was born. There are two murderers running around the same few square miles of woods. If I'm one of them, there is a chance—even if it's just a slim one—that a buried side of me knows who Dr. Goodnight is and where he's camping.

And if that hidden shard of me knows where Goodnight is, I'm going to find him and kill him.

I sit until the sun comes up, waiting for my ghosts to show. They don't. I stare at Rob's gorgeous bag. I can't take my eyes off it.

"What are you doing?" Rob asks muzzily. He sits up in bed, tousled and doe-eyed with sleep.

"I'm hungry, but I don't trust myself enough to go anywhere alone. Not even downstairs," I reply. "It doesn't matter that I'm on my meds again. I was still on my meds when I wrote most of this without knowing it." I gesture to my journal. "And maybe I did a lot more than write."

"I'll go with you," he says quietly.

"You sure about that? I'm dangerous, Rob. You're not safe around me."

Rob nods, his brow furrowed. "I'm not afraid of you."

I smile at him gently. "That's because you think you know me."

Rob leaves the room to allow me to bathe and dress. He waits outside my bedroom door. It doesn't leave me a lot of time to decide what I'm going to do next, but it's enough.

We join my grandparents downstairs and slip easily

into our most gracious facades. Rob handles them perfectly. He must have been handling them since I showed up three nights ago, or they wouldn't have allowed him to share my bedroom.

"How are you feeling, Magdalena?" my grandmother asks gravely as she serves out the scrambled eggs.

"Much better, thank you," I reply with a relieved smile. "I don't know why I thought I could do it without taking my medication. I felt better, so I thought—why keep taking them?"

My grandfather nods sagely. "I did the same thing with my blood pressure medication once."

"Almost died of a heart attack," my grandmother adds on cue.

"Magda has a condition, but it's manageable," Rob says. He offers me some orange juice, and when I decline, he offers it to my grandmother first, and then my grandfather, before serving himself. Ever the gentleman.

My grandmother beams at him. "Well, we're so lucky to have you, Rob. It was so brave of you to—"

"No, it's okay," Rob interrupts, hastily refusing praise. "We don't need to go back over it. Let's just put the whole thing behind us."

"Hear, hear," my grandfather says, raising his coffee cup like it's champagne.

And that's it. We eat our eggs and fruit salad, and drink

coffee, and talk about my grandmother's garden and what I'm going to do with myself for the rest of the summer.

We decide that stability is what I need, and that working at the shelter was good for me. If Maria still wants me to work there, that is. After breakfast Rob agrees to take me to the shelter so I can repair things with her. I bring my keys to the office and the walk-ins, just in case I can't repair things and Maria wants them back.

"You know, Maria called once while you were sleeping," Rob says as he drives his rare, classic car slowly down the winding, forest-lined road.

"Did you speak to her?" I ask.

Rob nods. "I told her you were really sick. She said she understood."

"Yeah, I'm sure she did," I reply, sighing. Now Maria thinks I'm using again. Which, technically, is true.

Rob glances over at me. "You don't have to worry about your job," he tells me. "She's cool."

I frown. "I didn't know you knew her," I say.

"I don't *know* her, know her," he fumbles. "I mean… I spoke with her. I've met her before. But, she's got to be cool, because look at what she does, right?"

I nod and watch him. Then I look out the window. "Right."

As soon as we walk into the kitchen through the delivery door, I realize I shouldn't have come back. I should have called and quit.

Gina walks past carrying a chafing dish. She sees me and Rob and freezes. Even with the painted-on eyebrows, I can see that she's surprised. She looks between the two of us, and then her eyes really land on me and turn down in sadness for a second before she whirls away and goes to hide from me in one of the walk-ins.

"What was that?" Rob asks.

"She's program. AA," I say shaking my head. "She took one look at my dilated pupils and knew I'm on frigging horse tranquilizers. This was a mistake."

"No it's not," Rob says encouragingly. "Just tell her that you have a condition. You're not an addict, like them."

He doesn't get it. But the way he said "addict" was surprising.

"I had no idea you had such a thing against addicts," I mumble as we make our way through the kitchen and toward Maria's office.

"It's why I broke up with Mila. She liked to do drugs, and I don't touch them."

I glance at him. "There's history there," I guess.

Rob's lips press together. "My mom had some issues with drugs when I was little," he admits stiffly. There's an edge to him I've never seen before.

"I'm sorry," I say, meaning it. "That's rough."

"Yeah," he says gratingly. "Mothers should put their kids to bed, not the other way around."

We stop in front of Maria's door. "How bad did it get?"

"As bad as it *can* get until my dad did something about it," Rob says. He knocks on Maria's door for me, ending the conversation.

Maria pulls open the door and she looks at Rob first. "What the hell are you doing here?" she asks him angrily, and then she sees me standing next to him. She gives a quick embarrassed laugh, and shakes her head, and waves us inside all at the same time.

"Sorry—he's with you?" she says, rolling her eyes. "I thought I was going to have to call Gina to help me throw you out. No men allowed in here, you know."

She gives me a hug. "Are you okay?" she asks.

"Yeah, I'm much better," I reply, feeling horrible for lying to her.

She reaches out a hand to shake with Rob. "We spoke on the phone?" she hazards a guess. "Rob?"

"We've met before," he reminds her. "But it was just for a second."

That was awkward.

"Oh. Well. Thank you for bringing Magda back." Maria turns to me. "When can you start working again?"

"Really?" I say, excited. "How about now?"

"Ah…sure," Maria says, thrown. She looks at Rob, who's shaking his head, and she stops.

"Magda's not really up to it yet," he says.

"Yes I am," I say. "I want to work."

Rob turns to me and puts a hand on my arm. "But I can't stay here with you. It's a women's shelter," he says pointedly. "Are you sure you're up to this right now? You'll be by yourself."

"No she won't," Gina says behind us. We turn and see her lurking just beyond the door frame. "I'll keep an eye on her."

I hold up my hands like I'm surrendering and smile. "I'm just going to sit and chop onions, Rob," I say. I look at him. "We decided this was good for me, right?"

"I just didn't think it'd be today." I see him grind his teeth for a second, but he relents quickly. "Fine. Call me later. I'll come pick you up."

"I can drive her home," Gina says, taking a step toward me. "It's no trouble."

"Thanks, Gina," I say. She won't let me do anything I shouldn't, and she's tough enough to flatten me if I try to do anything to hurt myself or anyone else. I should probably warn her, though. "Just keep an eye on me and don't let me go anywhere without you, okay?"

She gives me a strange look. "Okay," she says.

"Great," Rob says, although he's clearly anxious about leaving me with someone who doesn't know. He turns to me. "I'll see you later." He gives me a quick kiss on the cheek to mask him whispering, "Be careful," in my ear before he leaves.

Gina grabs on to my arm and steers me through the kitchen, walking fast. "How much Valium you on?" she asks in an undertone.

"It's not just Valium," I say, shaking my head. "I need these drugs, Gina. They keep me from seeing things that aren't there." I swallow. My hands are shaking. "They keep me from *doing* things without knowing I'm doing them. I have a condition..."

I take a deep breath to tell her—I mean, why not at this point? Gina won't judge me for being schizophrenic. But Maria calls out behind us.

"Wait, Gina. I needed to talk to you. Can you come back for a second?"

"I'll meet you at your prep station later," Gina whispers to me before turning and going back to Maria's office.

I go to my station, find my onion goggles, and get to it. I gratefully drop into the never-ending demands of the shelter's overwhelmed and understaffed kitchen. It's crazier than usual today. I keep expecting Gina to show at some point, but she doesn't.

I finish scrubbing my last pot and then wipe down my station slowly. Then I go and look for her. The kitchen is empty. That's not normal. I have to call out through the pickup window—the place where the kitchen and the front of the house meet.

"Hey!" I yell until the only girl out there looks at me. "Where is everyone?"

"I don't know," she says, looking lost. "I finished my side-work," she tells me, like I've got the authority to tell her to go home.

I recognize this girl, but I don't know how at first. Then I realize she was that pretty young thing I saw sitting on the steps with Taylor at that first barbecue Rob took me to. She looks skinnier than I remember. Her face is more angular, and the baby softness that was still clinging to her just a few weeks ago is gone now.

"Is Gina anywhere out front?" I ask her. "The cook," I clarify.

The girl looks perplexed for a second, and then she puts it all together.

"She left before lunch started," she tells me.

"Did she say why?" I ask.

"She just sort of took off her apron and left," the girl says timidly.

I realize I'm interrogating her and stop. "Did something happen?" I ask, like I'm looking for gossip, but really I'm starting to feel the first rolls of fear in my belly. Gina would never just walk out. And she'd never leave me. Not after I asked her to watch me.

"I don't know," the girl replies, conspiratorially. She's much more comfortable gossiping than being interrogated. "She left right after Maria. Like she was following her or something."

"Maria left? Before lunch?" I repeat disbelievingly.

"Yeah," the girl says. "I thought it was strange."

"It is." I glance behind me, but everyone's gone. It's late, but not that late. What the hell?

"Hey, can you, like, sign me out?" she asks.

"Yeah, sure," I say. "Come on back."

The girl meets me at Maria's office, and I dig into my pocket to get the keys. I pull out the keys, and something else falls out with them.

It's the dirty, wrinkled piece of paper that I placed under a rock once. On one side is my handwriting. I'm shaking as I turn it over, expecting it to be blank. But it isn't. In smudged, left-slanting handwriting are the words, *And the day after that, and after that, and after that...*

"Are you okay?" the girl asks. I feel her put a hand on my upper arm.

"Yeah," I say breathily. "I think so."

"Is that from your boyfriend?" she asks, stealing a glance at the paper.

"I'm not sure," I say. "I might have written it."

She gives me a confused look. I give her a confused look back. Why would I write this note to myself? If I was going to add something to my fantasy of Bo, I would have written it in my journal. I'm quite particular about that. I can't even start a new book of my journal until the old book is completed. This loose scrap of paper floating outside the neat edges of my journal doesn't fit. I need to check some facts before I take one more step. Luckily, I know a lady who can help with that. At least I *think* I do.

"Do you have a car?" I ask.

"Yeah," she replies.

I open the office. "After we sign you out, can you give me a ride to the library?"

"Sure..." she says uncertainly.

"Thanks," I say, taking out the logbook. "What's your name?"

"Amy," she says, pointing out her name on the time sheet.

I enter the time, 3:18, and initial it. I look her over like I'm going to write about her in my journal. Which means I *really* look at her. Pretty. Young. Tired, but hunting for sparkle anywhere she can find it. Too thin, too fast.

Just like Mila.

"Amy, are you paying for your drugs yet or are you still getting them free from Taylor?"

Her mouth drops open. "How did you—"

I wave her off. "Do you know who supplies him?"

"No." She can't look at me, but not because she's lying. It's because she's embarrassed. "He doesn't pay for drugs, either—just so you know. I'm not sleeping with him to get high. I'm sleeping with him because I want to."

"Where'd Taylor get them?"

"Some guy came to one of his parties a few weeks ago and gave him a ton of shit. Taylor said that guy had done that once before, and he never asked for money. Tay's not a dealer," she stresses. "He's never charged anyone for the drugs he gives out at his parties." She looks down. "It's just that now it's run out. And that guy hasn't come back. There's no way to reach him."

"But Taylor knew where to buy more drugs and sent you here," I say, gesturing to the shelter.

"He would totally buy for me if he could," Amy says, defending Taylor. "But only girls can work here."

And now I get it. I get how Dr. Goodnight did it and hid it for so long. I can see it all, probably because my mind is as predatory as his.

It's really a great system when you think it through. Gorgeous, fun guys reel in the cutest, youngest girls with free drugs. When the girls are hooked, the free drugs dry up, and the girls have to go get them. The girls tell their parents they're working at a shelter for the summer, and their parents overlook all the hours their daughters are spending out. With no net, the girls fall until they're in so far over their heads, they disappear. Great system, but only if the supplier is not interested in making money.

"Grist for the mill," I say. Amy has no idea what "grist" means. Doesn't matter.

I think about confronting Taylor, maybe even Liam, but

I don't think they're aware of the part they're playing in all this. That's the thing about parties and free drugs. Nobody asks questions as long as everyone is having fun.

I look at Amy and give her a sad smile. "Best summer ever, huh?"

"Not so much anymore," she replies quietly.

"I need to know for certain what's real and what's imagined. And I need to hurry," I tell her. She has no idea what I'm talking about. I turn Amy gently by the shoulders and give her a little push out of the office. "Library," I say.

August 4
Waning

"DO YOU REMEMBER ME?" I ASK THE LIBRARIAN.

I have no idea if I ever actually came here, or if I just imagined coming here. Right now, I'm not taking any of my memories for granted.

"Yes, I remember you," the librarian replies cautiously. "You checked out several survival guides."

And I read them? I ask myself tentatively. And it all comes back to me.

Just like with writing in my journal, I remember reading every survival book I could get my hands on, now that I think it through. Which means that everything I thought I learned from Bo could have come out of library books I read in bed at night. But the thing is, I remember reading about the edible plants, *and* I remember picking them with Bo. I have no idea what's real.

"Can I help you?" the librarian asks. She looks concerned. It's been a while since my last dose of meds, and I'm coming down. I feel sweat starting to slick my upper lip, and I can feel how dry my eyeballs are between my shrunken, peeled-back eyelids. I must look manic. I feel manic.

"Yes," I say, trying to pull myself together. "I need help with a bit of research. For a book. That I'm writing."

The librarian gives me a look. My lie sounded as clunky to her as it did to me. I just don't have the brainpower to make up a convincing lie right now. My artificially enhanced chemistry is flatlining.

"You're writing a book?" Amy asks, sounding surprised. I skip Amy's question and get back to the librarian. "The book is about assisted suicide. I'm looking into the lives of doctors who have euthanized dying patients."

"No way!" Amy says. "Is it a horror novel? I love horror. I will read anything by Stephen King."

I turn to Amy, impressed. "Me too," I reply. Back to the librarian. "Can you help me? I'm looking into one doctor in particular. His name is Ray Jacobson?"

"And you've tried the internet?" the librarian asks dryly.

I nod. "He disappeared around twenty years ago."

"Aha. Before everyone lived online." The librarian makes her way to her computer. She's past the point where she has an opinion about my search and is already diving into this intriguing challenge.

"Has this person been tried and convicted?"

"No. He ran," I reply. "He's been in hiding."

"Then the best place to start would be the FBI Most Wanted list."

I nod, and she starts typing. Then clicking. Then scrolling. Then refreshing. Then typing some more. Then frowning. Then shaking her head.

"No Ray Jacobson," she says, in that curiously detached way of someone whose mind is several places at once.

"Are you sure?" I ask. I sound plaintive. "He was an anesthesiologist." The librarian shakes her head.

So that's it. There was never a wild boy named Bo who lived in the woods and loved me, even though I am a broken, tainted, shitty excuse for a human being. I made him up.

"That's all you wanted to know?" Amy asks. She takes a little tin of lip balm out of the pocket of her jeans and dabs some across her lips. I get a whiff of the balm's scent.

"What's that?" I ask, suddenly thrown. That smell. I know that smell. Sage and lavender. Masculine and feminine. It's Bo's smell.

"You don't know about this?" Amy says, enthusiastically handing me the tin. "It's the best stuff ever. They're local, and they have a whole line of lotions and soaps and natural deodorants and bath bombs. They're amazing."

I stare at the cover of the tin. A wash of rainbow colors

subtly tints the lid. This particular product is called Raven's Pout, and the company is called Ray of Sunshine.

Okay. That could be coincidence.

"I love this balm," Amy continues, "because it's actually a lip plumper, but without the drying or the sting. Makes my lips look *insane*, and it's totally natural and organic and good for you. Try it. I don't have cold sores or anything," she assures me.

I lift it to my nose. This is Bo's scent. It was always there in the background when we were together. I loved it.

I could never smell Rachel or David, no matter how clearly I saw their dead bodies displayed in front of me. No matter how vivid a visual hallucination of mine has ever been, I can't recall there ever having been a smell.

I take out the note I found under the rock and look at the left-slanted writing.

My journal shifted from past to present tense, it even morphed from first person to third as my schizophrenia bloomed like a blood blister under the emotional pressure of Rachel's suicide, but I never, ever wrote with my left hand.

"Where did you get this lip balm?" I ask.

"You can only get Ray of Sunshine at the general store in Longridge. They're totally local and small, but they'll probably sell out to a huge corporation soon because they're too good."

I don't know what to do. I don't know what to trust anymore.

"Oh—hang on," says the librarian, still engaged in her task.

"What?" I ask, distracted.

The librarian turns to me with a triumphantly raised eyebrow. "There is a woman, née Maeve Jacobson. A former philosophy professor at UC Berkeley, she's wanted by the FBI because her husband, Ray *Walters*, a former anesthesiologist at Our Lady of Mercy Hospital, is wanted for helping seven terminal cancer patients end their lives."

I almost fall down. "No way." The librarian moves so I can see her screen.

"Yes way. Here's a picture of one of the men he euthanized," she continues when I don't respond. "This was taken moments before the man's death. I believe the victim's wife took the picture—yes, see? She's credited with the photo."

The librarian points down to the name in italics at the bottom of the picture, but I can't see to read right now. I wipe oily sweat off my face and focus my eyes well enough to make out a grave yet hopeful group of people surrounding a withered husk of a man lying in a hospital bed.

The dying man's hands are so twisted that his palms lie flat against the underside of his forearms. His head is bald, his skin a dry membrane stretched tight over nothing but agony. Even his attempt to turn toward the camera is obviously such a bone-breaking effort that my blank eyes sting with tears for all the suffering that man is enduring.

"That's his son, those are his two daughters, and—wow, twelve grandchildren standing around them," the librarian continues in a subdued tone as she points out the background figures.

"Oh my God!" Amy gasps. "That poor man."

"He's not poor, dear," the librarian reminds her. "He's surrounded by his family."

We linger on this photo for one more moment, and then the librarian decides we've looked enough and moves on to the next.

"And here's one where you can see Ray's face. This photo is also credited to the wife of the victim," she says in a low voice.

Ray looks a lot younger. Twenty or so years younger, but that's definitely him. He looks just like Bo. He's cradling the suffering man as gently as he can while he inserts an IV. Everyone else in the room looks grateful. Relieved. Like this is the moment they've fought for, waited for, even prayed for. But Ray looks abstracted while he works through the mechanics of death. Gentle, kind, reluctant. He takes no joy in killing, or in this justifiable death. He looks like a man apart.

And I know. Because there's a fixed line between people who have, and people who haven't. And I've killed.

I remember now. I remember everything.

"Do you want to see some more pictures of his victims?

Or the headlines? I guess an ex-husband of one of the euthanized women pressed charges. There was a manhunt spanning three states…" The librarian trails off.

"No. Thank you," I reply. I should be moving, but I can't. I need a minute to think, but I don't have a minute. The pieces are all here, I just need to put them together. I need someone logical and grounded to help me walk through all the steps. Amy's sweet, but right now I really wish she were Gina.

Wait.

Where the hell is Gina? What would make her leave me if she knew I needed her? Gina lives to save dumb-ass junkie girls who beg her to take care of them while they come down.

I can only think of one thing that could be more important to her.

The librarian hits a key, and the screen goes black. "This is a horror book you're writing?" she asks disbelievingly.

I feel my heart start to speed up. "For me it is." I grab Amy's hand and pull her after me.

"Good luck," the librarian calls after us.

We get back into Amy's little car, and she looks at me uncertainly, waiting for instruction.

There's a long pause while my brain pans through scenarios like eyes tracking trees as they whip by on the side of the freeway.

I didn't make up Ray. He's real. Maeve is real. So Bo is

real, and everything that happened between us is real, including tracking Mila's footprints and getting almost all the way to Dr. Goodnight's camp. That means I know most of the way to Goodnight's camp. I can find Gina, I tell myself, but it's less comforting than it should be.

Because Bo is real. That means Rob lied to me. He told me I made up a family in the woods, but I didn't. Why would Rob tell such a huge lie?

Did he even know he was lying, or did he just jump to the conclusion that Bo had to be fabricated because he knows I'm sick? He read my blog for the Cultural Outreach Club. He knows I lied about dozens of people I'd said I met, then befriended, and some I even became intimately involved with, like Ali Bhatti. My fifth best friend who was *so real* to so many people, but actually wasn't.

Did Rob think I must have made up Bo because I am, and have always been, a liar?

I turn to Amy. "Has anyone ever tried to convince you that you did something you didn't do?"

She frowns. "My big sister used to do something like that, but only when I was really little."

"Tell me about it."

Amy shrugs. "I was so young, I can barely remember, but there was this one time she left the refrigerator open and all the food spoiled and she tried to convince me that I did it because she knew my parents wouldn't punish me as bad. It almost worked, too. She told me how I did it so many times, I actually *remembered* doing it, even though I knew I hadn't." She screws up her face and shakes her head. "Weird."

"How did you know you didn't do it?"

"I wasn't tall enough to reach the handle," Amy says. "There was no way I could have done it. It still messes me up to think about it. Like, how could I remember doing something that I didn't do?"

I nod my head and look out the window. "I know exactly what you mean. Memory is a slippery thing," I mumble. I turn back to her. "But you couldn't reach the handle. So you didn't do it."

"No. *She* did it," Amy says bitterly.

I nod. "And blamed it on you," I say, barely daring to whisper it.

She doesn't want to talk about her sister anymore. Amy shakes herself and adopts a cheerful tone. "So, do you want me to drive you home?"

"Actually," I say, "can you bring me to Taylor's work first?"

Her eyes widen. "Why? You're not going to tell him I told you all that stuff, are you?"

"Hell, no," I reply. "Taylor has no clue what's going on. I want to go to the Outdoor Shop because I need to buy something."

"What?"

"A GPS." I narrow my eyes at her. "You need to drive fast."

Amy fidgets as she takes me home. I make her nervous. Probably because I keep forcing her to run stop signs and blow through lights.

She tries three times in seven minutes to put on the radio, and every time I shut it off like I'm waving away a fly.

It's her car, but she's not the kind of girl to get into an argument with a guest. She's a sweetie. The easiest kind of girl to get wrapped up in a pile full of other people's bullshit and go down as collateral damage. I'm angry about that.

When she pulls up to my grandparents' house, she actually says, "Nice," she's so impressed. Looking at the flowers out front, I see her too-skinny face light up, and I can see a glimpse of the delightful young woman she really is inside, and I swear to God, I love this girl. I couldn't love her more if I'd known her for years, and I don't even know her last name.

I take off my seat belt and face her, still thinking about what I need to say to her.

"Amy. If you ever, *ever*, get high again, I am going to find you, beat the shit out of you, and lock you in my bedroom until you either drown yourself in my bathtub or you get clean. We clear?"

She laughs like I'm kidding.

"This isn't a joke," I say. "I'm not your teacher. I'm not your mom. I'm not your friend."

Her face falls. It's starting to sink in.

I open my door and get out. "I'll know if you use," I say, talking over my shoulder as I jog past Rob's car parked in my grandparents' driveway. "And I'll find you."

Maybe she will get high again, because some people keep getting high no matter how low it brings them, but I doubt it for her. She's still capable of feeling fear.

And fear works. I learned that from Dr. Goodnight.

August 4
Late Afternoon

"I'm home," I call out as I charge through the front door. I hear my grandmother say something like, "*There* she is," as I enter the living room. Rob is sitting next to her.

I don't know what to believe, so first things first. I unfreeze my face and smile.

"I thought you were going to call me," he says, straining to keep the frustration from his voice.

"I know, but I got to talking with Amy—you know Amy, right? She's Taylor's girlfriend?" Rob makes a vague gesture, and I plow on. "We started talking after our shift, and I had some things I needed to do, and she was nice enough to drive me."

Rob looks put out. "You still should have called. I was really worried."

"Well, I'm fine," I say calmly, despite the fact that I'm sweating.

"You don't look fine," he says. "You should take your medication."

"Right! I'll be straight back down," I tell him when he tries to follow me upstairs.

He lingers at the foot of the stairs as I vault up them. I don't take my meds. I fill a glass with water. It clinks against my front teeth my hands are shaking so badly. I finish the water and look in the mirror.

"It wasn't me," I whisper. My reflection looks skeptical. I try again. "There's another killer in the woods, and it's not me. Dr. Goodnight probably has Gina by now. You have to move."

When I come back, he's still there, waiting.

"I need a shower before dinner. Can I see you tomorrow?" I say, walking toward the door to let Rob out.

"Magda," he says, taking my arm and stopping me. "You don't seem okay. Are you *sure* you want me to leave?"

I smile at him warmly. "Yeah. And thank you."

He leaves. But the look on his face lets me know he thinks leaving is a terrible idea.

I wave at him as he gets in his car. "Don't worry," I shout after him. "I'm really okay."

I watch him drive off and go down the street. I listen to his car disappearing into the distance.

Then I hurry inside. "Grandma? I'm probably going to nap after my shower," I tell her.

"Do you want me to wake you for dinner or is this another one of your long naps?" she asks.

"It'll be a long one," I tell her.

"It's those drugs," she says, almost as if she's on the fence about them, despite everything.

I don't have a reply for that. I go upstairs and turn on the shower while I change into hiking shoes and dark clothes. A metronome starts clicking in my head. *Move, move, move*, it demands, and I follow its orders without thinking. Is it strange that not thinking, only doing, soothes me?

I'm not manic anymore. I'm totally calm. I tuck the new GPS into my back pocket. I bring my phone even though there's no signal where I'm going. If something happens to me, they can use it to identify me. I turn off the shower, wait for my grandmother to go out to the garden to pick vegetables for dinner, and sneak out.

It's after five o'clock by the time I get out into the woods. I have about three more hours of sunlight, but I doubt Gina has that long. I run until I hit that steep, upward climb through thick and tangled brush, and then I climb as fast as I can. There must be an easier way to Dr. Goodnight's lab, but I don't know it. If I'd had time, I would have tried to find some kind of logging road that dates back to before this area was made a National Park.

Dr. Goodnight needs regular supplies, and I'm willing to bet he doesn't move his product out this way.

I don't know exactly how to get to the lab. I don't even know how close Bo and I came to it before the rain started and we gave up on Mila and turned around, but I'm hoping that once I get close enough, I'll be able to smell it. I've heard the fumes are a dead giveaway. I don't actually know what a meth lab smells like, but I'm sure it smells nothing like the forest.

I still haven't quite figured out how Gina finally put all the pieces together and realized that Maria was working for Dr. Goodnight, but I really wish she hadn't tried to follow her and find the lab. It definitely had something to do with me coming back. Maybe I'm on Dr. Goodnight's list, and Maria told Gina that I was dead already? No. That's too flimsy.

But something about seeing me flipped a switch in Gina, and she finally saw the shelter for what it was—a processing plant for Dr. Goodnight's victims. Of course, there are plenty of people who live and work at the shelter who have no idea where the generous donations that pay for everything come from. Gina is one of them. Maria never was.

Maria had to know. She's the one who had to turn a blind eye to the fact that guests sell drugs to the volunteers in order for it to continue. And she's the only one who sees the books. She's the only one who knows where the money is coming from.

I figured it out a few hours too late. It wasn't until I saw Amy slipping into Mila's place, like a new model coming off the assembly line, that it all came together for me. I could practically see the conveyor belt in my head. Picking up pretty young girls from town who had very recently acquired a habit and delivering them to Dr. Goodnight.

Mila's death wasn't an OD, though. Dr. Goodnight didn't kill her. She got off the conveyor belt, but she still died.

Did I kill her? I search for rage in me. I try to blur Mila and Jinka together so I can concoct a grudge, but it doesn't work. All I feel toward either of them is a softness that's like love but soured a bit by the memory of all I've done wrong by them.

This is the way she came. Bo said there were two sets of tracks, so I know she was following someone. She might have even been following Maria, just like Gina's doing right now.

After figuring out what the shelter was really about, Mila must have seen Maria entering the woods. She knew how to track, so she had time to go back home, get her gear, and then pick up Maria's trail and follow it out here, hoping to find Dr. Goodnight's lab. I'm sure that she had a GPS in her gear. She was going to do exactly what I'm trying to do, which is come back with exact coordinates for the lab and give it to the police or the FBI.

And Mila died trying. There must be traps out here, or maybe some kind of alarm system. Mila knew the woods. She could hunt. Bo said her tracks showed skill, and she still got caught. I haven't figured that piece of the puzzle out, either, and I need to, so it doesn't happen to me. Like it's probably happening to Gina right now.

I climb faster, but even if I get there while Gina is still alive, I don't know if I can save her. If she's been caught, I don't know if I *should* save her. If I do, Dr. Goodnight will know he's been found out. He'll torch his lab and disappear. The GPS coordinates will be useless. I'll have no proof that he really exists. And after a few months of lying low, he'll build a new lab, and the killing will begin again. Starting with Gina, most likely.

That's what I'd do if I were him. And as sick as it makes me to admit it, I know I'm a lot more like him than I am like normal people. He and I are both on the other side of that fixed line. I may have never actually cut a person to shreds, but there's plenty of blood on my hands.

But not Gina's. Not yet. Rachel died because I didn't show up. That's not going to happen to Gina.

I run.

August 4
Nightfall

I GET A WHIFF OF SOMETHING LIKE ROTTEN EGGS, BUT there's a burnt-plastic edge to it, so I know I haven't stumbled across a random sulfurous spring by chance.

I circle the smell as it moves on the breeze, fully aware that by doing so, I am increasing my chances of getting caught. As the sun lowers, the sweat on my back chills. Without light, the chances that I'll be able to find the camp today lessens.

Finally, I discern the crisp edges of human-made structures through the trees. I don't know what I was expecting. Probably a series of sheds or huts, but what's out here is much more high-tech than that.

It took me so long to find the lab because it's camouflaged. There are several soft-sided shelters that look like military tents or barracks right out of some jungle war. They look light and easy to move—ready to go in a moment if need be. No single shelter is excessively large, but there are several of them. I realize that, as I circled the area, I may have drifted too close to one without seeing it and already been spotted.

There are no dogs, though. I'd wonder why, but the stench probably answers that question for me. It's a painful smell. I can feel it burning the inside of my nose, so I can only imagine what it does to a dog. Maybe it ruins their sense of smell? While it's a relief that there are no dogs, it still leaves the question as to how Mila got caught.

I crouch down. I listen and wait. I hear a mechanical humming. Generators, I think. Behind that, I hear people—the thrum of voices, not the sound of bodies moving through leaves or the impact of footfalls. I take the opportunity to memorize the GPS coordinates.

I should go, but I stay. Darkness can only benefit me from this point on. I slip my pack off my back. When I'm sure no one is waiting for me to stick my head out so they can shoot at it, I move toward the voices. Stupid, I know, but I can't leave Gina without knowing if she's alive or dead.

When I hear her voice through the sides of one of the smaller barracks, my heart leaps with relief, then it falls. I *should* go. I should get the GPS location to people with badges and guns and the ability to stop Dr. Goodnight. Stopping him is more important than both our lives.

But I don't go. I'm not leaving here without Gina. I'm going to show up for her.

I skirt the outside, but there are no windows. I'm vaguely aware that I am afraid. My heart is pounding. I calm my rasping breath enough to hear what's going on inside the tent.

"She didn't tell anyone," Maria is saying to someone else.

"I don't snitch," Gina growls, her words garbled like she's drunk.

"What about that bitch? The hot one," says a male voice. I can't quite place it, but for some reason I think I've heard it before.

"I don't think Gina had a chance to say anything to Magda," Maria tells him. "Besides. We can't touch her. Goodnight wants her."

"Yeah, but we should still find out if she knows anything," he argues.

"She doesn't know shit, Langmire," Gina spits.

Officer Langmire. I always hated that guy. Now I know why no one questioned me, even though I was the last person to see Mila alive. The police already knew who killed her. I guess you can't get away with something this big without inside help. I wonder if the FBI are in on it, too.

That seems unlikely. But for all the talk of them being in town, I was never questioned by the FBI or heard about them coming to the shelter to interrogate people after Mila went missing. Just Langmire. Maybe he kept the FBI away.

"Where does she live?" Langmire asks.

"You can't touch her," Maria repeats loudly. "Goodnight will kill both of us if you do."

"Fine," Langmire says, backing down. "What are we going to do with *her*?"

"Go get Goodnight. He loves doing this shit himself," Maria replies tiredly.

I hear the plastic door swing open and close itself with a soft smack. Keeping low, I watch Langmire's figure move through the trees. He keeps going and going, toward one of the outlying buildings, I'm assuming.

Dr. Goodnight must stay far from the labs themselves, which makes sense. They don't just stink. Sometimes they blow up.

I watch Langmire disappear in the darkness. If I'm going to do something, I have to do it soon. Maria isn't going to conveniently leave so I can rescue Gina unchallenged. And the only way in is through the door, so I can't try to sneak in and take Maria by surprise somehow.

"It never keeps you up at night?" Gina says, baiting Maria.

"Shut up, Gina," Maria says, like she's not having any of it.

"How many girls have you sent out to him?" Gina persists.

I hear the *thunk* of a fist hitting a body, and a heaving sound, like Gina's about to throw up. Then the sound of clanking, like a chain moving.

"Just shut up, okay?" Maria says.

"I've been shut up for twenty years," Gina groans. Then she starts laughing, but it's a wheezing kind of laugh through pain. "Can't just be for money," Gina continues. "It's because you've been managing a habit all this time, haven't you? You traded all those girls for your high."

I hear the *thunk* of another hit, but this time a scuffle comes right after it. I hear cursing and the sound of toppled furniture. I stay down as I dart in through the door.

Gina and Maria are rolling around on the floor. Gina is handcuffed to an overturned chair by one hand, but she's managed to get ahold of Maria's neck. Maria is reaching up, trying to scratch Gina's eyes out, while Gina chokes her and curses at her.

Strangling Maria will take too long. I look around. There's all kinds of equipment in here—stainless-steel bins and gauges and tubing. Nothing I can use to end this quicker, though. Maria is flailing her legs, and the cuff of her jeans has rolled up enough for me to see a knife strapped to her ankle. I jump on her flailing leg and manage to get the knife out, but when Gina feels another person next to her, she startles and lets go of Maria.

"No!" I snarl, reaching after Maria while she scrabbles to her feet.

Gina recovers fast. She swings the chair still cuffed to her wrist over her head like a mace and knocks Maria down with it. Then Gina stands over Maria and thrashes her with the chair over and over, every blow accompanied by the name of a different girl.

"No time," I snarl. I grab Gina to make her stop. "Where's the key?"

Maria lies on the ground, bloody and unconscious, but still breathing. Gina spits on her.

"Langmire has it," Gina replies. She looks at me. Her face is a mess. She sighs like she's sad to see me. "What are you doing here?"

I shake my head—no time to explain—and start trying to pull apart the damaged chair. Gina motions for me to stand back, and then she holds her bound wrist as far out of the way as she can while she stomps on the armrest. I take a moment to get the ankle sheath off Maria and strap it to myself, and then I go to help Gina. Stomping together, we manage to break the chair enough to get the cuff off.

We run for it, not even bothering to check outside the door first. At this point, they're either out there or they aren't, but we have to go now, or we'll be trapped.

I grab Gina's shirt and start pulling her the way I came, but she stops and yanks me in the other direction.

"The cars are this way," she whispers harshly.

We run uphill though the trees. It's too dark to see more

than a few feet in front of our faces. There isn't a trail, but the underbrush isn't as thick as it is the way I came. Gina's breathing is heavy and wet. She's also clutching her ribs. After only a few minutes of climbing, she's struggling. I come alongside her and put one of her arms over my shoulder.

"Are you sure this is the way?" I'm whispering because we're barely outside the ring of Dr. Goodnight's labs.

"Yeah," she pants. "Up to the ridge." She pants some more while she digs in the pocket of her jeans. "Cars are parked up there. Go on," she says. She hands me her keys and shoves me forward. "I'll catch up."

I ignore her lie and haul her along with me. "How did you figure it out?" I ask. "About the shelter and Dr. Goodnight?"

She turns her head to look right at me. "Because his son looks just like him."

We stop dead.

"His son?" I repeat. "You saw Dr. Goodnight's son?"

"Yeah. With you. You don't know, do you?" Gina sinks down on to a log, grimacing and holding her side. "Maria called me back into her office. Tells me to tell *you* I can't drive you home," she says, exhausted. "Then she tries to tell me that boy you were with didn't look anything like Michael. She knew Michael better than I did. Shit. We both have eyes." Gina spits blood. "I knew she was lying, so I followed her."

"Michael *who*?" I ask. I need to be sure.

"Michael Claybolt. He's Dr. Goodnight. That boy you were with today is his son."

I hear a loud crack, and I jump, ready to run, but Gina topples forward on to the ground in front of me.

"Someone's always got to ruin it," Rob says, coming out of the shadows. He's dressed in dark camouflage gear and he's holding a gun. "Hi, Magda."

August 4
Pitch-Dark

TWO KILLERS.

One clean. One bloody.

Dr. Goodnight. And his son.

I back away from Rob. I almost knew this was going to happen. Almost.

"Or is it Lena?" he asks, coming toward me. "I've noticed you like to be called Lena out here in the woods. Or is it just that you like it when Rain calls you Lena?"

I keep edging back slowly.

"It's always been hard to keep track of your different personas. You were one person here in the summer, and another person in New York, and then someone else entirely online. You taught me I had to be more than one person to do whatever the hell I wanted and get away with it. Thanks for that. It's been so much fun watching you all these years." His expression suddenly darkens. "Not so much fun watching you cheat on me with Rain, but I'm sure we can get past that as a couple."

I see Gina's hand twitch, and I don't know if that means she's still alive, or if it's a dying reflex.

Rob jerks his head toward me expectantly. "No questions? Nothing you want to ask me?" When I don't respond, he smirks at me. "Come on! Aren't you curious about the fact that I've been following you the whole time I was supposed to be with my mother—which would be tough because my dad killed her when I was thirteen."

He laughs at that, but it isn't funny to him. He wants me to ask him about his mother's death. He's wanted to tell me about her since our first date when he showed me that picture in his wallet. I don't ask. I don't want to listen to his origin story, but he isn't going to be denied this moment.

"He killed her in front of me. He made me *help*. But it was easy because she deserved it," he says simply, though there's nothing simple about it. "That's when I realized what I really was inside."

He pauses, allowing himself to catch up with his feelings. Whatever they are, he pushes them down and adopts an airy tone.

"Coincidentally thirteen was the year we met, and I fell in love with you, but you went for Liam that summer. You didn't like woodsy boys back then, did you? So I changed for you."

Let him blame me. Let him tell me I made him. I'm not going to fight it. I'll eat his sins and add them to my own if I can just get him away from Gina. Her breathing has sped up, and I think she's coming around. I edge ever so slightly away from her.

"Still nothing?" he snaps, following me. "You don't even want to know how I convinced you that you were the murderer? That was pretty amazing."

He pauses to congratulate himself, but when I still don't react, I feel his frustration mount.

"Don't you want to know how I came up with the idea? Your journal," he answers his own question, annoyed that I'm ruining his catharsis. "You had no idea you were writing in it. If you didn't know that, what else didn't you know about yourself? That, plus I found all those bloody clothes in your closet. I figured if gaslighting you didn't work, I'd cram a whole bunch of pills down your throat. Works for my dad."

Now it's not just Gina's hand that's moving, but her face, too. I keep leading Rob away from her.

"Sorry about Mila, by the way," he says, still fishing for a reaction. "She saw me go into the woods by your house, and she followed me because I *never* go into the woods, right? I started setting that up when I was thirteen, like you taught me. You need to be at least two people in order to get away with doing whatever you want." He pauses, but I don't react. "But Mila caught me. She was going to end up on my father's table sooner or later anyway. Fucking junkie. I don't like the table. I like the hunt. Like you."

He finally gives up on toying with me and sighs.

"Where are you going?" He gestures widely to the forest around us with his gun. "I grew up out here—with *Rainbow*." He says the name mockingly.

So. Rob is the childhood friend. The dickhead who hurt Bo when they were thirteen.

"We were inseparable once. Rain and Rob. But he was strange. You don't date guys who get within ten feet of strange, or so I thought. Turns out you like strange, don't you?" he says, sneering. "Don't think Rain taught you something that I don't know. You could have an hour's head start, and I could still catch you before you made it back to town."

I smile at him. It's a little smile and full of secrets.

Then I run.

I have no chance of getting away from him. I know that. Getting away isn't my goal. I want him to catch me. I hear him curse behind me. I surprised him. That small victory doesn't last long. He tackles me from behind and lands on top of me, nearly knocking the wind out of me. He flips me over to face him and grabs me by the shoulders to slam me down again. He hits my head against the ground. Everything goes black for a moment as I almost lose consciousness. He pins my hands above my head.

"What the fuck are you doing, Magda?" he screams in my face. I laugh wildly and wrap my legs around his waist.

"Harder," I say.

"You're fucking crazy," he says, but he likes it. "Seeing me kill that woman made you hot, didn't it?"

I arch up against him and give his lower lip a little nip.

"You really are perfect for me," he says. He kisses me, but he's not dumb enough to let go of my arms. I pull my knees up his sides and grind against him.

"Come on. Hit me a little," I say, writhing under him. "Wait—take my clothes off first."

He falls for it and lets go of my hands to undress me. My knees still cocked up, I reach one hand up and thread it through his hair. My other hand goes to my ankle. In one motion, I pull the knife out, yank his head back, and pull the blade across his throat.

He throws himself back, his mouth a surprised O and his eyes so wide there's a complete circle of white around his irises.

But I couldn't get the angle to sink the blade deep before he moved. I only grazed one side of his neck. And he's still got his gun.

I jump up and kick him as hard as I can before I run to get Gina. She's made it to her hands and knees. Tough as nails.

"Get up," I snarl at her. She tries to wave me off, but I drag her to her feet and scream, "Get up or we're both going to die!"

She staggers to her feet. The bullet is somewhere in her back. Her left arm hangs down, totally useless, so I swing her right arm up over my shoulder and start hauling her uphill.

Rob fires a couple of shots behind us, but we're already covered in darkness.

I'm carrying most of Gina's weight. My legs shake. I can still taste Rob in my mouth, and I feel like I'm going to throw up. I almost do, more than once, but I keep climbing until we crest the ridge.

I see the shadowy shape of cars way down the dirt road. Gina's head is lolling. She starts mumbling, "Go. Just go."

"I can't," I reply, laughing bitterly with shock and sheer exhaustion. "I don't know how to drive."

I hear a zipping sound and feel a bee sting my leg. I swat at it instinctively and find a metal cylinder sticking out of my thigh. I pull it out and look at it.

It's a dart.

I'm warm all over. I see the ground rushing up, but I never feel it catch me.

August 4?

THERE'S A HELD BREATH IN MY CHEST THAT MAKES MY heart beat too fast.

I gasp awake.

"Too much adrenaline?" a man asks.

I lift my hands and hear a clank. I try to sit up, and something stops me. I kick my legs, and they go nowhere. Every fiber of me is trying to run, but I'm tied down to a bed—or a gurney, more likely. I decide it's a gurney, based on feel. I focus my eyes. The camouflage ceiling tells me I'm in one of Dr. Goodnight's barracks.

This isn't the first time I've woken up strapped down, so I don't try to scream. There's no point, although the adrenaline makes my heart flutter, and I want to scream. I take a shivering breath to steady myself, and the man smiles.

"You look so much like your mother," the man says, studying my face. "I don't blame Rob. He said you were special. That you were one of us. Before you cut his throat." Michael Claybolt is a handsome man still, although older than he was in the picture Rob has in his wallet.

He's big and he's stayed fit. Even the graying hair suits him.

He stands up from the chair next to my gurney and turns his back on me to go to a countertop along the side wall. As he does, I see a long needle in his hand, and I feel the corresponding ache in my chest from where that needle burrowed into my heart. He drops the needle in a stainless-steel tray.

I hear rasping breaths, and I turn my head. Gina is strapped to a gurney next to me. There's an IV bag dripping fluid into her arm. I notice I'm hooked up to an IV, too.

"Rob says you have a taste for it," Michael continues. He speaks to me with his back still turned. "He said you've killed more people than he has."

"I don't know about that," I say, trying to talk through a chattering jaw. "How many people has he killed?"

Michael faces me. "You know how many," he chides.

And now I'm afraid of him. Stark terror adds more icy adrenaline to my blood. I shake all the way down my body.

"Three that have been found," I say, forcing myself to answer because I can tell an answer is expected. "There could be more, though."

Michael shakes his head. "Rob likes to make a show of his kills. He thinks gruesome equals fearsome." He smiles indulgently. "He has a theatrical nature. In fact, he came up with the Dr. Goodnight moniker. I'm not really a doctor—he borrowed the title from your boyfriend's father. Said it made me more intimidating." He thinks, and then shrugs. "He's still young."

I hear Gina mumbling incoherently as she starts to come around. Michael notices as well and starts busying himself with medical equipment.

"He tells me that you've managed to kill four people without even touching them," Michael says. He lifts a vial, sticks a needle through the membrane, and draws a viscous liquid into a syringe. "He says you're so good, you convince them to kill themselves."

"Not all of them," I correct. "One of my kills didn't commit suicide, but she was overdosed by a nurse *because* of me. I've also put two people in comas that they haven't come out of yet."

"Interesting," he says, thinking. Like this is an interview to see if I'm worthy of joining his and Rob's club.

"The two I put in comas probably won't make it," I say, trying to pad my résumé. "Neither of their families have the patience to keep watering vegetables."

Michael pauses and studies me. I went too far with the vegetable comment. He didn't like it. He wrinkles his nose distastefully and shakes his head.

And that's it. The interview is over. I'm going to die.

Dr. Goodnight brings a tray over and puts it down on a short table between my gurney and Gina's. On the tray are two rows of three syringes. He pulls the chair over to her side and picks up the first syringe in the top row. He watches Gina deliriously rolling her head back and forth on the pillow for a while. Then he injects the first syringe into her IV line.

Her eyes flick open. "Hi, Gina," he says.

She rolls her head to face him. After a moment, she seems to recognize him, and she starts pulling on her restraints, trying to get away.

"I remember you," he tells her. "And it looks like you remember me."

He picks up the second needle.

"I never had any reason to come after you. You were smart. You were there when my son was born. You survived and got clean. You kept your mouth shut." He's speaking fondly to her, seemingly oblivious to the fact that Gina looks like she would strangle him if she could. "I'm wondering what changed."

He injects the second needle into her IV.

"Was it her?" he asks, gesturing to me. "Did she get in your head somehow?"

Gina's already bruised face turns red. It's like fire is crawling under her skin. She bites down on her lips to keep from screaming, but I can see her back bending, her fists clenching, until finally a broken shriek comes out of her.

"It'll be over soon," says Dr. Goodnight. "But first, tell me. Did this girl get in your head? She has a habit of doing that. She even got into my son's head."

He locks eyes with Gina, but she doesn't answer him yes or no. Froth boils from between her lips. A clicking sound coughs out of her melting lungs. I don't look away. She needs me to stand witness. I showed up, and I'm not leaving early. I lock eyes with her, and I give her whatever I have. It isn't much. It isn't enough. She's still going to die, but I'll be with her when she does.

"I can make it end," he says, holding up the third syringe. "Just say yes. Tell me if Magda convinced you to come out here and play the hero."

I nod to tell her it's okay. I want her to take the easy way.

She works her jaw like she's trying to speak. Dr. Goodnight leans in close, and Gina spits on him. Before I can stop it, a shocked laugh flies out of me.

She smiles at me.

Dr. Goodnight's head snaps around at the sound, and black hatred fills his eyes. He turns back to Gina, jabs her IV with the third syringe, and her body locks up. Then it convulses over and over for what seems like forever.

And then it's done.

Dr. Goodnight turns to face me. The look on his face is clear. I'm next.

He never needed any information from Gina. He just wanted me to know what was coming for me. There was never an interview, although he wanted me to think I had a chance. I look at Gina. Tough old broad. He tortured her to scare me. It worked. I'm scared and I'm crying now, but I won't beg because I'm not crying for me. I'm crying for Gina. She was probably the best friend I've ever had. I didn't know that until just now, but it doesn't matter because nothing I can say or do is going to change how this is going to end.

It's going to hurt. And he's going to take his time. "Ha." I force myself to laugh. He doesn't like it when people laugh at him. "She spat in your eye. Good for Gina."

He turns around, holding up a syringe. "This won't be very funny to you in a moment."

"You're not going to let Rob do it?" I ask. I narrow my eyes at him, smiling. "Or maybe you know he can't?"

"I'm doing my son the biggest favor of his life by killing you," he tells me as he flicks the syringe with his middle fingernail. "His obsession with you makes him vulnerable."

"He'll hate you if you kill me, you know. Or maybe that doesn't matter. Maybe I managed to kill him after all."

Michael Claybolt can't give me the satisfaction of thinking I've won that. "You didn't kill my son," he snaps. I'm actually getting under his skin.

"Then where is he?" I taunt. "He's been obsessed with me for five years, and now he's suspiciously absent at my death."

Dr. Goodnight leans in with a gleam in his eyes that tells me he knows he's about to get the last laugh.

"He doesn't know I've got you. He's on his way to Ray's camp to catch you," he says. "And when you don't show, he'll kill all of them."

Then he plunges the first needle into my IV.

I'm surfing flame.

You have to be very careful when you do that. The fire hurts, and you want to jump away, but you can't because there are dark holes in between the fire. If you fall into one of those, you don't come out. So I stay in the fire.

I crest a wave of pain and see...

White mounds. Sheets. Beyond that is my hand. I'm lying on my side, so I'm no longer tied down. I'm telling myself to run, but my body isn't listening to me. I hear the clank of metal things being gathered together, and then the dunking sound of them being dropped into liquid. I can't close my eyes. Then I see Dr. Goodnight's figure, but he's blurry. I can't even move the muscles in my eyes well enough to focus them, but I can smell. I smell bleach.

He reaches for me. His hands are on me.

I hear him make a heaving sound, and the room wheels around my fixed field of vision, and then all I see is the fabric of the shirt covering his back.

Dangling over one of his shoulders, I sway with every step he takes.

We pass a sudsy, soaking sink full of stainless-steel needles. And more sharp things, still unused and filled with venom. My hand nearly brushes the long, thick needle that injected adrenaline into my heart. I can't move my hand enough to grasp it.

I'm trapped in my cocoon.

Dr. Goodnight carries me outside into the warm, damp dark of the forest.

The ceiling fan goes woop-woop.

Gina is lying next to me in bed at the hospital. We're both looking up at the fan, watching it spin.

"That's far," Gina says, judging the distance to the fan.

"I know," I reply. "David was super tall, though."

"Yeah, but still," Gina replies doubtfully. "He must have really wanted to die. It wasn't your fault, you know."

"Maybe not. But I still feel like it was." I turn my head to face her. "I'm sorry I got you killed, too," I say.

"You didn't get me killed," she replies, rolling her eyes. She turns her face to mine. "Whatever you used to be, you aren't that anymore."

"I'm still a killer," I say. "Which is too bad, because now I'm dead and I can't kill any of the right people."

Gina laughs. "You aren't dead," she says. "Goodnight has never tried to kill a junkie like you before. You recognize that taste in your mouth, don't you?"

"Yeah," I say vaguely. "Phenobarbital. I was on it for weeks at the hospital after I killed Zlata. To keep me from screaming." I look around. "So that's why I imagined us here. The taste reminded me."

"Yeah," Gina says, looking around. "Your body built up a tolerance. It would take more than what he gave you to kill you." She turns her head to face me again, but now she's Rachel. "But you have to wake up or Bo is going to die," Rachel says. "Wake up!"

I open my eyes and see Gina lying next to me.

Her face is streaked with blood and phlegm, and her eyes are filmed over with death. She rests on her side, her cuffed hand next to her face, like she's sleeping. There's dirt under her cheek. There's dirt under my cheek, too, and all around us.

I flex my hand. It moves.

I listen. I can hear some motion above me, and the sound of someone grunting. Something heavy and warm lands on top me, nearly crushing me. I do not react when it rolls and flops across me.

Maria.

There's a bullet hole in her forehead. I dare to move my

eyes enough to see walls of dirt around us. We're in a pit. And now I can smell them. The bodies rotting under me.

I hear footsteps moving away from the edge of our mass grave. I wait. The smell is unbearable. The spongy feeling of decay beneath me is unthinkable. But I wait.

When the footsteps have gone, I turn my head to make sure there's no one standing up there. Then I start to push Maria off me.

My body doesn't work very well. My vision keeps blurring, but that's a blessing. I can't really see what's under me, covered by only a few inches of maggoty dirt. My stomach heaves. I swallow the vomit down and stand. The ground beneath me rolls and shifts like logs on water. Legs, arms, torsos, turning under me. I steady myself against the wall of the pit. The edge is just at my head's height.

Slowly, I raise my eyes over the edge and look. I see no one.

I have to stand on top of Maria to climb out. The effort makes my heart pound and my ears ring. I crawl away from our grave on my hands and knees. I'll never make it to Bo's in this condition. I need a jolt. I'll have to crawl back to the barracks where Gina died to get it. So I crawl.

My back and my neck feel vulnerable. Any minute as I crawl, I could be found. I wait to feel the shot or the stab that will kill me as I put one hand forward, then a knee, then the other hand.

I force myself to go faster. By the time I'm inside the barracks, I'm sweating. The counter. I see the stainless-steel dish on top of it, and the syringe still inside it.

I haul myself up and grab the adrenaline shot. There's about an inch of fluid left inside. I don't know how much is too much, or how much is enough. I turn the syringe toward my breastbone and feel for the hole it made before.

I close my eyes and stab myself in the heart. I push the plunger down before it hurts.

My insides grow wings and try to fly out of my mouth. I stick out a hand to catch myself as the world tips and tilts. The sweat covering me freezes, and I shiver violently. I get my legs under me. They shake, but they hold me up.

I drop the used syringe into the bleach-filled soaking sink. I grab a rag and wipe away my handprints that trail up and across the counter. I look behind me at the gurney I was strapped to. The sheets have already been stripped and put in a bucket filled with more bleach.

He likes things clean. And he's thorough. That's good for me.

I need a weapon. My teeth chatter as I look around. My brain unclogs and thoughts shoot through it. Knife. Ankle.

I reach down and, miraculously, it's still there. He either didn't notice it while he was strapping me down or he knew I'd never be able to reach it and didn't bother to take the time to unbuckle it. It's a good knife. I hold it in my hand and leave the barracks.

My body feels hollow, it's so light. I move quickly but silently to a dwelling I know is somewhere on the outskirts of this camp. I need to go to Bo. I know that. But first, this. The thing I was made for.

Weeks in the woods have taught me how to move without sound. But it's more than just practice. It comes naturally to me. Bo called me a hunter. Close. But not entirely right. I walk in Michael's footsteps to cover my tracks. I leave no trace.

Michael doesn't hear me enter his tent. He doesn't see me as I cross his spartan room to where he's standing, beside another bucket of bleach, holding his dirty shirt. I wait until he drops the shirt with my DNA on it into the bucket and turns around.

There must be ghosts in his eyes. I know what that's like. He probably thinks I'm one of them, because even though he's facing me now, he hesitates for a moment. All he does is squint and look at me as if he knew me long ago but can't remember from where.

That split second of hesitation is all I need. I stab him in the neck. I touch him with nothing but the blade.

He seems to wake up. Clutching the wound with one hand, he lunges for me, spraying blood through his fingers. I step back, evading him. If this turns into a brawl, I've lost. I have no illusions about that. I plant a foot and brace myself. I know from butchering the deer how tough it is to get even the sharpest knife into a body. I push off my back foot to stab him in the chest.

He doesn't know which wound to grab. Confused from the rapid blood loss, he goes back to the bucket and reaches for his dirty shirt. He drops it and makes a move toward a chair that's supporting a pair of night-vision goggles and a large rifle with a red-feathered dart in it—the same night goggles and dart gun he used to take me down earlier, no doubt.

I stab him again before he can get to the chair, and he stiffens like a real boy turned back into wood.

And it's done. I should be horrified by what I just did. Soul-sick with the thought of killing a human being. I've killed a man with my own hands, and all I feel is relief. The monster is dead. I tiptoe away from the dark, syrupy blood fanning out before me.

I know what I am now. No more lying to myself. No more tearing myself in two so I can hide one half of me from the other. I am a predator. But just because I have this sick gift doesn't mean that I have to misuse it the way Michael did. The way Rob does. I can do better. I can be better. Bo will show me how.

Bo and Rob. They're both waiting for me.

I exit the tent and take the briefest of moments to orient

myself. I've never tried to navigate through the woods in the dark. I almost take the night-vision goggles but think better of it. I've killed a man. I can take nothing and leave nothing, or it may become evidence against me. I can't get lost. I can't stumble and break a leg.

I can't fail.

August 4
Dead of Night

I RUN WHEN THERE'S ENOUGH MOONLIGHT PIERCING THE canopy to see, and I walk fast with my arms out when there isn't.

I'm not sure how much time has passed. I don't know when Rob set out, or what condition he was in when he left. I don't even know if Michael was telling me the truth. Rob could be dead. He could have bled out after I cut him. But I doubt it.

Adrenaline doesn't last forever. As the shivers turn into the shakes, my legs get heavier and clumsier. Bitter-smelling sweat soaks through my clothes, mats my hair, and smears tracks through the combination of pit filth and sprayed blood caking my skin. My heartbeat is erratic, and my breath is wheezy. Branches whip me. I fall. I get up. I keep going.

I wasn't afraid when I faced Michael Claybolt. If he died or if I died, at least the world would be less one miscreation. Now I'm terrified, because the world can't afford to lose someone like Bo.

My vision is blurring, and I don't know if I'm still going the right way. I slow down and pivot. I think I see the place I hid after overhearing Sol accuse Bo of murder. Poor Sol. She was just copying Raven, but she's only seven. Following Bo, and then seeing him and me having sex must have scared her to death.

Rob. He's waiting for me. He wants me to find him. I see firelight flickering ahead, and I stagger toward it.

I force my fumbling body to move silently. I have to crouch down and crawl the rest of the way up the rise that surrounds Bo's camp. I lie on my belly as I look over the rise and down into the bowl of Bo's camp.

The firepit in the center is blazing high with what looks like books and furniture. They must have run out of firewood, and Rob wanted to keep the blaze big so I could see it. Most of the family is huddled together, clinging to each other. I can hear some quiet sobbing.

Set apart from the rest, I see Bo on his knees with his hands clasped behind his head. Rob paces in front of him, holding some kind of rifle across his chest, military style. There's a big bandage on his throat from where I cut him, and another in the crook of his arm. He was either given an

IV or maybe some blood while I was unconscious. Michael fixed him up and sent him out after me on a wild-goose chase so he could kill me without Rob there to complicate things.

Whatever it was, Rob doesn't look like he's injured.

He looks energized, while I can barely stand.

He also looks impatient. Across the bowl a twig snaps, and Rob whirls toward it. Everyone freezes.

"Mag-da," Rob calls in a singsong voice. "Come out, come out." He waits a few more seconds and then whistles sharply. When there's still no reply, he shouts, "Mag-da! Le-na! Magdalena!"

"It's not her!" Bo snaps. "I told you. She's gone. She doesn't want to see me anymore."

Even though he's scared and angry and probably hates me right now for dragging his family into this, I can hear how much saying that hurts him.

"That's because she thought you killed her friend," Rob says, like he's repeating himself. "And then she thought you weren't real." Rob takes a moment to laugh. "But now she knows the truth, and she'll come to you." He raises his voice again and shouts to the rim of the bowl. "Because she knows I'll kill you if she doesn't!"

I can barely hold up my head. I let it drop on to the ground while I think. But with my eyes closed, I feel like I've got bed spins, so I pick up my head and open my eyes. If I don't go down, he'll start killing them. If I do go down, he'll start killing them. That's why he's here. To kill them in front of me. He needs me to know what he's done. He needs the attention.

I've got a knife and the high ground. I don't think I can throw anything far enough to hit Rob accurately at this distance. Besides, I don't know how to throw a knife. I back down the rise knowing that one snap will give me away. Rob doesn't have to shoot to kill. He can always just start maiming them to get me to come out. But as long as he's not entirely sure I'm out here, he'll hold off on that.

I skirt the camp, picturing the buildings in my head. Which one of them would have the family rifle in it? Or a bow and some arrows? More important, how can I get to any of those buildings without being seen? They all surround the firepit.

Except for the shed with the clean room in it. That's outside the bowl. The stump outside had an ax in it the last time, but what am I going to do with an ax? The only thing it's good for is to pull focus. Axes are pretty flashy. They make people forget about things like concealed ankle blades.

I heft the ax over my shoulder as I walk unsteadily toward the bowl—not to look tough, but because I don't have the strength to carry it any other way. No point in trying to conceal my footsteps now.

Someone is going to get shot.

It's the only way to create an opening. Rob wants to kill

me, but he wants to do it last, so he won't aim for my head. Hopefully the rest of the family can rush him and overpower him before he has a chance to aim true at them in the flickering firelight.

This is a terrible plan.

"There she is!" Rob says triumphantly. "I told you she'd come."

I walk into the bowl on shaky legs. I'm putting all I have into not stumbling, but everyone can see what condition I'm in. I pass the family huddle and glance down to see if they're all there. Hoping one got away. Maybe Moth is running to get help. But no, they're all there, even little Moth. She's wet herself.

As I pass, I see Raven is in the center of the huddle. Aspen and Karl are blocking her. They're keeping her from Rob's sight on purpose. She pulls the collar of her button-down flannel shirt aside for a moment. Something's under there. I have to turn my head back to Rob before I can see it clearly so I don't give whatever she's concealing away. Please let it be a firearm.

"Stop right there," Rob tells me. I'm halfway between where he stands with Bo kneeling at his feet and the family huddle. Rob is looking me over, reveling in this moment. "Magda, you look like utter shit. Did your friend bleed out on you before you got her to the hospital?"

I glance down. I don't have to fake my indifference. "No, actually, most of this is your father's blood."

He chuffs disbelievingly. “No it isn’t. You got away. He didn’t catch you.”

I shake my head. “He lied to you, Rob. He caught me. Then he sent you out here to get rid of you while he killed me—or *tried* to kill me—but I stabbed him four times…no, three times? I don’t know. A bunch of times. He’s dead.”

I swing the ax down to lean on it. This is no act. I can barely stay upright. Rob tilts the muzzle of the gun my way for a brief second while the ax is in transition, but it’s not a serious move in my direction. He’s either too stunned by what I said about killing his father, or he thinks I’m too weak to attack him with an ax. Which I am. The world tips. I lean forward and take deep breaths, trying not to throw up or faint.

“Magda?” Bo says, worried.

“Stay there,” I tell him.

Rob aims his gun at Bo again. “I don’t believe you,” he decides.

I right myself and pop my ears to stop the ringing before I look at him. “I don’t really care, Rob. I’ve never really cared what you thought. You’re just background noise to me.”

Come on. Shoot me, you prima donna with your bespoke bags and your Patek Phillipe watch and your classic cars and your showy murders. There’s nothing you hate more than being overlooked, and I’ve been overlooking you from day one.

He points the gun at me, but Bo makes a move to defend me, and Rob remembers why he's here. He's here to make me suffer. The gun is back on Bo. And Rob is laughing.

"Almost," he says. He's nodding at me, acknowledging that I nearly got him off his purpose. "Drop the ax," he orders.

I do it.

"Kick it away from you."

I do my best, but I really can't kick it far.

"And choose which one of them you want me to kill first."

Thank you.

I hear Maeve begging me quietly, "Please, Lena. Pick me or Ray. It's okay, honey—you don't have to choose. I'll go first."

That's a *mother*. She's even trying to mother me.

I block out Maeve's voice and speak over her. "I've never liked Raven," I announce.

"*What?*" Bo nearly shrieks. "Lena, don't play along with him."

I shrug. "Would you rather I pick Moth?" Bo looks like he's going to be sick. "He said pick *someone*. I pick Raven."

Bo hates me. In this moment, he hates me.

"Raven. You're first," Rob calls out.

Raven stands up haltingly. She's hunching her shoulders, probably to hide whatever it is she has under the long, untucked shirt she's wearing. I turn and face her, raising my eyebrows as if to ask, *Are you ready?*

She doesn't look ready. Her face is a blank page. She has no idea what I want from her, and there's no way for me to prepare her. Whatever weapon she's got under there, I hope she knows how to use it. Her knees barely bend as she stiffly walks forward. She's so brave.

"Stop right there," Rob tells her. "Magda. Back up. You're too close to her."

I move away from Raven, but not that far. Let him think I want to be in the splash zone. My body is still facing her, but I turn my head around to look at Rob. I catch sight of Bo glaring at me. He loathes me for this, but that's okay. I just wish he were paying better attention to the important things. Like the rifle.

I look at Rob. "Do it," I tell him.

I see his eyes flicker with suspicion. All he knows is that he shouldn't want what I want, but I'm following his rules, so he's stuck. I toss my head back around and look at Raven.

"It'll be okay," I whisper. I'm ready for this.

I know if I wait to hear the shot, it'll be too late. We're grouped too closely together. Instead, I listen to something else. I'll call it predator's instinct. I turn and step into the path of the bullet as Rob fires. Raven is about three inches shorter than me, so the shot he meant to put right between her eyes grazes the top of my left shoulder.

Even though it just nicks me, really, the power behind it is startling. I feel it throw me back, and I hit the ground.

Oh, Bo. All he can think of is me. He shouts my name and lunges for me, when he should be turning around and getting that rifle away from Rob.

"Raven!" I scream, hoping she has something good hidden down the front of her shirt. I reach for the knife at my ankle.

I see a tiny arrow fly past Rob, but Raven misses. He raises his rifle and takes aim at her.

I've never thrown a knife, but if I hit the rifle with any part of it hard enough, it might throw off his aim. I rear up and pinch the blade between my thumb and forefinger. Then I chuck it from some muscle deep down in my belly.

Rob staggers back, shocked. The knife sticks out of the back of his trigger hand. I landed it. Killing things always came naturally to me.

Bo has the sense to dive for the rifle, but it's still strapped high and tight across Rob's torso. They struggle with each other. They're two guys who grew up wrestling each other. They're evenly matched, but Bo has more to lose. He gets Rob in a hold, lifts him right up off the ground with his gorilla strength, and slams him down on the ground.

Bo is stronger, but Rob is a piece-of-shit murderer like me. He's not looking to subdue his opponent, like Bo is. He's looking for the kill. I know this. Even though Bo is on top, Rob knows how to kill from the bottom. Like me.

Bo won't kill Rob. That's why I love him. Before Ray can make it over here to help overpower Rob, I make a choice. I snatch the tiny bow and the remaining arrow from Raven's uncertain grip. At the same moment, Rob notices the knife sticking out of the back of his hand.

He yanks the knife out, as I draw back the arrow in Moth's training bow.

"Rob," I call gently as I stand over them. When he looks at me, I shoot him in the eye.

It's like hitting a switch. Everything stops. I made a clean kill, which is more than he deserved. Rob is dead. My arms fall. I drop to my knees. Bo pushes himself up off Rob's corpse and reaches for my head to cushion it as I fall to the ground.

Bo's face is over mine. His big, tender eyes. I try to reach up to touch his mouth, but holy shit my shoulder is killing me, and I can't move. I'm so cold.

"Is anyone hurt?" I ask him.

"Yes," he whispers, breathing a laugh. "You are."

I think I smile. "I'm sorry I was late."

"I waited for you." He grins. "Good thing you're worth it."

"She's in shock, and she's losing blood fast!" That's Ray speaking. "Karl, get blankets. Raven, go to the storeroom and get the emergency kit. Aspen, boil water. Rainbow, let go of her so I can treat her."

I'm so cold.

"No," I protest. "Don't let go..."

August 6
Before Noon

I KNOW I'M SAFE, BECAUSE I CAN SMELL BO.

Every inch of me hurts. I open my eyes but stay where I am, absorbing Bo's room. I have no idea how they got me up into one of those tree house dormitories, but I'm glad they made the effort. It's beautiful to me. Probably because it's his.

The small room is circular with a peaked ceiling. There's a trapdoor skylight that's open to let in a breeze. The wooden walls are covered with posters of the periodic table of the elements, star charts, and a foldout anatomy print of the human body. The floor is covered in a handmade hook rug.

The sheets on his bed are mismatched, clean, and worn to softness. The bottom sheet has big yellow flowers on it, and the top one has sailboats. I notice I'm clean, my hair has been washed, and I'm wearing a long cotton nightgown. I can still feel a hot rock at my feet, but the piles of blankets that they had to put on top of me when I was in shock are gone now. Bo keeps me warm enough. It's small and cozy, and I love it here, mostly because I can feel the length of Bo's body pressed up against my side. I hear him turn the page of a book, and I have to move my head to see what it is. Something mathematical. He reads math books. That's adorable.

"How long have you been awake?" he asks, putting his equations aside.

"I just woke," I say. My voice is really scratchy.

I remember IV bags and catheters while Ray fought to flush out my system and keep me from bleeding to death. My body is ultrahydrated right now, but none of that fluid went down my throat. My mouth is gritty.

Bo picks up a mason jar of water and helps me sit up to drink. It's so good. I finish the whole thing. Bo watches me drink, smiling, as if my moving and drinking on my own is a pleasure to him.

I give him back the mason jar. "Will you help me with something?" I ask him.

"Anything," he replies immediately.

"I have to go back into town."

Bo frowns suddenly. "Can it wait? There's no way out of this camp except on foot."

"I know," I say quietly. "And no. It can't wait."

He shakes his head. "You were poisoned and shot a day and a half ago."

"I've been getting poisoned for a year now—and, ironically, that's why I'm still alive. And I didn't get shot; I got *grazed*. On the shoulder. I promise I won't walk on my shoulder." I get him to smile, at least, but he's still worried. "Please, Bo."

He nods gravely. "Okay." Then he gives me a half smile. "I went into town to look for you, you know. But I had no idea where your grandparents lived, and at the shelter they said no one named Lena had ever worked there."

I give him a matching half smile. "Well, *Rain*, I always preferred Lena to Magda."

He grins at me sheepishly, and we share one of those rare moments when you not only understand someone else, but you see yourself in them. We stay like that for a while.

I take his hand. "What did you do with his body?" I ask. He knows I mean Rob.

"My dad and I buried him deep," Bo replies, his voice low and rough.

"And his cell phone?" I ask carefully. I don't know if Bo knows enough about electronics to have considered it. "What did you do with it?"

"I took it back to his father's camp and left it there. Don't worry, I wore gloves." Bo's face is pale and frozen.

"So you saw."

He nods. "We had no idea, you know. We knew the Claybolts were drug dealers, and my mother hated them, but we didn't *know*." He stops. He swallows. "I thought about taking Rob's body back to his father's camp, too, but…" He looks away and lets out a long breath.

"But if his body is ever found, I could go to jail for killing him," I answer for him.

"It was self-defense—more than that. You were defending all of us," he says, his anger mounting.

I smile and pull his hand against my chest, holding him to my heart. "You don't have to tell me I did the right thing. But thank you."

He gathers me to him in a careful hug, avoiding my shoulder. "I know you did the right thing," he says.

We stay like that until I can cry.

Bo gets me down by having me sit in a hammock that's attached to a rope, which is swung over a branch right outside the tree house and counterbalanced by a big rock. He holds the hammock as I get in and then lets me swing down slowly. It's fun, actually, and it answers the question as to how I got up there in the first place.

"She's awake!" Moth screams, and then her tiny body is hurling toward mine.

Bo intercepts the preschool projectile. He tosses her up in the air playfully and reminds Moth that she needs to be gentle with me. Moth settles for a one-armed hug and an Eskimo kiss.

Sol gives me a tortured look. I smile, but I skip over her because the conversation we need to have can't happen now.

Karl and Aspen are simultaneously too fascinated and too terrified by me to come any closer than ten feet, so I just wave at them to let them know that I see them.

Raven stops in front of me. She's trying to say thank you, but I'm not going to make her.

"Good thinking to hide that training bow," I tell her. "You saved my life." Before she can argue about who saved whom, I move on to Ray.

"You're a great doctor," I tell him. He looks at his feet and gets angry at them because he's not good at hearing compliments.

"Your blood salts were so high and kidney failure was definitely a worry, and I didn't have everything..."

His eyes are blinking rapidly. I interrupt him before he can go into genius mode and get all technical on me. "Ray. My kidneys are applauding you right now."

He laughs, and shuffles, and tries to disappear, so I let him.

And then, Maeve. She folds me into a deep, soft-bodied, sweet-smelling, everything-is-going-to-be-okay mommy hug. I just let myself sink into that for a while. Strange how quickly the unknown can become second nature. The strangers in the crowd are now my family.

"Where are you going?" she asks, all business now.

Because of course she knows I didn't drag myself out of Bo's bed before I was totally healed for nothing.

"First I have to get my pack. I left it outside the Claybolts' camp. Then I have to visit an old man," I reply.

Bo and I hold hands as we walk to Whispering Pines.

We enter, and I go to the nurse's station and sign us in as Aura-Blue and Guest. The nurses here don't really check those things.

Francis Tanis is sitting in his usual spot, reading the paper. I smooth the cute patchwork dress I borrowed from Raven and squeeze Bo's hand as we go over to him. "Mr. Tanis. Do you remember me? I'm Aura-Blue's friend," I say. He looks at me blankly, and for a moment I think all is lost.

Then Mr. Tanis stands. "Of course I remember you. Magda, wasn't it?" he says in his hale and hearty way.

I shake his hand, relieved, and introduce Bo by his first name only. The old sheriff asks us to join him.

"What can I do for you?" he asks, giving me that knowing smile.

I get right to it. "I found Dr. Goodnight," I say. "His real name was Michael Claybolt."

"Michael Claybolt?" Mr. Tanis repeats, obviously recognizing the name.

"He's dead," I say bluntly. Mr. Tanis's eyes flash, but he

keeps his mouth closed. "I've written down the GPS coordinates for his drug lab in the forest. His body is in his tent." I stop. This was always going to be hard. "There's also a mass grave. It's just a pit, really." My voice cracks, and I clear my throat so I don't start crying. I hand the piece of paper to Mr. Tanis.

He takes it. "Do you need some water?" he asks. I nod, and Mr. Tanis goes to the nurse's station to get it for me.

"You okay?" Bo asks quietly when the old sheriff leaves.

I shrug with my good shoulder.

"Do you really think this guy can help?"

I shrug again, and he laughs. He leans toward me. We touch our foreheads together, eyes locked.

Mr. Tanis returns with a small paper cup for me. I take a sip and continue.

"In the pit is the body of a woman with a police-issued handcuff around her wrist. The keys for those cuffs belong to Officer Langmire."

Mr. Tanis jerks forward suddenly as if he's about to leap out of his seat. "Are you sure?" he asks.

"Oh, yes," I say. "I'm very sure. He didn't kill her, but he was involved. And I'll bet he's not the only one at the local level who is."

"What makes you say that?"

"He's an idiot. Why would he be the only officer

handling the disappearance of a teenage girl, unless people higher up in the food chain needed a fall guy in case everything went sideways with the FBI? I know you're friends with the new chief, but..."

He looks devastated, but he nods. "I figured it had to be something like that, even though I didn't want to admit it." He looks out the window. "If it was just about the drugs, there'd have been as many men dying as women. But only women? It never made sense."

I give him a moment before asking, "Can you get this"—I gesture to the GPS coordinates—"to the FBI?"

"Yes, I can," Mr. Tanis replies quietly. "I'll go out into the woods myself if I have to and take pictures for them if they don't listen."

"One more thing—I'm giving you this information anonymously," I tell him. "I don't want to be brought into this in any way." He narrows his eyes at me, gauging how serious I am about that. "If the FBI shows up at my house, asking me to testify, I'll say you're a senile old man I visited once with a friend."

His eyes widen momentarily, but then they settle into something like respect. "You have my word," he says in a way that tells me his word is worth something.

"Thank you," I say, standing up. "The women's rehab shelter was involved, too. But I think the FBI will be able to figure that out once the dirty cops are taken in."

Mr. Tanis nods again, but he seems too overwhelmed to speak.

"Goodbye, Mr. Tanis. You were right."

"Doesn't feel right." He looks at me, his eyes sad. "How did you get away from him?"

I smile, but I don't answer.

"Okay, then. Good luck." He shakes hands with Bo and me, and he waits for me to turn before saying, "Take care of that injured shoulder." Clever old buzzard.

"I will," I tell him.

Before we leave, I send a text to Rob's phone: ***Where are you????***

With the last bar on my battery, I call my grandparents. I tell them a convoluted lie about having been out looking for Rob, who's gone missing. When they pick us up, I introduce Bo as one of Rob's childhood friends. They invite him over for dinner, and when that goes well (and how could it not after Bo admits he's been accepted to seven colleges), they invite him to stay the night in the guest room.

My grandparents have always been good at getting back to normal.

August 19

THIS WILL BE MY LAST ENTRY.

What's left of the summer is a circus for this small town.

TV crews, true-crime writers, talk-show hosts, and religious leaders looking to recruit new followers descend on this pretty little pocket of the world, all of them wailing about the social issue closest to their hearts and looking for anyone to talk to them.

Despite the fact that I dated the son of a serial killer and work at the shelter that same serial killer funded and used to cultivate his prey, no one has shown up on my doorstep yet, which isn't surprising considering the mess the FBI is dealing with. They may come to ask me about Rob's whereabouts eventually, but it's likely they've already written me off. On his phone, which they have, it's clear from our text messages that Rob was lying to me and I had no idea he and his father were killers.

I'm not worried. I was careful. It's not like the police have my DNA or even my fingerprints on file. I've never been arrested and booked. If any physical evidence of me were left behind, it would be in the genetic soup of the pit. Good luck sorting that out. As long as I'm not placed on the scene, there is no way anyone will know. So far Mr. Tanis has kept his word, and then some.

The local police force has been gutted.

The FBI is trying to close down the shelter, but a few of the kitchen workers (all clean and sober) are putting up a fight to keep the doors open for the women and small children who have no place else to go.

The TV cameras have come in handy in that respect. Every day the kitchen circle stands outside in the parking lot holding hands in protest at closing down the shelter. Every evening after they go home, I go to the office, get the books straightened out, pay the electric and water bills, and call in stock orders for the upcoming weeks. That may sound overly optimistic, but I already know which way public opinion will swing this decision. I don't want one of my walk-in refrigerators warming and wasting weeks' worth of produce.

The fact that the shelter is the sole beneficiary of an offshore account controlled by a non-taxable, nonprofit organization that has millions of dollars in its coffers means that it won't have to close down for financial reasons in the foreseeable future, either. Dr. Goodnight made quite a lot of money as a drug manufacturer, but it seems after what he gave to Rob to live comfortably or used to set up his own camp in the woods, he put the rest of that fortune into this account. And in that way, he left one tiny cove of purity in the catastrophic oil spill that was his existence. I'm not letting this shelter go under. If I do, I may as well have stayed in the pit.

I'm going to make something out of the rest of my life. I may never be able to atone for what I am or what I've done, but I'm going to try. There are piles of drug money stashed in that account—enough to open and run several shelters. This isn't the only town where women are chewed up and spat out.

Amy will run things here when I'm gone. She's surprisingly good at accounting, she's reliable, and the kitchen likes her because she's recently joined AA. She'll keep the lights on when I'm not around.

I found a new doctor, and I'm on meds again, but gentler ones. We're still working on getting my dosage right, but I'm feeling better every day. I am mentally ill, and I need help. I've accepted that. Medication is a part of my treatment, but it's a delicate balance. I'm still discovering mine.

Bo and I have gone to visit a few colleges, but I already know where he wants to go. Berkeley has always held a fairy-tale fascination for him. And he already dresses like half the hippie love children that go there, so that works. I have no preference. I would live on Mars if Bo asked me to. I'm sure there are plenty of women in Berkeley who need a safe place to get clean and sober. I'll start there.

I won't keep a journal anymore. I'll write. I'll write every day. But not in a journal. If I have something going on in my life that I need to figure out or express, I'll talk to Bo.

I may never be a butterfly. But I'm finally free from the cocoon.

Author's Note

If you've been affected by any of the issues raised in this book, you can find help at any of the below organizations—you're not alone.

National Alliance on Mental Illness

nami.org

1-800-950-NAMI

info@nami.org

National Crisis Text Line

text HOME to 741741

Acknowledgments

For those of you thinking that this was a very odd book for me to write, all I can say is that I totally agree. I have a good explanation, though. When I came up with the idea I was really high.

Let me start over. I had cancer.

Treatment for cancer spans a whole range of possibilities, but it usually involves a fair bit of pain. My treatment was blessedly short compared to what some go through, but it still delivered on the pain part because cancer is an asshole. While I was lying in my hospital bed, I looked gratefully up at my morphine drip knowing full well I couldn't get through the week without it, and the thought crossed my mind that I might end up like so many others and not be able to get through any subsequent weeks without it, either. That's when

I got the first inkling for this book. I was afraid, and when I'm afraid of something I turn it into a monster (hello, Doctor Goodnight) and put it in a book.

But I was lucky. Not only did I come out of the hospital cancer free, I came out with no dependency on opiates. For that I have to thank my surgeons, Dr. Babak Moeinolmolki and Dr. Andreas Keiser, and the incredible nursing staff at USC's Keck Medical. They took amazing care of me while I was in hospital, and then when I got home, they checked on me many times to make sure that opiates were not destroying the life they'd worked so hard to save.

I also have to thank my friend Barbara Stepansky for her notes and support, and my brother Germano Angelini for walking me through the dual diagnosis of drug addiction and psychosis. A special thank-you goes out to my new editor, Steve Geck at Sourcebooks, and of course, the usual suspects: my husband, Albert, my daughter, Pia, and my agent, Mollie Glick. I couldn't do any of this without you. I love you all.

About the Author

Photo © Marc Cartwright

Josephine Angelini is a theater graduate from New York University, specializing in the classics. Originally from Massachusetts, she now lives in Los Angeles with her screenwriter husband and their daughter. You can find her on Instagram @josephine_angelini, on Twitter @josieangelini, and on Facebook @josephineangelini.

She is the author of international bestsellers *Starcrossed, Dreamless,* and *Goddess*, as well as the WorldWalker trilogy (*Trial by Fire*, *Firewalker*, and *Witch's Pyre*).

FIREreads
#getbooklit